AWAKE

Best always!

James M. McCracken

AWAKE

James M. McCracken

Cover Design by J Caleb Design

CONTENTS

DEDICATION

To my father,
John Michael Huff,
forever my Superman.

ACKNOWLEDGMENTS

Special thanks to Dennis Blakesley, Michael Anne Maslow, Anthony Huff, Pushpa Huff, Kathleen Mooney, Pamela Bainbridge-Cowan, Chris Forcier, James Logan, Betsy Jones, Phyllis Jensen, Ruth Bradley, Bill and Carol Ray, and Jane Blake for all of their encouragement and support.

EPISODE I:
FINDING DAD

The drive to the old farm on the west side of Hillsboro was depressing. The grey sky continued to refuse to give up its moisture. Once-green fields were nothing but dry stubble and dirt. Trees resembled dead sticks that someone had stuck into the ground. It was a far cry from the summers of Timothy Stone's father's childhood. Philip used to tell his son how much he loved playing in the branches of the leafy oak trees and running barefoot across his family's lush, green lawn.

Tim turned into the driveway. The front yard was just dried, cracked dirt, no flowerbeds. The trees were long dead and gone. He drove past his parents' two-story farmhouse and parked his Volkswagen Bug in the barn. Grabbing a tarp from the workbench, he covered his car, careful not to harm the solar tiles on the roof. They were a gift from his best friends and neighbors, Godfrey and George Bjorge and their father, John, when Tim had graduated from Lewis & Clark Law School in Portland. He closed the barn doors and snapped the padlock secure.

When Tim turned toward the house he was struck by what

he had just done. He looked back at the padlock and shook his head at the pointlessness of it. He glanced at his watch. The bus would be arriving in an hour to pick his parents and him up. He hated to admit it but he was beginning to feel nervous and a bit scared.

I can't believe I'm doing this, putting my trust—no my life and the lives of my parents—in the hands of total strangers. It's not the same as going to the doctor. With the doctor there is a relationship, a trust that was built up over time. No, this is the government. There is no relationship, or even a hint of trust. We don't even know if this insane plan is going to work. What proof is there that this planet can save itself if we weren't around?

Stop it! It's too late. What's done is done, just accept it.

Tim walked across the gravel driveway to the back door of the farmhouse. Opening the door to the enclosed back porch, he went inside, making sure to close and lock it securely behind him. The air smelled musty and stale and yet, familiar and comforting. He walked past the shower room and remembered the day it was built. He was about ten at the time. It was his mother's idea. She was tired of his father and him tracking the outside inside after working in the fields.

Just beyond the shower room was the back door. Tim gave it a knock before opening it and walking into the kitchen. His mother was standing in front of the sink. She had her long, auburn hair that was streaked with grey pulled back in her usual bun. Over her housedress she wore a blue and white floral-patterned apron. She didn't look at her son. She stared out of the window above the sink at something, possibly the dirt yard or the grey sky, on the north side of the house. Tim could tell she was worried.

"Hi, Mom," he greeted her and kissed her cheek.

"Hi, Timmy."

"Mom, Timmy? Really? I'm twenty-eight years old. Can't you just call me Tim?" he teased, trying to lighten the heaviness that hung in the air.

"Let's not talk about that right now," she answered. "Is your condo ready? All the perishables and garbage taken out like they told us to do?"

"Yes."

"Did you cover the furniture with your sheets like I showed you? You don't want to have to do a lot of dusting when—"

"Yes, Mom, I covered everything," he assured her.

"Good." She nodded but still hadn't taken her eyes off whatever she was looking at outside.

"Do you need me to clear out the refrigerator or take out the garbage?" Tim asked.

"No, it's all done. I emptied everything in the compost heap behind the barn by the old garden and let the chickens loose. It just doesn't feel right. How will they survive?"

"Instinct?" Tim suggested but honestly had no clue. It was another scathingly brilliant idea by the all-powerful government. *Release all the animals.*

Tim looked around the kitchen. Everything was neat, clean and in its place. "How's Dad?" he asked.

"He's in the front room. He's a bit more confused this morning and a bit agitated. He doesn't remember what's happening today but I think he senses it deep down. He keeps taking the sheets off the furniture—" Her breath caught and for a split second she looked as though she was going to cry.

Tim gave her a hug. "We'll be okay, Mom, I promise. I'll go check on him."

"Okay, dear."

The front room was through the dining room and off the small foyer. Tim had never realized how many sheets his mother had. The dining table and chairs sat beneath one large sheet. The sideboard had been covered with another. The grandfather clock in the corner, its pendulum stopped, was covered. Even the large mirror on the wall had a sheet over it. Tim couldn't shake the creepy feeling he had. The room reminded him of one in a horror movie. Any moment he expected to see a vampire or Frankenstein jump out at him from the shadows. He shrugged off the thought.

Tim found his father seated in his overstuffed rocking chair. A crocheted afghan that Tim's mother made for him covered his lap. Philip pointed the remote at nothing in particular and pressed the buttons. The TV switched from the news channel to a blank screen with static.

"Hi, Dad."

Philip looked up at Tim and smiled, then pressed a button on the remote and tucked it away. The television was still on the non-channel but was no longer making any noise.

"How are you doing?" Tim asked.

"Everyone I can and the easy ones twice," his father answered and laughed.

"Good," Tim said and pretended to laugh at the joke he had heard every time anyone asked his father how he was. Inside, Tim's heart broke a little more.

When he was a boy, Tim thought his father was Superman, fast, strong and fearless. He worked hard all day plowing fields, sowing seeds, reaping the meager harvest the parched land offered. Every evening he would come in covered in a layer of thick dust that reminded Tim of his mom's talcum powder that she kept in the bathroom cabinet. After dinner his father would go out to the barn and spend another hour or more working on one piece of equipment or another before coming in and resting in his chair.

But Philip looked different now. His skin was as pale as the talcum powder; his broad shoulders were slumped; his eyes, once as dark as fresh coffee had faded to the color of weak tea. He smiled and stared at Tim, but his eyes reflected confusion. Tim could tell his father was trying to figure out who he was. Again, Tim's chest ached deep inside.

The memory of the first time his father forgot him was scarred into his memory. It was almost a year ago. Tim had come over for dinner on his twenty-eighth birthday. His mom brought out a cake and his dad looked baffled. He asked her what it was for. She answered, "It's Timmy's birthday." He looked around and said, "Well, shouldn't we wait for him to come home from school?" Tim was sitting right beside him. It felt as though a knife had stabbed his heart; but, time dulled his pain just as it faded his father's memories. Even though his wasn't aware of it, Philip needed his wife and son more now than ever before.

Tim bent down and gave his father a hug and felt his father's shoulders tense.

"It's me, Dad, Timmy," he whispered. His father relaxed and hugged him back.

When Tim stood up he noticed his father looking around the room at the sheets covering the furniture.

"What's going on? Why is the laundry lying about?" he asked.

"We're going on a trip."

"We are? This is the first I've heard of it. Who said we're going?"

"We're just going uptown for the afternoon," Tim explained trying to calm his father's growing fear.

"What for?"

"We have an appointment."

"For what?"

"We need to take care of some business."

"Okay." He seemed satisfied with that answer. He looked around the room again. "What's all the laundry doing lying about?"

As Tim launched into a repeat of the previous conversation, his mother entered the room.

"It's time to change your clothes, Philip," she told her husband.

"Change my clothes?"

"You need to put on some clean clothes."

He looked at his flannel shirt, pulling it away from his chest so he could see it better. "These are clean."

"Honey, I need you to put on the new shirt and pants I bought you."

"But these are fine. I like these."

Tim could tell his mom was becoming frustrated and that no amount of trying to convince his dad was going to work, but he didn't know what to do. So, he remained silent.

"Well, I'm going to change my clothes. I can't go to town looking like this," she said. She turned around and headed for their bedroom off the dining room.

"Dad, why don't you go give Mom a hand?" Tim suggested.

"Okay," Philip said and pulled himself to his feet with the aid of his twisted walking stick. Years ago, while plowing the lower field he came across a fallen branch, six feet long, twisted and gnarled. He stripped the bark, sanded it down smooth and put three coats of varnish on it, making himself a walking stick.

Tim followed his father into the dining room and watched him disappear into his bedroom, a room that had been off limits to Tim since as long as he could remember.

Moments later they both emerged, dressed in clothes that looked as if they were going to church on Sunday. In actuality they hadn't been to church in years, not since Philip was diagnosed with early stage Alzheimer's and the pastor, realizing he wasn't going to inherit anything from them, stopped making house calls.

"You both look beautiful," Tim said.

"Thank you, Timmy," his mother smiled.

The sound of a bus pulling to a stop on the gravel at the edge of the road sent Tim and his parents scrambling. While his mother grabbed her coat and purse, Tim helped his dad slip on a jacket. He sent his parents ahead, out the front door, while he rushed to the back porch to turn off the main circuit breaker to the house and the well out back. Going back into the kitchen, he turned the water on to drain the pipes. With the house secure, Tim hurried after his parents, locking the front door behind them. He slipped the key into the pocket of his jeans and the thought occurred to him, the next time he'd unlock the door it would be twenty years from now.

After a bit of arguing about whether or not his father needed his walking stick in order to get around and that it was not a weapon to be used in some fit of confusion, the driver relented and let him board the bus with it. Three young boys Tim didn't recognize jumped up and moved to seats toward the back of the bus, leaving the front seats for them. Once everyone was settled, the bus turned around and headed back up the street. It rattled and shook with every bump in the road, jarring Tim's already frayed nerves. He looked at the faces of the others on the bus. He could tell they were just as worried and nervous as he was. No one said a word to each other. Tim glanced at his parents. They were holding hands. His mother's blue eyes looked damp but Tim knew she wasn't about to cry, especially not in front of strangers. He looked out the window.

It's been two years since the President made her address to the nation; an address that would affect the lives of every living person in the country and around the globe. "Due to the depletion of the earth's natural resources, the leading scientists of the world have come up with a plan: If the earth could rest from human interference for a short twenty years, it would renew itself. The oceans, rivers and streams would cleanse themselves from the pollutants we've dumped into them. The air would also become fresh and clean once again. The land would become fertile; crops would be plentiful. All of this because we would not be interfering with it, polluting it, ruining it."

Madam President continued, "To accomplish this, the entire population of the world will be placed into suspended animation." She explained that Suspended Animation Centers, or SACs, would be located in every city and town in the country. "In every Center, two trained attendants will remain awake to maintain the computers and all of the systems that are needed to monitor the population. They will be on hand to awaken everyone at the end of the twenty years."

She then introduced a man in a military uniform who looked older than Tim's dad. He stood up and explained how, by working together on this global crisis, the nations had set aside their differences and agreed to disarm their weapons so that no *accidents* would happen while everyone slept. It was a nice thought, but Tim didn't put much faith in anything the man said. After all, for over six thousand years men and women in power had been trying to accomplish world peace, why would it suddenly happen now?

Madam President next asked one of the scientists to step forward. He introduced himself and said he was forty-six years old. Tim was surprised. The scientist looked to be Tim's age. The man explained that, for the last twenty years, he had been in suspended animation as part of the testing that was done on the process. He tried to reassure everyone that they would be safe. "It's like going to bed one night and waking up the next morning, only it's actually several years later," he chuckled. Tim didn't think it was funny. What proof did anyone have that this guy was telling the truth? For all anyone knew he could have been lying. The man launched into a detailed explanation of the process which left Tim confused.

When he returned the podium to the President, she called another scientist forward. This woman discussed the issue of food storage and safety. "To prevent an infestation of rodents and other non-desirable invaders, all perishable food stuffs should be disposed of and not left in cupboards." She then assured everyone that hoarding food was not necessary. The government would see to it that food storage facilities would be set up in each city and town. These would house safely preserved foodstuffs to be used to cover the gap between the time when everyone was awakened and when food production would be restored. The locations of these facilities would be kept top secret to prevent looting and only a handful in each town or city would know their location. Amid the barrage of shouted questions from the reporters present, the scientist backed away from the podium and returned the conference to the president.

After that announcement, it seemed like overnight the Suspended Animation Center in Hillsboro sprang up. The SAC in Hillsboro was built across from the Washington County

Courthouse on Main Street, on the site where the old Washington County Museum and Civic Center once stood. It was the tallest building in town at fifteen stories high. The building took up two entire blocks from First Avenue to Third and from Main Street to Washington Street. It was an impressive building, Tim thought.

The bus pulled to a stop outside the SAC's main entrance. The driver opened the doors but no one moved. He looked in his rear view mirror.

"Come on, people. Get going. I have other people to bring in."

Philip stood up first. He started for the door. Tim and his mother quickly followed him.

Standing on the sidewalk, Tim looked up at the outside of the SAC building. Thick ribs of steel covered by stone and concrete rose out of the ground and reached to the top of the building. Between the ribs were walls of smoke-tinted glass. It reminded Tim of the old Wells Fargo Tower in downtown Portland, only a lot shorter, but for Hillsboro it was a skyscraper.

Tim put his hand gently on his dad's back and ushered him up the steps to the tinted-glass doors.

"What's this?" his father asked.

"This is where we need to go," Tim's mom answered.

"What are we doing here?"

"We have an appointment," she said, her voice quivered slightly.

"We do?"

"Yes."

"Why didn't anyone tell me?"

"It's okay, Dad. Come on,"

They entered the SAC. Inside, the lobby looked like any

other professional building. A large, circular reception counter sat in the center of the room, directly in front of the doors. Four women in white lab coats stood behind it, one facing in each direction. Tim and his parents walked up to the counter.

A young woman looked up.

"Your names and addresses?" she asked without a smile.

"Philip and Della Stone, 33133 SW 331st Avenue," Tim's mom answered.

"And you?" the woman asked and looked at Tim.

"Timothy Stone, 1450 NE Orecno Station Parkway," he answered matching her cold, unemotional delivery.

She took a breath and then waited for her computer to respond.

"You may have a seat. We will call you up when ready." She motioned toward the seating area to the right.

Obediently Tim escorted his parents to the waiting lounge and took a seat on a rather surprisingly comfortable, leather sofa. The sofa faced a large flat screen monitor on the wall. It played a video of some guy in a white lab coat touring the SAC while explaining what was about to happen. Every few minutes a different ad interrupted; the same ads that had been bombarding the television for the last two years. One ad, videoed in black and white, showed chimneys pumping black smoke into the air; drain pipes empting dark goo into a stream; and barren farmlands. Then it switched to color and showed a clear, blue sky, clean streams and rivers, lush green fields—*obviously computer generated*—with the miserable jingle Tim couldn't get out of his head, "Get ready to hit the SAC and have the best rest of your life."

"What's that nonsense?" Philip asked and motioned toward the monitor.

"It's a commercial," Tim answered.

"Well, turn the channel."

Neither Della nor Tim said anything.

When the program returned, the man in the lab coat continued his tour of the building. He showed everyone that in addition to the fifteen stories above ground; there were five basement levels that housed the ventilation system, the fuel cells for the electrical power system, the large computer system and a floor designed to look like a town square complete with two apartments where the heads of the SAC would live. Tim found the whole video to be a bit unnerving.

Just get on with it, he thought and tried to calm his uneasiness.

"Mr. and Mrs. Philip Stone, Mr. Timothy Stone," a woman with a clipboard called out.

Tim and Della stood up and helped Philip to his feet.

"Come with me, please."

They followed her into an elevator and up to the fifth floor. The doors opened onto a lobby that looked like a hospital ward. A reception desk sat directly in front of the elevator with two men in white scrubs seated behind it. Their escort announced them before she returned to the elevator. *Probably to take other people to their doom,* Tim figured.

"Right this way," one of the men said and led the trio to a small room beside the elevator. The room had no windows. Four chairs, two against one wall and two on another, sat beneath a framed picture of green farmlands and another of a thick forest. The man in scrubs motioned for them to sit down.

"Good morning, my name is Robert. I have a few questions to ask you." He looked at his clipboard. "First of all, do you answer to Phil, Philip?" He looked at Tim's father who didn't answer.

"Philip," Della said for him.

Robert gave her a confused look.

"My father has Alzheimer's," Tim explained.

"Oh." Robert wrote something down on his clipboard. "What about you, Mrs. Stone."

"I'm fine."

"No, I mean, do you go by Della or Del or—"

"Mrs. Stone," she answered abruptly.

Again a look and more writing.

"I go by Tim," Tim offered in order to move things along.

"Very well," Robert said. "Do any of you have any allergies to medications?"

"No," Della answered for all of them.

"What about eggs?"

"No." Again she answered.

"Hay fever or any environmental allergies?"

"Just mold and wet dirt," Tim spoke up.

"Well, there won't be any of that here," Robert smiled at him and made a check mark on his clipboard. "Now, so you know what to expect, in a moment you will be fitted with wireless electrodes that will be used to monitor your vital signs. Then I will be back to escort you down the hall to one of the sleeping rooms."

"Sleep?" Philip said. "I'm not tired."

"It's okay, Dad."

"This is crazy. I'm going home." He started to stand up but Della took his hand.

"In a few minutes, dear," she said. Philip sat back down.

"Mrs. Stone," Robert spoke. "If you would come with me for a moment, we will fit you in another room."

"I'll stay with Dad," Tim assured her. "We'll be okay."

Reluctantly she left the room with Robert.

"Where's your mother going?" Philip asked.

"She has to go to another room for a moment. She'll be right back."

"Oh." he nodded. He looked around the room and then back at Tim. "Where's your mother?"

"She had to go to another room. She'll be right back."

Again he looked around the room while they waited.

Right when Philip opened his mouth to ask again, the door opened and a woman in colorful, teddy bear-patterned scrubs entered pushing a cart with a small tray.

"Hello, I'm Julie," she smiled and greeted them. "If you wouldn't mind unbuttoning your shirts, please—"

"Why?" Philip snapped.

"So I can put these on you," she answered holding up two half-dollar sized discs with a small wire sticking out on one side.

"Like hell you are!"

"Dad, please. It's so the doctor can check your heart. That's all."

"There's nothing wrong with my heart."

"I know, but please, let them check."

Julie looked at Tim and gave a slight smile. He hoped she understood what was happening.

"Okay," Philip relented. He unbuttoned his shirt and lifted up his t-shirt.

Julie quickly stuck the four electrodes on his chest and torso. She then did the same on Tim's.

"You can button up again," she said and left the room.

Before Philip could say anything or peel the stickers off, the door opened and Della entered the room. She gave Philip a kiss on the cheek and helped him button his shirt before she sat down beside him.

The wait wasn't long. The door opened again and Robert

invited the three to follow him. He led them down the hall to the right of the reception desk. The hall was well lit by wall sconces. It looked more like a nice hotel than what Tim had imagined for a place like this. Robert stopped in front of a door about halfway down the hall and opened it. Tim and his parents followed him inside.

White sheets hung from the ceiling like curtains and formed a hallway, shielding whatever was behind them from view. The Stones followed Robert to where the curtains stopped and where two men in blue scrubs stood, one behind a portable podium and the other in front. Beyond them on either side of the narrow aisle, Tim could see large, glass, pneumatic tube-like things that were tilted back slightly.

"Hello, Mr. and Mrs. Stone," the man in front greeted them.

Tim could feel his heart beat faster while his anxiety grew.

"If you would please step into your chamber," the man said to Della.

"No, Philip first, please," she protested. Tim could tell by her voice she was frightened.

The man looked at her.

"Mr. Stone has Alzheimer's," Robert whispered to the attendant.

"Oh, of course," he said. "Mr. Stone, would you stand in here please."

"What is it?"

"It's a sl—"

"It's a new x-ray machine," Tim interrupted. "It will only take a few seconds."

The attendant gave Tim a look that said he wasn't pleased that he interrupted him but Tim couldn't care less. This was his father and if they wanted his dad to cooperate, they needed to let his mother and him, the people he trusted, handle him.

Della gave Philip a kiss and then Tim helped him into his chamber. At first Philip tried to stand straight up.

"It's okay, Mr. Stone, just lean back and relax," Robert said in a kind tone. Philip did as instructed, resting against the padded back of the tube.

"I need to take the walking stick," the attendant said.

"The hell you will!" Philip said. He tightened his grip on it and pulled it away.

"Will it hurt if he kept it?" Della asked Robert. "It's sort of a security blanket for him."

"It will be okay," Robert told the attendant who didn't look pleased.

That brief interaction made Tim realize Robert was more than just another assistant but what his exact role was in the SAC was still unknown.

"Now, Mr. Stone, close your eyes and continue to take slow, deep breaths," Robert instructed in a gentle tone. "You will be okay, I promise."

Philip closed his eyes. The glass door slid shut. The lights above the tube began to flash.

Tim stood watching his father, expecting him to open his eyes, but he didn't.

"Okay, Mrs. Stone," Robert said and directed Della toward the chamber beside Philip's.

"That's it?" Della said looking back and forth at Philip and then Robert.

"Yes, he's asleep." Robert answered with a nod.

"Oh," Della said faintly. She looked at Tim before stepping into her chamber. Tim rushed forward and gave her a quick hug and kiss on her cheek.

"I'll see you when we wake up," he told her.

She leaned against the back and gave him a nervous smile.

"I love you," Tim said.

"I love you more," she answered.

She closed her eyes, the door slid shut and she was asleep.

Robert looked at Tim and smiled as though he knew how frightened Tim felt.

"It's okay, Tim. It doesn't hurt," he tried to reassure him.

"But I don't like tight spaces."

Robert smiled. "It'll be okay, just close your eyes and keep them closed. You'll do fine."

Tim tried to smile but felt his lips quiver. He stepped into the tube across from his mother's and leaned against the padded back of the chamber. It felt spongey, like memory foam. He took a deep breath and closed his eyes. There was a whoosh sound as the glass door close. Tim fought the urge to open his eyes. *I wonder what being put into suspended animation feels like? Will I dream? What if I have a nightmare? Worse, yet, what if I need to use the bathroom? What was I thinking I...*

Tim opened his eyes. The glass door in front of him was still shut. Immediately he felt a rush of panic. *Let me out of here!* He put his hands up and felt the cool surface of the glass door. His heart began to beat faster. He couldn't get enough air. He looked through the glass and saw Della still asleep in her tube. His breathing began to slow. He looked to her left, expecting to see his dad but instead the tube was empty and open. Panic rushed back. His heart thumped harder and faster in his chest. A red light above his head began to blink. He felt the glass start to vibrate and quickly took his hands away. The door slid open with a hiss, like a seal being broken. Tim gasped as though starved for air. Once breathing normally again, he took a step out of the tube and his legs gave beneath him. He fell to the floor.

"What the hell?" he said but no one was listening. He looked up and down the aisle, at the rows of tubes with people still fast asleep in them. *They're still asleep?*

Slowly he pulled himself to his feet, using the door of the tube to steady himself. His legs felt weak. *What's the matter with me? I only closed my eyes for a second.* He took a few deep breaths. The air smelled strange, like perfume. He looked around to see where it was coming from and noticed an air vent in the ceiling. *They must be piping in scented air, how strange.* Tim took another deep breath and felt something pinch his chest. He pulled his shirt up and peeled off the electrodes, throwing them on the floor of his chamber.

He decided to give walking another try. With his hand still holding fast to the tube, he took a step. *So far so good.* He took another step, let go of the tube, and crashed to the floor. *You've got to be kidding me. What is going on? What did they do to me?* He noticed a door at the end of the aisle and decided to crawl toward it. *Maybe if I could get outside I would feel better and steadier on my feet.*

Tim reached the door and used it to pull himself up again. His legs felt a bit stronger. *What I wouldn't give for dad's walking stick right now.* With a bit of effort, he managed to get the door open. *I don't remember it being so heavy.* He stepped out into the hall. *That's odd, where did all this dust come from?*

A layer of thick dust dulled the green-tinted concrete floor making it appear grey. Cobwebs hung from the wall sconces. Using the wall again to brace himself, Tim made his way toward the elevators beneath a flickering sign.

"Please let them be working," Tim said out loud. His voice was faint and raspy. His throat felt dry.

He pushed the button and heard the familiar whine of the cables as the car was brought to his floor. The doors opened and the light in the ceiling of the car flickered. Not wanting to fall again, he carefully stepped inside and leaned against the wall. He pressed the button for the first floor. The doors closed. While the car descended, Tim noticed footprints in the dust on the floor. *Other people are awake!*

The elevator doors opened and Tim stumbled out. The lobby was deserted. The monitor that had so proudly played the video tour and commercials was dark and silent. The reception desk, and even the marble tiled floor, looked as if they could use a good dust mopping. *How can this be right? I closed my eyes a second ago. How could this get so dirty this fast? Where are the people running this place?*

Something moved outside and caught his attention. *What's that?* Slowly he headed for the tinted, glass doors. They opened by themselves as they had when he and his parents arrived. Instantly blinded by the bright sunlight Tim staggered back a step and the doors closed.

What's going on? What's the matter with me?

After giving his eyes a few minutes to adjust to the light he tried it again. Using his hands as a shade, he walked out the door and stood on the steps of the SAC. His mouth gaped while he looked across the street at the courthouse. Ivy covered the once bare façade of the historic, old building on the right and spider webbed its way across the newer half on the left, covering windows and walls alike. Trees! There were trees on the front grounds. Grass! Green grass covered the once barren landscape in front of the courthouse and even grew in the cracks of the pavement of Main Street.

This is crazy! Twenty years couldn't have already passed. I couldn't have slept twenty years… wait a minute, those trees look too big and too old for only twenty years. What's going on?

Tim staggered down the steps using the handrail for support. He walked out into the middle of the street. Turning around he looked back at the SAC building. Some of the windows were cracked; others were shattered. *Maybe a bird flew into them—birds! I hear birds!* He looked around for the source of the chirping and noticed birds perched high in the trees in front of the courthouse. That's when he saw the clear blue sky. It was beautiful, like staring into a blue sapphire. Tim had only seen a sky that color in paintings and pictures his father showed him when Tim was a young boy.

Dad! I have to find him, but how long has he been awake? Where would he go? He must be frightened and confused. Maybe he headed for home. Tim started walking. The farm was only three miles away. *It would take Dad awhile to walk that far but he could make it.*

Tim started down First Avenue and headed toward Baseline. Everything was quiet, uncomfortably quiet. He looked around, peering into the shadows for any sign of his father or anyone for that matter. *Surely I can't be the only other person outside. I saw the footprints. Where is everyone?*

He made it to Baseline and looked toward the east, toward the center of town, nothing. There were no cars on the road, no people. It was a ghost town. He turned toward the west and headed out of town.

Trees covered in thick leaves of every shade of green imaginable lined the street. Overgrown bushes and tall grass reclaimed the parking lots of the old Elmer's café and the county sheriff's office and jail. A sudden feeling of fear engulfed him at the thought, *What if the prisoners are awake?* Tim quickened his pace.

He reached Dennis Avenue before he slowed down and felt calm returning. The traffic lights weren't working but he heard a clicking sound in the control box mounted on the pole by the walk signal. He looked up at the lights. The lenses were broken. *But there's still power. What do you know?* He smiled and felt comforted by that. *I guess that old military guy knew what he was talking about after all.*

Tim couldn't get over how eerily quiet it was while he continued. Usually Baseline, the highway to Forest Grove, was noisy with cars, trucks and buses. He began to feel more worried for his father. *He must be so confused.*

The Hillsboro West strip mall was a few blocks up on the left. Tim remembered the old Buttercup Restaurant he frequented as a teen. The food was horrible but cheap and all of the popular kids went there after school. The Buttercup was torn down a couple years after he graduated from high school to make room for an auto parts store and some other smaller shops.

The sound of breaking glass, a window shattering, startled Tim. He searched for the source. At the Oak Street end of the Green Bamboo Restaurant building he spotted two people. One appeared ready to throw something at the building. The other was standing back. Both were dressed in jeans and dark jackets and looked to be teenagers.

"Hey!" he shouted to them and waved. His throat still felt dry and scratchy; his voice, hoarse.

The two froze and looked at Tim for a second before ducking around the end of the building.

"No! Stop! I only want to talk to you!" Tim shouted and coughed. The need for something to drink became stronger.

Maybe that's what they were after. Tim looked along the side of the building for a hose bib. *Damn those in-ground sprinkler systems!* He started walking again. *I'll get some water when I get to the farm.*

Tim came to a wall of laurel on his right. He remembered his father telling him that at one time a hedge separated the pioneer cemetery from the highway, but all Tim remembered was a row of twigs. He felt the smooth waxy leaves and looked up. *It must be over twice as tall as me.* That was the moment it hit him. He turned around and looked across the street at the bushes, green grass and wild flowers. *They are all so vibrant and beautiful.* He couldn't remember ever seeing so much color.

Distracted by the scenery, Tim reached the top of the hill west of Hillsboro and almost missed his parents' street. The sign marking SW 331st Avenue was nothing more than a rotted wooden post with a faded stop sign hanging upside-down by one bolt. The two-lane, dead-end street was narrower with shrubs and vines creeping across the pavement in an attempt to reclaim the land beneath.

I'm almost home; just a mile and a half more.

Tim stopped when he reached the neighbors' driveway and stared at the house. He wondered if he should check to see if they had awakened and were home and if they had seen his father. All of the windows were dark. There was no movement outside by the barn. He decided to keep moving and continued on to his parents' farm.

When he reached the edge of the farm he froze in shock. Tall fir trees, shrubs and grasses had overtaken a large portion of his dad's field across the street from the house. In the front yard of his parent's home, oak trees with huge green leaves had grown tall, shading the house. He looked down. *There's grass growing!*

Beyond the trees Tim could see that the house was still standing. Other than in desperate need of a fresh coat of paint, it didn't appear any worse for wear. The driveway entrance to the left of the house was partially blocked by overgrown blackberry vines.

There might be enough room for me to get my Bug through. My car!

Tim looked at the barn. The roof sagged in the center and appeared ready to collapse at any moment. The windows on the side facing the house were all shattered. He rushed to the door. The lock was rusted and broken and laid on the ground next to a rock the size of a softball. The hasp was loose, hanging by a single screw. It came off in his hand. He threw it aside and slid the door open.

Cobwebs and dust coated everything. The smell of mildew and dirt was strong. Tim noticed footprints leading to the workbench and around his partially uncovered car. *Dad?* He turned away from the barn and looked at the house.

"Dad!" he called out and ran to the back door. He pulled the key from his pocket but saw it wasn't needed, the door had been jimmied. *Dad wouldn't have done that.* His heart pounding and adrenaline coursing through his veins, he slowly opened the door. It creaked. Tim cringed. Slowly he stepped into the back porch. He tiptoed passed the shower room and noticed the electrical panel door was ajar. He checked it. Some of the breakers were flipped but the main breaker was still off.

Quietly he opened the back door and went into the kitchen. There was a noise in the other room.

"Who's there?" he called out.

There was no response. Slowly he headed into the dining

room. The sheets over the table and chairs had been disturbed. His heart pounded loudly in his ears. When he entered the foyer, he looked in the corner for his dad's old baseball bat. It was gone. Unarmed and still shaken, he peeked into the front room. The sheets that covered the furniture were removed. His dad's chair was empty and slightly rocking as though someone had jumped up.

"Dad?" he called out even though he knew it wasn't him.

"Don't come any closer!"

"Okay," he answered. He felt his body relax a bit. The voice sounded like a frightened young girl.

"I mean it. I have a gun!" she threatened.

"It's okay. I won't come any farther." Tim looked at the mirror hanging on the front room wall across from the foyer. He felt another rush of adrenaline. In the glass he could see the stranger pressed against the wall beside the doorway just inches away from him. Her face was shadowed but he could see the gun in her hands.

"I'm not going to harm you. I just want to talk to you," he said, speaking slowly and softly hoping to ease her fear. "My name is Tim Stone. This is my parents' house." She dropped her hand a little and Tim could see she was holding his father's pistol. He felt his fear melt away. The gun wasn't loaded. They haven't had ammo for it for years, since his dad was diagnosed. "How long have you been awake?" he asked keeping his eyes on her reflection.

"Forty-eight days. You?"

"I just woke up today. What's your name?"

"Lily. Lily Evers."

"Hi, Lily, may I come in? I would like to sit down. My legs are still a bit wobbly."

There was silence while she appeared to be thinking it

over.

"Okay, but don't try anything. Remember, I have a gun," she warned.

"I won't forget."

Cautiously, with his hands raised, Tim entered the front room. He kept his eyes on her reflection while he inched his way across the room to his mother's chair. Sunlight was coming through the window and by sitting in his mom's chair he would be able to see the intruder more clearly.

Lily moved slowly over to the sofa against the inside wall across from him. She sat down on the arm nearest by the foyer, staying as far as possible away. She held the pistol with a tight grip in her trembling hands. It worked. Tim was able to see her face. She was young, seventeen or eighteen, tops. Tim found her attractive. Her hair was light auburn and long, past her shoulders. There were bits of straw grass tangled in it. Seeing her he suddenly wondered what he looked like. He felt his hair and face. *That's odd.* His face still felt smooth as if he had just shaved and his hair didn't feel as though it had grown either. *How can that be after—however long I had been asleep? Does suspended animation include stopping the growth of hair?*

"So, Lily, where did you live, I mean, before?" Tim asked.

"My family lives—lived on Northeast Montgomery Street by the airport."

"Lived? What do you mean, isn't it still there?"

She shook her head. "It's all gone. No houses."

"Gone? I don't understand."

"The place was overgrown with vines and bushes and stuff. I found piles of charred bricks and rusted, twisted metal. There must have been a fire."

Her hands began to tremble more. She gripped the gun

harder and pressed her hands into her lap.

"It's okay," Tim tried to reassure her. "There's plenty of room here for you to stay. You don't have to leave."

She looked at him as though she didn't believe him.

"I mean it. There are two bedrooms upstairs. It's a big house." After hearing what he said, he guessed he didn't need to tell her. Since she found the gun that was hidden upstairs she'd obviously already seen for herself.

"I'll think about it. I mean about letting *you* stay here," she said, holding the gun up again.

Instantly Tim felt his anger ignite. *Who does she think she is, breaking into* my *parents' home and trying to dictate to me, who stays or who goes.* He fought the urge to snap at her.

"How did you end up here?" he asked instead.

She appeared to think for a moment. Tim assumed she was trying to decide whether or not to answer his question.

"I spent a few days walking around town, trying to find where my other family lived but I got kind of lost. I ended up by the cemetery and spent the night in the laurel hedge. I figured I would be safe there but that's where they found me." She looked down at her lap and turned her head as though struggling not to cry.

"They?"

"Some guys."

"Boys?"

"Men," she corrected herself.

"Did you know them?"

She shook her head.

"What did they look like?"

"I don't know," she answered and shrugged her shoulders.

"Do you remember what they were wearing?"

26

"Two were wearing orànge jumpsuits with Washington County printed on the back. The other two were in regular clothes, jeans and shirts. At first they were nice. They gave me some food and water. But then they wanted something in return." She pressed her hands and the pistol into her lap and began to cry. "There were too many of them," she said, her voice strained. "I couldn't fight them." She pressed her hands deeper into her lap and began to cry.

Oh my god! What Lily was trying to tell him and at the same time, not, came through loud and clear. After years of seeing a therapist about his OCD and other issues, he knew that her saying something didn't necessarily mean she trusted him. It was more about her need to tell someone. Still, he instantly felt a connection with her and wanted to protect her.

"It's okay. You're safe here. No one is going to hurt you again. I'm not going to hurt you, I swear."

She looked at him. The dust and dirt on her cheeks was streaked with tears. "That's what *they* said," she snapped and held the pistol up, aiming it at him. "You're just like them."

"No," Tim answered and held up his hands. Even though he knew the gun wasn't loaded, he still hated having it pointed at him. His father repeatedly told him while teaching him to use a rifle, "never aim a gun at anyone you don't intend to shoot."

"Lily, I'm not like them. Please, you gotta believe me."

She looked at Tim with a suspicious eye. "Promise?"

"Yes," he nodded. "How did you get away?"

She lowered the pistol and Tim felt his body relax again.

"One of the guys broke into the liquor store just off the main street and stole a bunch of bottles of some old stuff. They sat around drinking it and offered me some but I only pretended to drink. I waited for them to pass out and then I ran away."

"Did you see anyone else around?"

"A few people, old people, but they wouldn't help me. They seemed too scared and wouldn't open their doors." She shook her head.

"Where? Where were they?"

"One was right up the street," she said glancing over her shoulder at the foyer. "But the others were in the houses near the cemetery."

"I see." Tim nodded and wondered if by up the street she meant the Bjorges next door? "So you ended up here?"

She nodded. "I figured since this was the dead end of the street, no one would come by here. I'd be safe."

"Well, you *are* safe and as I said, you are welcome to stay here. Have you found anything to drink?"

"The water's not working so I put some pans out to catch rain water but I'm afraid I drank the last of it."

"That's okay." He started to stand up. She jumped and raised the pistol, pointing it at him again. Tim froze then sat back down. "I only want to check to see if the pump is still working."

"Pump?"

"For the well out back. The house uses well water."

"Oh, okay" she said. He could tell she still didn't trust him. She stood up and pressed her back against the wall at the end of the sofa. She kept the pistol pointed in his direction.

Slowly Tim stood up and walked past her, staying as far away as he could. Once in the foyer, he headed to the back porch. He was aware that she was following him and felt the pistol aimed at his back. He opened the door on the electrical panel box and flipped the main breaker on. Instantly the light above the box by the kitchen door came on.

"Ah-ha!" He couldn't help but grin. He flipped the breaker for the pump out back. "Come with me, I'll show you where the pump house is."

Tim didn't wait for her to reply. He headed out back behind the barn. The pump house was a small wooden shed his dad had built after drilling the well. It was about the size of an outhouse. The wood looked grey, sun bleached, but it was still standing. He unlatched the rusted hasp and opened the door. After a few minutes of manually pumping to prime the machine, it kicked on and began working.

"Run back to the kitchen and turn on the cold water faucet. Let me know if you get anything," he told Lily without looking at her. He heard her run off.

Moments later, "The water is dirty and rusty," she called out from the back door.

"Good!" he answered and closed the pump house door. He headed back to the house.

"We can't drink this," she said showing him the dirty water that poured into the kitchen sink and down the drain.

Looking in the sink Tim noticed about five partially eaten apple cores. From the amount of browning he guessed Lily had only been here a couple days.

"It's okay. These old pipes are notorious for being a little rusty at first. If we leave the water on for a while it should clear up. Let's give it some time."

With all the excitement over the water, Lily dropped her guard and actually stood beside him watching the water pour from the faucet. That's when Tim noticed the pistol was lying on the counter. He smiled and began to relax.

"How about we sit down for a bit, my legs are still a bit shaky." Tim walked across the room to the breakfast table and pulled out a chair. He motioned toward the other chair across the table for Lily and sat down. Still a bit wary, she eventually walked over and sat down.

"I heard you before you came in, you were calling for your father?" Lily started the conversation. "Is he awake?"

"Yeah, I think so. When I woke up, his chamber was open and empty."

"Well, if he's awake, wouldn't he have come back here?"

Tim nodded. "I thought he might, but he has Alzheimer's and with everything looking so different, I'm not sure he'd be able to find his way. He's probably out there wandering around lost and confused."

"Well, what about your mom?"

"She's still asleep."

"Oh," Lily responded sounding like she was at a loss for what to say next.

"It's okay," Tim assured her and smiled. "What about your parents, your family?"

Suddenly her expression changed and she looked down at the table in front of her. "They didn't wake up."

"Well, they will," he said trying to sound positive.

She started shaking her head slowly. "No. They won't. Something must have gone wrong. When I woke up, I saw—" Her face contorted and she began to cry.

Instinctively Tim jumped up and wrapped his arms around her. Her body tensed for a moment and then she buried her face in his chest and held onto him.

"It's okay," he said and let her cry. "It's okay. We'll be okay."

She continued to sob and Tim continued to hold her. He glanced over his shoulder at the sink.

"Hey, look, it's cleared up."

Lily lifted her head so she could see. Tim felt her arms

relax and slip from around him. He let her go. She wiped the tears from her eyes.

Tim opened the cupboard and took out a glass. After rinsing the dust from it, he filled it with cold, clean, clear water. He smelled it to be sure. There was no odor. He took a sip, tasting it for anything foul. A smile spread across his lips and he held out the glass to Lily.

"Here."

She grabbed the glass and quickly drank its contents, spilling some down both sides of her face.

"Oh, that's good," she sighed and held out the empty glass. "More, please."

Tim filled it up again and handed it back to her before grabbing another glass from the cupboard for himself.

His thirst quenched, he felt his stomach growl to be fed.

"Let's see if we can find something to eat," he said.

"There's nothing here," Lily spoke up looking around the kitchen, "Just some green apples by the barn."

"Let's go take another look."

They walked outside. Tim was still not used to how bright the sunlight was or how fresh and clean the air smelled. They rounded the back corner of the house and found the apple trees. He picked a few of the larger apples and handed them to Lily. Then he had a thought. He headed to the back of the barn where his parents' compost pile used to be. The weeds and grass had grown tall, to his knees. He found several familiar plants and felt excitement bloom in his chest.

"Stay right here, I'll be right back," he told Lily.

"Where are you going?" she called after him.

"I'll be right back."

He ducked into the barn and moments later emerged with his father's potato fork.

"These are potato plants," he explained and plunged the tines into the ground. "My dad showed me pictures of them from when he was a kid." He turned the clump of dirt over. Immediately potato bulbs, from the size of large pebbles to softballs, became unearthed. He eagerly gathered them up, handing them to Lily.

"Hang on a second," he said noticing another cluster of plants. "If these are what I think they are," he said taking hold of the base of the green stalks and pulling. "They are!"

"Carrots?" Lily asked.

"Yes, carrots."

That evening they dined on fresh potatoes, carrots, a few beets and some green apples. It felt good to eat. Tim tried to remember the last meal he had before he went to sleep but came up blank. It didn't really matter.

Later they sat on the front porch and watched the sky over Mt. Hood in the distance darken as the sun set on the other side of the house. Without the pollution, there weren't the bright reds, purples and oranges but it was still so incredibly beautiful.

"Mr. Stone—"

"Please, call me Tim."

"Okay, Tim," Lily started again. "Where do you think your father would go?"

"I have no idea. It's hard to say what he's thinking or feeling. I just hope I can find him before—" he stopped himself before he spoke the words and made it real. While he stared out at the trees in the yard, he tried to push the thought from his mind.

"I'll help you find him, if you want," Lily offered.

Tim looked at her and smiled. "I'd like that, thanks. What do you say we go check to see if the water heater still works?"

They left the sun to finish setting on its own and went back into the house. Tim turned the hot water on in the kitchen sink. It was clear. He felt it. Cold. He let it run for a while and felt it again. It was warm and then hot.

"We have hot water!" he announced.

After finding a bar of soap still in its wrapper in the linen closet outside the shower room, Tim grabbed a clean towel. He handed both to Lily. "Since you're my guest, you can either shower or bathe. I'll wait until you're finished."

"Thank you," she said and smiled. She slipped into the shower room and closed the door. Tim heard the lock click and the shower come on. He headed into the house and to his parents' bedroom.

Switching on the light, he was surprised that the LED bulb in the ceiling fixture still worked. *I guess they do last a long time.* The blankets and pillows on his parents' bed were disheveled. *This must be where Lily's been sleeping.* He turned toward the closet and pulled out an old pair of his mother's gardening jeans and held them up. *They look about the right size.* Grabbing a blouse, he was about to close the closet door when he noticed an old scrapbook on the shelf. He took it too.

Standing outside the shower room door, he knocked softly and listened. The water shut off.

"It's me, Lily. I found some clean clothes I think might fit you. I'll leave them by the door."

She didn't answer. Tim returned to the front room.

Settling into his mother's chair, he opened the album. Carefully he turned the pages that were fragile and brittle. His mother's handwriting was still legible beneath each picture. He continued to turn the pages. Suddenly he stopped. He stared at a photograph of an old house with a boy in the yard. The writing beneath the photo read: Philip Stone, age 13, outside his parents' home on East Walnut Street.

Tim was so caught up in his thoughts that he didn't hear Lily walk into the room.

"What do you think?"

Tim jumped, nearly dropping the album.

"I'm sorry. I didn't mean to startle you. What are you looking at?"

"It's my parents' old photo album. I think I may know where to find my father."

Day Two. Sleep eluded Tim. He dozed off and on seated in his dad's chair in the front room. Thoughts of his father, lost and confused, wandering around like a homeless person filled his head. He was anxious for daybreak so he could go searching.

The sun was still behind the mountains to the east but it was light enough to see. Tim and Lily started out for the house that used to belong to Tim's grandparents. Even though it was on the east side of town, it wasn't all that far. While they walked, they both continued to marvel at how different the world looked. How bright the colors were. How clean the air smelled. *Those scientists were right, the world did cleanse itself.*

"So, what did you do for a living?" Lily asked.

"I'm a—was as a paralegal in a law firm in Portland."

"Oh?"

"It's not that exciting. The lawyers handled family law cases, divorces mainly," Tim explained. "I spent most of my time doing research on the internet. It's amazing what people put on there and the pictures they post of themselves; some really bad stuff that doesn't help them in their divorce case."

"I bet," Lily responded but sounded a bit distracted and

distant.

"What did you do?" Tim asked to change the subject.

"Nothing much," she answered with a shrug and kept looking around.

The pair made it to the Hillsboro West strip mall and Tim could tell Lily was becoming uneasy. She walked closer to him and became very quiet. He wondered if this was where she was attacked and if the two he saw yesterday had anything to do with it.

"You doing okay?" he asked her.

She nodded her head and wrapped her arm in his. Tim couldn't help but smile. He felt proud. He was walking through town with a rather hot girl holding his arm.

"No one will hurt you. I'll protect you," he assured her, although deep down he wasn't sure how or with what.

They headed east along Oak Street, figuring it was best to stay off the residential streets and more on the main drag. There was less chance of running into trouble. They passed the old, Catholic Church. Tim noticed that some of the stained glass windows had been smashed. They stopped and listened but didn't hear anything.

"Guess whoever did that is gone," he reasoned out loud.

They continued down past the Miller Education Center. Same thing, windows smashed. *What would anyone expect to find of use or value in an old school? What's the point?*

Tim noticed cars covered in dust parked along the curbs of some of the side streets. Some had the solid, "never a flat" tires. The cars that didn't sat on rims with rubber shards. Tim wondered if their fuel cells still worked.

Three more blocks and they came to Tuality Medical Center. Lily tightened her grip on Tim's arm again.

"It's okay. We're almost there."

The streets were eerily quiet. The hospital, even though it was normally as quiet as a library inside, was always bustling with traffic, both vehicles and pedestrians outside. Seeing it like this was a bit creepy. Subconsciously Tim quickened his pace and they reached SE Tenth Avenue before he realized it.

"Only a couple more blocks," he told Lily. She let go of his arm.

They crossed Tenth Avenue in the middle of the block and headed south toward Walnut Street. Tim's heart beat faster with anticipation of finding his father. Inside he was flooded by different emotions: anxiety, fear, sadness, pity. He imagined his father had to be feeling the same and more, frightened, confused and lost.

When they turned the corner onto Walnut, Tim spotted the house. Even though the rhododendron bushes were overgrown, nearly covering the large front window, it was unmistakable. He had seen the house, inside and out, many times while growing up.

"Dad!" Tim shouted when they reached the front door. He tried the doorknob, locked. He pounded on the door with his fist. No response. He could see that someone had been there because the tall grass had been knocked down, leaving a path. "Dad!" Tim shouted again and disappeared around the side of the house. The path led around to the back door by the garage. He tried the door. It was locked tight.

After making a thorough search of the garage and property, he was sure his father was no longer there. That is, if Philip ever was.

"I'm sorry," Lily said when Tim rejoined her on the sidewalk in front of the house.

"It's okay," he said, trying to sound hopeful. "We'll find him. Since we're in town, let's go by the SAC. I want to see if anyone else has awakened." The reality was Tim only wanted to see if his mother had. She would know what to do.

They made it to Main Street without seeing a soul. Lily seemed relieved by that. Still, Tim wished there were someone he could ask, someone who may have seen his father, maybe even taken him in.

When they reached the Cultural Arts Center Tim heard an alarm bell ringing. It grew louder the farther up Main Street they walked, making Lily more afraid. She wrapped her arm in his again. When they reached the middle of the block, between Fifth and Fourth Avenues, Tim realized it was coming from the bank on the corner just ahead.

"You've got to be kidding me," he said and nearly laughed. "Someone is trying to rob the bank?"

"I don't like this," Lily said and tightened her grip.

"It's okay, no one's going to hurt you." Tim smiled at her. She relaxed a bit but still held fast to him. They continued on their way.

When they reached the corner of Fourth Avenue and Main Street, Tim saw him, a man dressed in an orange jumpsuit. He looked young, but at that distance Tim couldn't be sure. The guy had just crawled out through a broken window on the front of the bank. In one hand he clutched a canvas bag and in the other he gripped a walking stick. Tim didn't think first. He charged across the street.

"Hey, you!" He shouted in an angry tone.

The young man's eyes widened. He fidgeted for a moment not knowing which way to run, then, suddenly he bolted toward Fourth Street. Tim chased after him.

"Stop! I just want to ask you a question," he called to the crook. The guy kept running, passed one block and then another. He turned left on Edison and headed west toward

First.

Damn, this guy can run. He must have been awake for a long time.

"Please, stop!" Tim shouted again, nearly out of breath. He felt his legs slowing down and hope of retrieving his father's walking stick slipping away.

Just when Tim thought it was over, Lily bolted past him. She closed in on the guy right when he reached Second Avenue. She shoulder blocked him, knocking him into the power pole. He hit hard and fell to the sidewalk, dropping the walking stick and the bag. He groaned and rolled over onto his back, stunned. Winded but still able to move quickly, Lily straddled him and pinned his arms down. She began to pummel him with her fists.

"I hate you! I hate you!" she screamed at him.

"Stop it! Stop it!" he cried out and twisted under her. "I never touched you! It wasn't me!"

"You were there!" she said and punched him in the jaw. His head jerked to the side.

When Tim caught up with them, he grabbed the walking stick which was lying just out of the thief's reach.

"Hey, that's mine!" he protested and with renewed strength rolled over, knocking Lily off him.

He scrambled to his feet. Instead of retaliating, he quickly retrieved the canvas bag he took from the bank. He turned around and glared at Tim. That's when Tim realized just how young the guy was. He had to be at least eighteen since he was in jail but his face looked as if it had never seen a razor, it was smooth. The guy lunged for the walking stick but Tim pulled it away just in time.

"Where did you get this?" Tim demanded.

"What's it to ya'?"

"This belongs to my father," Tim answered. "Where did you get it?"

"Chill man, I didn't steal it!"

"No one said you did. I only want to know where you found it."

"Why should I tell you; you aint no police."

"How do you know?"

He cocked his head and slowly grinned but didn't answer.

"Let's just say if you tell me, I'll forget that you stole that from the bank." Tim nodded at the bag.

The boy thought about it for a moment. Tim hoped he wouldn't think too much because, he had no back up plan.

"All right," he answered. Tim silently sighed in relief. "I found it by the cemetery off Main. It was just lying on the ground."

"When? When did you find it?"

"Man, I don't know, two, maybe three days ago?"

"Thanks."

Before Tim could ask anything else, the young man took off running and disappeared up Second Avenue.

"Three days ago," Lily repeated sounding a bit worried, which Tim thought was sweet of her. "You don't think—"

"Let's go check it out," Tim said. They headed back toward Main.

"What would your dad be doing at the cemetery?" Lily asked while she kept pace beside Tim.

"Maybe he remembered his parents are buried there? I don't know. With Alzheimer's he sometimes has moments of clarity, so maybe he went there. Or maybe he became lost on his way back home.

"Oh, before I forget, you were quite something back there."

She looked at him with a slight bit of confusion.

"The way you took that boy down," Tim said. "I also heard what he said to you while you were hitting him."

"Yeah, well, what can I say, he had it coming," she explained and took his arm again.

Tim smiled and they pressed on.

When they reached the entrance to the cemetery they stopped to catch their breaths.

"How will we find him in there?" Lily asked. "This place is so big."

"We'll start at my grandparents' graves then search from there, I guess."

That's one thing about cemeteries, Tim thought, *there aren't a lot of trees to block the view*. Although, without the groundskeeper's interference, a few wild trees had sprouted and grown up over the past twenty-whatever years but the view was still pretty clear.

They followed the broken blacktop road to the top of the hill by the mausoleum. Tim stopped and his breath caught. A dark figure was curled up near his grandparents' graves.

"Dad!" he yelled and rushed toward the curled up figure.

When Tim drew nearer, the man slowly raised his head and looked at him. Tim knelt down beside him.

"Dad, it's me, Timmy."

Philip looked at his son without any sign of recognition.

"Where's your coat, Dad?" he asked while he looked his father over. The knees of Philip's slacks were torn and stained with grass and dried blood. His shirt was torn. There were bits of leaves, twigs and pine tree needles in his silvery grey hair. He had a bruise on his cheek and Tim instantly thought of the boy.

"Are you hurt?" he asked out of habit but realized his

father wouldn't answer. Tim touched his dad's hand, Philip felt cold. Quickly, Tim slipped off his jacket and put it around his father, sitting him up.

"Do you think you can stand up?"

Philip started to make an attempt and Tim helped him to his feet. Lily held out his walking stick. Philip grabbed it and stared at her. Tim recognized the look; his father was trying to figure out whom she was and if he should know her.

"Let's find him something to drink," Tim told Lily. He looked around and spotted the water faucet by the side of the road. "There!"

"I'll check it," Lily volunteered and ran ahead. She turned it on. The water sputtered at first then turned into a steady stream. Tim could see it was rusty.

"Let it run a while," he instructed while he ushered his father toward it.

Philip moved a lot slower and seemed stiffer. They inched across the grass. By the time they reached the faucet, the water was running clear. Tim looked around for something to use as a cup but Philip stepped forward and stooped down a bit. With one hand on his walking stick and the other on the water pipe, he began drinking straight from the spout as if it were a drinking fountain. After he had his fill, he straightened up. Water dripped from his chin but he didn't seem to notice.

"Better?" Tim asked.

Philip nodded.

"Let's go home." Tim held out his arm to his dad. Philip grabbed hold.

"We can cut across the cemetery," Lily suggested. "I know a shortcut."

"That would be great."

Tim and Philip slowly made their way across the

cemetery following Lily. She led them through a narrow stand of trees and across the pioneer section of the cemetery. They bent down and made their way through the laurel and out onto the highway. At that point, Philip stopped to rest. The trio made it back to the farm just when the sun had started to set.

While Lily took Philip into the house, Tim grabbed the potato fork and rushed out back. He dug up a few more potatoes and found some other wild vegetables. As he walked onto the back porch, he remembered his mom's secret hiding place built into the wall across from washer and dryer. She once told him, after Dad was diagnosed, that she hid knick-knacks and other mementoes in there that she feared might get broken.

Tim set the vegetables down on the top of the dryer and turned around. To everyone else it looked like an ordinary wooded plank wall. Tim reached out and gave it a slight push. He heard a click and the door popped open. To his surprise but as he hoped, instead of trinkets, he found food. She had been hoarding a secret stash of food. *Thank you, mom,* he thought and quietly laughed.

The cupboard was organized, just as Tim expected. The top shelf was filled with jars of dried beans, lentils, rice and macaroni noodles. The next shelf had jars of canned corn, string beans, beets, peas, squash, spinach and even a couple jars of local honey that looked dark as molasses and appeared to have gone bad. On the next shelf were cans of Spam, corned beef and tuna fish. The cans of tomato sauce on the bottom shelf were bloated and rusted. *Those are definitely bad.* Before closing the door, Tim grabbed a can of corned beef and a can of spam to see if they were still good. For now, he decided to keep the cupboard a secret.

When he entered the kitchen, Tim was greeted by the

sound of television static. He set everything down on the counter beside the sink. The can of Spam fell onto the floor. Lily walked into the kitchen just when he stood back up. She immediately spotted the can.

"Wow! Where did you find that?"

"In the barn," Tim lied.

"Guess I should have looked harder."

"So, what's my dad doing?"

"He found the remote and is flipping through the channels. They're all like that, nothing but static."

"That's okay, I don't know if he really watches it or if it's just a habit to have it on for the noise."

After washing the vegetables and putting them on the stove to cook, Tim searched the cupboards to see what spices he could find. He found an unopened jar of pepper and another of salt. After digging a bit more, he also found a bottle of Mrs. Dash's Imitation Butter Sprinkle. He pulled off the foil seal and sprinkled a little out to taste it. It wasn't too bad. Next he opened the can of corned beef. Lily made a face and cringed.

"You don't like corned beef?" he asked her.

"When was the expiration date on that?"

Tim looked at the label. "I don't know." He gave the contents a sniff. "Still smells okay. Here, you want to try some?"

"No!" she shrieked and took a step back.

"What's the worst it could be? If it tastes bad, spit it out."

"You try it then."

Tim took a fork and cut off a small piece. He smelled it again. It smelled like corned beef still. He touched it with his tongue to get a taste. "Seems okay," he reported. "Here goes nothing." He put it in his mouth and chewed it before swallowing. "Tastes good." He smiled and held out the fork to her.

"No, I'll stick with the veggies," she said, still leery.

That evening while they sat in the kitchen and ate their meal, Philip didn't put up his usual argument that he wasn't hungry. He ate and then went to his bedroom and closed the door. Tim did notice that his father didn't ask about Della or say anything at all. It worried him. *Was his Alzheimer's getting worse?* Tim waited a little while before going to check on him.

Standing at the bedroom door, Tim knocked lightly.

Philip didn't answer.

Quietly Tim opened the door a crack and looked in. Philip was fast asleep under the covers. Tim closed the door and returned to the kitchen. Lily had already washed the pans and dishes.

"How is he?"

"He's asleep. I don't think he's been awake all that long."

"What makes you say that?"

"If he were awake as long as that boy said, he would be in worse shape. People can go without food about three weeks, but without water a person would die in three days. No, I think that guy was lying and judging from the bruise on my dad's face, I think he stole the walking stick."

"Well, he's home now," Lily said and leaned against sink. "And no one's going to hurt him. So, what's next?"

"I don't know. My mom is still in that place," Tim answered and sat down at the breakfast table. "I just don't understand it. Why hasn't everybody been woken up? The plan was that we would be in suspended animation for twenty years. From the looks of things we were asleep a lot longer than that."

Lily's face registered shock as though she hadn't thought of that before. She glanced out the window over the sink and then turned back to around. "You really think so?"

"Yes, I do," Tim answered. "Another thing, where are the two people who were running the SAC?"

Lily shook her head and shrugged her shoulders.

"You know what also doesn't make sense; we still have electricity and yet there isn't anything on the TV. No news reports. No nothing. There aren't even cars on the road or people from outside Hillsboro passing through town."

"Hey, you're right," Lily said sounding surprised. She walked over and sat down in the chair across the table from him. "What if you go back and wake everyone up—"

"Me? I don't know anything about it."

"Well, maybe you could check around. See if you could find those guys or maybe there are some instructions somewhere? I can stay here with your dad."

Tim looked at her and couldn't help but remember when he was her age. Life was so simple then. He wished it were that easy now.

"Okay, I'll go have a look."

Day Three. The next morning, just after sun up, Tim headed off to the SAC, leaving his dad at home with Lily. Philip was still asleep.

When he reached the end of his parents' road, he realized he was either becoming more used to the walk or his strength had finally returned. Still, he wished his Bug was running. Everything on it that he knew to check, the solar tiles, the solid rubber tires, appeared fine. It just didn't have any power. Before leaving Lily helped him push it out into the driveway. *Maybe a few hours the sun will reenergize the fuel cell.*

Walking up to the SAC Tim noticed that someone had broken out the windows on the First Avenue side. Inside he found a landscape brick lying on the lobby floor amid shards of glass. Someone was either upset over something or had a strange way of getting their kicks. Either way the act didn't make any sense to him.

Tim pressed the elevator button and the doors opened immediately. He stepped in and touched the button for the fifth floor. The doors closed and he felt the car start to rise. To his surprise and horror, it stopped on the second floor. Feeling a bit fearful, Tim stepped to the front corner by the buttons. The doors opened but there was no one waiting. He decided to have a look around.

The hallway looked the same as the one on the fifth floor. A reception desk was directly in front of the elevators. It was covered in dust but he noticed there were finger prints. Someone had gone through the drawers already.

He headed down the hallway toward the back of the building and opened the first door on the right. It was a large room filled with sleep chambers. He decided to have a look. Down the first aisle, he saw people still asleep in suspended animation in their tubes. Above each tube lights pulsated.

When he reached the end of the first aisle, Tim rounded the corner and started back up another. Immediately he noticed something that didn't look right. A couple of the tubes were empty, the lights above, dark. *The people must be awake.* Then he noticed the tube across from them. The lights above it were out. The glass door looked as if someone had tried to pry it open and inadvertently knocked it off its track. Tim looked at the little girl inside. She lay crumpled at the bottom of the chamber, her head resting against the glass. Tim's breath caught as the realization hit him. He stumbled back and bumped into the unoccupied chamber behind him, his eyes fixed on the little girl.

Stop looking at her! She's dead. He heard a voice in his head shout.

Pulling himself away, he kept walking, looking up at the lights and then at each person asleep inside. He didn't recognize any of them. Even after reading the nameplates beside each chamber, still no recognition. At the end of the row, he noticed another tube where the lights above were dark but there was still someone inside. The man appeared to be sleeping but his skin is pallid. *He's dead.* Tim looked at the tube. It appeared to be fine; but then he noticed a small hairline crack in the glass about half an inch long near the top. *Possibly from someone stumbling and falling against it,* he reasoned. Whatever happened, it killed the man. He thought of the row where his mother still slept. There were chambers with people asleep beyond hers. He quickly hurried to the elevator.

While Tim waited he made a mental note: *Trying to force open the tube is not the way to wake the occupant.*

When he reached the fifth floor, he nearly ran to the room where he left his mother. He needed to see her; to be sure she was still okay. To his relief, he saw the lights above her tube were still blinking. Her skin still had its normal pinkish shade. He touched the glass and wished she would wake up.

After a few minutes of staring at her, hoping her eyes would open; he turned away and decided to have a look around. He found four empty tubes one aisle over and read their nameplates: John Bjorge, Anna, George and Godfrey. He recognized them immediately. John was not only a friend of the family but his parents' neighbor. He owned a mechanic shop in town. If they'd gone home and were still there, maybe John would help him get his Bug going.

He started back to the lobby feeling excited and hopeful. Once in the elevator he noticed the buttons for the five basement levels. Still wanting to find the people who were supposed to wake everyone, he pushed the button for the lowest level.

The elevator stopped and the doors opened. Immediately he was hit by the sound of machines running. He took a quick look around but there wasn't anyone on this level, just the ventilation systems doing their job and huge generators that sat idle. He took the elevator up to the next floor.

The fourth basement level was different. The elevator doors opened to a large room. Black leather office lounge chairs and a small couch sat against the wall opposite the elevator. On either end of the wall was a door. The one on the right was the men's room and the one on the left, the ladies room.

Tim stepped out. It was quieter but there was still a humming sound coming from a door to the right. He noticed a sign on the door and went to check it out. Mainframe Room Authorized Personnel Only, the sign said. *Oh, that's right, this is the computer level.* He headed up to the third level.

When he the elevator doors opened Tim was struck by a faint, putrid odor. It brought back memories of finding a dead possum in the field behind the barn when he was a kid. He decided to check it out even though he was a bit fearful of what he might find.

Lower Level Three seemed to be set up like the floors above. A reception counter sat in front of the elevators. A hallway stretched in both directions running parallel to Main Street outside. At the end of the hall, he noticed a door that didn't look right. The odor became stronger the closer he came to the broken door. He covered his nose and mouth with his coat sleeve but the stench was still gut-wrenching.

The lock on the door had been pried open. Tim gave it a

gentle push and it swung open freely. Inside was a sleep chamber room unlike those on the upper floors. This room was more opulent. The sleep chambers that lined the walls faced the center of the room. The floor was carpeted but Tim couldn't tell the color through the dust. A large, round, dark green velvet, tufted sofa-bench sat in the center of the room. A large arrangement of fake flowers sat on top of the center back. Above it a crystal chandelier hung from the ceiling. *I could have used that when I woke up.*

Standing in the doorway, Tim knew right away that everyone was dead. Whoever had broken into this room had smashed the glass of every tube. *Why would they do that?* Holding his breath he entered the room to check the brass nameplates affixed to the wall between each chamber. He tried to avoid looking at the bodies but he couldn't help not seeing them. Some were children and women. He read each nameplate and finally found one I recognized: Jose de Angelo. *The Mayor!* He found another, Franklin Green. *The chief of police.* Then another, Donald O'Rourke. *The Washington County Sheriff.*

Tim began to panic realizing this was no random act. These defenseless people were targeted specifically. He started to back out of the room when he tripped on something and fell. He dropped his coat when he hit the floor but grabbed it and covered his mouth and nose. He looked around to see what had tripped him and noticed a three foot long metal pipe. He felt his stomach churn and scrambled to his feet. He reached the hall right when he became sick.

How could this happen? Where were the heads of the SAC? Why didn't they stop this?

Tim didn't wait for the elevator. He took the stairs to the second basement level. Judging from the undisturbed dust on this floor, it appeared that no one had ventured there. *Perhaps whoever murdered the city's officials knew where to find them?*

The second basement level surprised Tim. It was different from the others. The hallway seemed wider and was made to look like a narrow street with a sidewalk on either side. It was all an illusion, just creative painting. When he saw the mural on the inside wall he realized this was the floor he was looking for, the one where the two heads of the SAC lived and worked. He remembered seeing it in the video but seeing it for real was more impressive and intriguing, like walking down Main Street at Disneyland.

Fake façades of old houses lined the outside walls complete with windows with curtains and lights by the front doors.

Windows, how odd.

Tim stepped up to the first window and peeked inside. To his surprise it was a bedroom. He quickly backed away, feeling like a Peeping Tom. Then he noticed a sign above the door, "Wilson's Fine Furniture." *It's not an apartment. It's a furniture store.* He felt less embarrassed. He took a look in the next window and saw it had living room furniture. *What great attention to detail, they thought of everything.*

In the central core on this level, he found a small movie theater, a fitness gym, library and a grocery store that required a keycard to enter. The outer wall on the east side, beside the furniture store, was a locked door with a façade that looked like a real house complete with a mailbox with the name, Dr. Robert Anderson on it. The outer west wall had a house façade also and the mailbox read, Dr. Michelle Dever.

Tim still had not found anyone. He knocked on the doors of both residences but no one answered. He turned the corner along the south wall and saw an office sign hanging above a door almost in the center. He practically ran to the door.

The wall around the door was decorated to look like a country doctor's office. A paned glass window with curtains hid the wall behind it. The sign above the door had the name of Dr. Michelle Dever painted on it.

He tried the doorknob and was surprised to find it was unlocked. "Hello?" he called and opened it and immediately fell back a step. Lying in the middle of the office floor were the skeletal remains of a body. Unlike downstairs, there was no putrid odor to warn him. When he recovered from the shock, he slowly approached the office.

The carpet beneath the bones was dark and discolored. The body's clothing was nothing more than remnants of rotted fabric. He noticed a plastic ID badge and kicked it, flipping it over. It was discolored but he could still make out a few letters. It was Michelle's. *The bones must be all that's left of her.*

He noticed an interior doorway across from the entrance. This time he approached it with caution.

This must have been her private office. A large desk stood in the middle of the room. A lamp and a computer monitor sat in one corner; a framed photograph in the other. There was an opened log book and a pen in the middle of the desktop. *She must have been working on something.* On the wall behind the desk hung a dusty painting of a narrow river with jagged mountaintops in the background. Tim looked down at the carpet and his breath caught again. On the floor, behind the desk, were the remains of another body and a corroded pistol nearby.

Tim approached to the desk, careful of where he stepped. He took the book to read later. When he closed it, a paper fell out onto the floor. He picked it up and read its one line message: Oh God, what have I done? *What an odd thing to write.*

He turned around to leave and noticed a bookshelf behind the door filled with large blue binders. He read the labels on the spines. They were manuals about the computers, the ventilation system, and other important topics but nothing about the suspended animation process that he could find. He noticed binder fourteen was missing. How long, he had no way of knowing but the absence of dust where it was supposed to be made him think it had been removed fairly recently. He took a few minutes and searched the office, checking the desk drawers but nothing. It wasn't there. He searched the outer office and its bookcase as well but came up empty. He was about to leave when he heard the elevator bell ping. The sound sent a wave of panic through him. Still clutching the log book from the desk, he grabbed both ID badges and rushed back into the hall. The elevators were about twenty feet away. He spotted the door leading to stairwell in the opposite direction and made a dash for them. He ducked into the stairwell and raced up the stairs, not looking back.

He didn't stop running until he reached Dennis Avenue. He wanted to put as much distance as possible between him and whoever that may have been. After catching his breath, he walked back to the farm. While walking he thumbed through the logbook, reading random entries.

December 25th, Day 2606. Today is our seventh Christmas. Robert and I had an argument. I think the solitude is getting to him. He wanted to wake up some of our guests. I suggested he call Chuck in Forest Grove if he wanted to talk to someone else.

January 17th, Day 2629. A strong thunderstorm is battering the building. I checked the cameras and there appears to be a fire by the airport. I don't think it will pose any danger to us here. The heavy rains should take care of it.

April 21st, Day 2720. It's been three days since we have had any contact with the Forest Grove SAC. Robert tried to raise them using Skype and his cell but to no avail. I contacted Aloha. They made an attempt but no response.

November 10th, Day 2927. We still haven't had any word from Forest Grove and now we have lost contact with Aloha as well. Portland Downtown is not responding either. I sent an urgent message to Washington, D.C. and am waiting for their instructions. Robert thinks we should take a drive to check it out but our orders are that we not leave the building.

December 17th, Day 2964. Robert took the Hummer and drove to Forest Grove. I don't know what repercussions this will have on the environment. I guess time will tell. He was supposed to be back an hour ago.

December 20th, Day 2967. Robert finally returned. The news isn't good. It appears that an explosion on the ventilation level ripped through the Forest Grove SAC followed by a fire. There were no survivors. The entire population of Forest Grove is gone. God rest their souls.

February 13th, Day 3022. Robert is beginning to show signs of mental fatigue. He's on edge most of the time and I've caught him talking to himself while he's making his rounds.

March 1st, Day 3037. Robert has snapped. I've had to give him a sedative to calm him. I sent another urgent message to D.C. but still haven't heard from them. They haven't even responded to my first message sent last November so I don't hold out much hope.

Tim was nearly home when he stopped reading. He couldn't believe the government wouldn't have tested these people to make sure they could handle being alone for this long or at least given them a backup plan. He decided not to tell Lily what he'd seen. *Well, at least not everything.* There was no sense in frightening her until he found out more.

"We will have to wait until I find the missing binder or everyone wakes up on their own," he explained at dinner. "If we try to wake them, we risk killing them."

"Where's your mother?" Philip asked, catching Tim off guard.

"She's away for the night," Tim answered and hoped his dad would be okay with that. Two minutes later Philip asked again and then again. Tim reminded himself that his father had put up with his asking the same question over and over when he was little, so he could to show the same love and patience. For the most part, Philip didn't seem aware of what happened to the world outside. Tim imagined it is one blessing of his father's disease.

EPISODE II:
ALOHA

Tim wiped the sweat from his forehead and leaned against the shovel handle for support. His back ached and his blistered hands stung. Burying the dead was hard work even with the use of the backhoe they borrowed from the Kubota tractor lot next door to the cemetery. John Bjorge was a miracle worker when it came to fixing engines and his twin sons, George and Godfrey, were equally good with the new technology of power cells and solar tiles.

Eighteen years before everyone went to sleep oil wells around the world had dried up. For decades the auto industry had been gradually switching to electric engines but they still relied on gasoline. It wasn't until the invention of a new power cell and the lack of sufficient gasoline that they were forced to make a complete switch.

Everyone was thrilled. The new power cells were smaller than the previous batteries that were used and lighter. They also lasted longer and didn't require a gasoline back-up system. Still, there were old hybrids out there and some gas guzzlers but even in Hillsboro, Power Cell Stations, PCS's, had begun to replace the old gas stations.

The whole subject of engines mechanics seemed way too complicated. Tim never understood how it all worked. When he was a kid his father tried to teach him using a simple lawn mower engine. Even though Tim grasped a few things, most of what his father said went over his head. He preferred to pay someone to work on his Bug instead of attempting to do it himself.

"Do you think we should say something?" Anna Bjorge, John's wife, asked when the last square of sod was put back in place over the mass grave.

Anna was a gentle lady, kind and soft spoken. She was pretty in her day but time and a life of hard work had taken its toll. The same could be said of John. He was a burly man, six foot two and barrel chested. His thick black hair was nearly gone. He and Philip were the same age, mid-sixties, though since being placed in suspended animation for God knows how long, how old any of them were, was still up for debate.

Even though Anna and John immigrated to the states right after they were married, Anna retained a heavy Norwegian accent. John's accent was faint. Tim suspected that working with the public in his mechanic shop had helped to soften it. Either that or Tim had become used to hearing him and could understand him better.

Instead of answering his wife, John looked at Tim.

"Uh, sure, I guess so," Tim answered, giving a shrug and feeling a bit awkward. Tim wasn't an overly religious sort. He stopped going to church when he was twenty-four, about the same time his dad was diagnosed and the priest quit coming to visit.

While the others bowed their heads and Anna said a prayer, Tim looked at the mass grave. They had searched the main office for the map of the cemetery in order to find unused land but the only map they found was too faded to read. So they decided to dig the huge grave in the lawn in front of the office. John figured no one would have been buried there and he was right. Anna logged the names of the dead and left the list in the office for the caretaker, for whenever he woke up.

That evening when Tim returned to the farmhouse, Philip was sitting on the porch steps with Lily. He hadn't mentioned Tim's mom again or said much of anything since Day Seven. It worried Tim to think that maybe the stress from waking up from suspended animation and the world looking so different caused his Alzheimer's to progress; or that something happened to him between the time he woke up and when Tim found him. Physically, however, Philip seemed to be doing fine. The bruise on his cheek had faded but was still visible.

Lily jumped up when she saw Tim. "Hi. Is that the last of them?"

"Yeah," Tim nodded. "Hi, dad."

Philip looked at Tim with his faded eyes and nodded. Tim thought he even saw a slight smile.

"Have you two eaten?" Tim asked Lily.

"I fixed him some of those dried beans you found but he only took a bite and then wouldn't eat anymore," she answered. "Would you like some?"

"Sure."

Lily went inside. Tim turned and looked at his dad.

"You want to come inside, Dad?"

Philip stared at him. He appeared to be thinking over what Tim had said, but Tim couldn't be sure. Without saying a word, Philip tightened his grip on his gnarled walking stick and stood up. Slowly he climbed the steps to the porch, opened the door and went inside. Tim noticed his father's left foot seemed to drag a bit.

"Dad, are you okay?" he asked while Philip shuffled across the front room to his chair. He turned and sat down.

"Please, Dad, say something."

"What do you want me to say?" he asked with shocking clarity.

It caught Tim off guard. He stammered. "Nothing, I was just wondering if you were feeling okay?"

Philip patted his chest and stomach. "I guess so," he answered.

"Good." Tim said with a smile. However, the foot thing was new. He worried it was a sign of something more serious. *Mom, I wish you were awake. You'd know what to do.*

When Tim turned to head to the kitchen, he heard the television click on and the sound of static. *He's found the remote.*

Standing in the doorway to the kitchen, Tim watched Lily. She had proven to be such a godsend. Not only had she helped him find his dad but she also looked after him while he made his daily trips to the SAC. That was why he picked a nice spot in the cemetery for her family, away from the mass grave. He wanted to give them as proper a burial as he could, a sort of thank you to her.

It took a moment for Tim to wash up before he sat down to the kitchen table. The aroma in the kitchen smelled delicious and Tim's stomach growled with approval. He looked at the bowl of red beans and eagerly took a bite.

"Tell me what you think," Lily said.

A sudden feeling of déjà vu struck him, only this time he was his dad and Lily was him.

"What's wrong?" Lily asked, dropping down in the chair across the table from Tim.

Tim picked up a napkin and discreetly spit the beans out. "How long did you cook them?" he asked.

"I let them boil for a minute or two."

"I knew it," Tim said with a laugh. Lily looked horrified. "It's okay. I'm not laughing at you. I'm laughing at myself. You see, when I was a teenager my mother had to go to California for a week to help her parents. While she was gone, I was in charge of the cooking. On Sunday, I invited my dad's parents over for an early dinner of beans and cornbread, Dad's favorite. I took out a big pan and filled it with water and dumped the beans in it. While they cooked I made the cornbread. It all took less than an hour.

"Everyone sat down to eat. I brought out the bean pot and set it in the middle of the table. I was so proud. I watched them each dish themselves up a big bowl. When they took a bite, you should have seen their faces."

"Why? What happened?" Lily asked.

"Grandma asked for some butter for the cornbread and while I was gone, she secretly dumped their bowls back into the pot. When I came back with the butter, they all pretended to be finished. I sat down and dished up a bowl and took a bite. That's when everyone broke out laughing. The beans were not cooked. Grandma explained that dried beans like these need to cook for hours."

"Hours?" Lily repeated and glanced at the stove.

"Yeah." Tim nodded and they both laughed.

Day Fifteen. Tim woke early, right as the sun was coming up over Mt. Hood and the Cascades. He was beginning to enjoy watching the morning sky while sitting on the front porch with a cup of hot water. What would make it perfect would be if he had a cup of *real* coffee. What he found in the cupboard didn't survive. It had lost most of its flavor and only lasted a few days.

Lily walked out on the porch. "Morning."

"Morning," Tim answered.

"Your dad still asleep?"

"Yeah. Oh, I'd like to go back into town today. I want to check on my mom and look around the SAC some more for that missing book. Are you good to watch my dad?"

"Of course," she answered and smiled. "It's not like I have anywhere I need to be."

"You do know, Lily, if you ever need or want to go anywhere, you just have to tell me. It's fine if you'd rather not stay here."

"Oh, I know. I'm fine. I like it here. Besides, finding that book and waking everyone up is more important."

"Thanks." Tim wanted to lean over and kiss her but stopped himself, remembering what she had told him.

Before heading into town, he stopped next door at the Bjorges' farm to see if John or George were able to figure out what was wrong with his VW Bug. Letting it sit in the sun didn't recharge the power cell as he had hoped.

Tim paused when he saw the three of them, John, George and Godfrey, laughing and working in their barn. A flood of memories filled his head. George, Godfrey and Tim had gone all through school together. They were best friends but seeing them with their dad who was healthy and strong, stung a little. Tim hated it but he was jealous. He would give anything to have his dad back the way he used to be. Even if it meant being reminded that he never quite measured up to the son his father wanted. At least his dad would be okay.

Anna, Mrs. Bjorge, came out of the house and saw Tim standing in the middle of their driveway.

"Morning, Tim. Why are you just standing there? Come in." She called and waved.

When they were at the cemetery, Anna had told Tim that she was the first in their family to wake up. Listening to her explain what she did made Tim think she was unfazed by the changes in the world. At least she never mentioned any of the differences. Tim was still in awe over them. Anna explained after regaining her strength and seeing John and the twins still asleep, she walked back home and resumed her normal routine of cleaning and cooking. A day or so later the twins woke. They joined her at the farm and waited for their dad. He woke up thirteen days ago, two days after Tim had.

Come to think of it, none of them talked about how they felt or what they thought about being placed in suspended animation. Even when Tim asked them for help with burying the dead, they just treated it as any other odd job they did and kept their feelings and thoughts to themselves.

John reopened his auto repair shop in his barn and as far as Tim knew, he was John's first and only customer.

"Hi, Mrs. Bjorge," Tim greeted. "I just stopped by to check on my Bug."

"John's in the barn," she told him. "Be sure and stop by for some biscuits before going home."

"I'm going into town but if it's okay, I'll stop later."

"Sure," Anna smiled and went back into the house.

"Hey, Tim," John said, looking up from under the hood of the VW. "I thought I heard your voice."

"How's it coming? Think it'll run again?" Tim asked and walked over to the barn.

"Oh sure," he laughed. "As long as I can get a good charge in this old power cell, it should be running like new. I found some solar tiles to replace the ones that didn't make it."

He nodded at the roof of the Bug. "I haven't reconnected them yet. We'll know more in a couple days."

"Great

The sound of metal grinding caused Tim to look up from his Bug. In the back of the barn, George and Godfrey were working on what resembled an old flatbed truck. Tim recognized it immediately. John used to drive it up and down the street all the time. He built it from the chassis up. There was no outer shell, just wooden planks for a floor and a bench for a front seat. The old engine, built from scrap parts, sat next to a large trunk-sized first generation, power fuel cell. Two large solar panels covered it all like the hood on a truck. *A grown man's go-cart*, Tim thought with a silent laugh.

"Sounds like they're getting close to getting her started," he commented.

John looked over his shoulder at his sons, or his truck, Tim couldn't be sure, and grinned proudly. His round, grease-smudged face and stocky build made Tim think of the Michelin Man from the old tire commercials. John scratched his head beneath his black wool cap.

"If anyone can get ol' Bessie going again, those boys can," he said proudly. "There. We'll leave this hooked up to the charger for a couple days. Be sure to say a prayer the power holds out."

"What do you mean, holds out? Isn't the power company back up and running?"

"Not necessarily," John answered. "Do you see any power company trucks out checking on the lines?"

"No."

"That's my point. If the company were up and running, the first thing they would do is send out trucks to check on the status of their lines. No, I think we're running on back up cells and reserves from the solar panels and wind turbines the power company set up. Right now we are feeding off them but the more people who wake up and the more power they draw, we run the risk of losing power all together. Should that happen before everyone wakes up, I'm afraid our grave digging days aren't over."

Suddenly Tim felt sick.

Walking to town, all he could think about were John's last words. *Surely the government would have thought about that and made some provision.* The memory of seeing the generators on Lower Level Five popped in his head. He made a mental note to check on them when he reached the SAC.

As had become his custom, Tim took a tour of each of the fifteen floors of the center checking each suspended animation chamber and marking the empty chambers to keep track of any new people who had awakened. It had been three days since the last person woke up.

Tim headed back to the fifth floor to visit with his mom.

Della looked so calm and peaceful. Her cheeks still had their pinkish hue. Her grey streaked, auburn hair was still neatly pulled back in a bun the way it was when she went to sleep. Tim glanced at the blinking lights above her tube for reassurance. They were still working.

When he first came to visit, he just sat on the floor of his chamber across from her. He couldn't remember when he actually started talking to her. Even though he knew she probably couldn't hear him through the glass, it still brought him a measure of comfort. Besides, no one else was around.

"Hi Mom," he said and took his seat. "I'm still looking for a way to wake you and everyone else up. Oh, Mr. Bjorge is trying to get my Bug running again. He thinks maybe in a day or two. Dad's doing okay. He's still dragging his left foot a bit.

I'm not sure if he's tired or if it's something more serious. I haven't noticed anything else, other than he's been a lot quieter since he woke up. Lily is with him right now.

"Oh, Mom, I can't wait for you to meet her. She's really nice and has the cutest laugh. She has been a real help to me. She watches Dad while I'm here. Oh, I suppose I told you that, already? Dad seems to be okay with her. Though at first he would just stare at her and not say a word."

Tim stood up and walked over to his mother's chamber. He touched the glass of the tube. "Well, I have to go. I'll come back and see you again. I love you, momma."

Once in the elevator Tim pressed the button for Lower Level Five, he wanted to check on the generators. The carriage vibrated while it started to descend. Tim felt it in his stomach. He hated elevators as much as he did heights, another thing he talked to his counselor about.

Nervously he fumbled with the ID badges in his pocket while he watched the lighted numbers above the button panel count down. Changing his mind, he reached up and pushed the button for Lower Lever Two just in time. The carriage stopped and bounced a bit causing Tim to grab the handrail attached to the wall. The doors opened to the level that housed the apartments and offices of the two administrators of the SAC. He headed back to the office where he had found their remains and the log book. Remembering the binders, he wondered if one of them would have information on the back-up system.

The outer office still gave Tim the creeps. Even though Doctor Dever's remains were gone, there was still the dark stain on the carpet where she lay for who knows how long. He carefully stepped around it and headed into her back office. The bookshelf was against the wall behind the door. It didn't take long to find what he was looking for. He flipped through the yellowed pages. The government had anticipated a possible power failure and had indeed installed generators and additional back-up power cells in the lowest level of the building.

"Good," he said out loud.

Slipping the binder into his messenger bag, he decided to check out the two apartments. The missing binder had to be in one of them.

When he reached the first door, he pulled Dr. Robert Anderson's badge out of his pocket and held it up to the magnetic sensor. He heard a click and the lock released.

The door opened into a tiled entryway. Tim switched on the lights.

"Oh my god," Tim gasped when he glanced to the left into the small kitchen. "This guy was a real slob." Dirty dishes were piled high on every flat surface and in the sink. A layer of dust coated the greasy cabinets and ceiling.

"Cleanliness means different things to different people. Not everyone is as particular as you. However, for you it's more about needing approval, your father's approval to be exact," Tim's therapist's words filled his ears. To a degree she was probably right. Tim wasn't interested in farming. It seemed like a lot of work for so little a reward. Nor was he into fixing engines and stuff like his dad was. He wanted a more secure job and one that didn't follow him home or consume his life. His dad never understood and would shake his head and give Tim *the look*.

Tim fought the urge to start cleaning and pulled himself away from the kitchen. He headed into the apartment. The small entry hall opened up into a large dining room/living room.

"Oh my god," he gasped again.

It was worse than the kitchen. Clothes, loose pages torn from binders and books and other trash covered every inch of the floor about two inches deep. Tim had to step up to enter the room. Near-empty bookcases lined the walls to his left and right in the dining room portion. Torn books were piled high on a large dining room table and overflowed onto the floor. In the living room, a sofa and strange leather chair sat facing an electric fireplace with a flat screen TV mounted on the wall above it. A few knick-knacks peeked out from under the dust and cobwebs on the narrow mantle. A stereo with an old turntable sat to the right of the fireplace. Bits of broken vinyl records were scattered among the rest of the trash on the floor.

Through a set of French doors, off the living room, Tim found the large master suite. An oversized king bed sat against the far wall on a platform with drawers on either side that had been pulled out and emptied. It appeared to Tim that someone had been looking for something. Clothes and more books covered the floor. Tim's foot slipped on something beneath the papers and clothes. He fell to the floor, hitting his head on something hard that was also buried. Curious as to what he hit, he dug through the clothes and found a strange, green, wooden box with a handle on the top and a lock on the side.

Could this have been what the person was looking for?

He stood up, grabbed the box and set it on the bed while he continued to look around the room for the missing manual. Right when he was about to give up, he spotted something blue peeking out from behind the dresser. With his heart beating faster with anticipation, he pulled the binder out. Most of spine label was torn off along with the number. He just knew this was the binder he was looking for. He opened it. A few loose papers fell out. The rest were gone. He looked at the papers that covered the floor. There were so many. *There was no way*

I could sort through all of them and even if I could, there was no guarantee the pages I needed would be there, he reasoned. *But I have to try.* He scooped up an armful of papers and dropped them on the unmade bed. Trying hard to focus and not think about how dirty the mattress must be, he began reading the headers on each paper and sorting them into piles.

Tim didn't know how long he spent sorting but he felt it was a long time. His eyes were starting to hurt. He looked around and realized he needed help. There was no way he could do this alone.

He grabbed one last armful of papers and noticed he had uncovered a laptop. It was in rough shape. The screen was cracked. There were spills of something on the keyboard. He stuffed it into his bag. *Maybe George will be able to get something off it.*

He started to leave the bedroom when he remembered the box. He grabbed it. It was heavier than he thought and with the walk ahead of him, he decided to look inside to see if it was worth lugging home. He tried the lock but it was strong. *I need to find the key. If what is in this box is important the key would be hidden.* He searched the room and didn't find anything. Feeling time slipping away, he decided to take the box and pry it open at home.

Back in the main hall outside the apartment, Tim breathed a sigh of relief. He tucked the box under his arm and headed down the hall. When he reached the corner, he stopped at a façade that look like an old-time gas station. Curious, he tried the ID badge. The lock clicked. Cautiously, he opened the door.

Lights switched on automatically. *Motion sensors.* To Tim's surprise, he found himself standing in an underground garage. Two, black Hummers were parked in the center of the room. Along the wall to his left was a long workbench with tools, what appeared to be engine parts and wiper blades hanging on hooks above it. To his right, a wall of metal shelves with boxes stacked on them. He took a closer look at the boxes. *Power cells! There must be twenty of them! I have to tell Mr. Bjorge.* Across the room were more shelves with solid rubber tires. Behind the Hummers, on the outer wall that faced First Avenue, were heavy steel garage doors and a man door.

Remembering that the doctor had taken one of the Hummers out for a spin, Tim walked over to the nearest one. The windows were tinted so he couldn't see inside. He tried the driver's door. It was unlocked. *Of course it is. Who's going to steal it? Me,* he heard his voice in his head answer.

Tim stopped and looked at the box in his hands. The realization that he was indeed stealing, taking something that didn't belong to him, hit him; but equally hard was the realization that he felt nothing, no remorse, no guilt, nothing. *What has happened to me? I would never have done this before. But is it really stealing if it's to help everyone?* He pushed the thoughts from his head. This was a conversation for a later time.

Before he talked himself out of it, he climbed behind the wheel. *Impressive. Nice leather seats, CD player, radio, lots of room in back. The government sure knows how to spend tax-payers' money.* He smiled when he imagined the look on George's and Godfrey's faces when they see him drive up in this. He found the keys hanging from the visor. He tried to start the engine. *Nothing.* He tried it a couple more times and still nothing. *Damn it!* Climbing out he made a mental note to talk to John about this place. The spare parts might come in handy if they were still good.

Deciding he had done enough sleuthing for one day, Tim headed back to the lobby. The sun had already begun to set. He had to hurry if he was going to make it back home before dark.

Carrying the box out in the open made him nervous. The gang who raped Lily was still out there and from what she told him, they had no qualms about stealing. With no way to conceal the box, his only option was to hurry. He picked up his pace. After a brief stop at the Bjorges' for biscuits to take home, he made it home as the last sliver of light dropped below the hills to the west.

Day Sixteen. The scent of brewing coffee woke Tim from a sound sleep. Sunlight was already pouring through the curtains of his bedroom window. He threw off the covers and headed downstairs.

"Good morning, sleepy head," a familiar voice greeted him when he walked into the kitchen.

He froze in the doorway.

"Mom?"

"Yes?" she answered and smiled at him.

She was standing in front of the stove dressed in her cherry patterned apron over her blue housedress. Her hair was neatly pulled back in a bun. She cracked another egg and emptied it into the frying pan.

"You're awake," Tim said in shock.

"Of course I am. I've been awake for hours. I thought you were going to sleep the day away. Sit down. Would you like some coffee?"

"Uh-h, sure," Tim said. He couldn't believe his eyes. He sat down at the kitchen table. Three plates with silverware were set in front of the three chairs. "How did you get home?" he asked.

"Don't be silly. Cream?" she smiled while she filled a cup with steaming hot coffee.

Tim poured a bit of cream into his cup and watched as it turned the dark brew into a warm brown. He stood up and wrapped his arms around her.

"I'm so glad you're awake," he said while tears streamed down his cheeks.

"Of course, dear," she said. "Now be careful. Don't spill the coffee."

"Tim," he heard a voice behind him.

"Lily?" Tim said and turned around but no one was there.

"Tim." He heard the voice again.

Suddenly he felt himself being shaken. He opened his eyes to see Lily standing over him.

"Wha—" he looked down and realized he was holding a pillow.

"Did you sleep on the couch all night?" she asked.

An overwhelming sinking feeling engulfed Tim's chest and brought tears to his eyes. *It was only a dream.* He sat up and put the pillow back on the sofa where it belonged.

"I guess so," he answered and dried his tears. "Any coffee?"

Lily crossed her arms in front of her and gave him a look that said, *really?*

Tim took an extra-long shower, letting the water wash away his tears. The dream had felt so real. He could have sworn he could taste the coffee, smell it. He felt his mother in his arms and then felt her slip away. *What could it all mean?* Tim turned the water off. He had to get back to the SAC and check on her, make sure she was still okay.

Toweling off he remembered he hadn't checked the

kitchen cupboards in the doctor's apartment. *Maybe there was something of use in them.* He decided to check it out.

"Feeling better?" Lily asked when Tim walked into the kitchen.

"A bit."

"If it helps, I know how you feel. I still dream about my parents and brothers. Then when I wake up to reality, it hurts all over again."

Tim suddenly felt foolish. Here he was lamenting over his mother still being asleep and there was Lily with her family who would never wake up. He gave her a hug while she stood in front of the sink.

"We'll be okay," he assured her.

"Yeah," she agreed weakly.

"I'd like to go back to town this morning? I want to check on a couple things I forgot. I won't be as long as I was yesterday. I should be back in a couple hours. Do you mind?"

"No, go. Your dad won't be awake until around noon anyway and I want to see if I can catch some of those chickens that are hiding out back by the pump house. I fixed the old chicken coop so if all goes as planned, maybe we'll have eggs again."

"Sounds good."

The SAC was quiet. Tim skipped his tour and headed straight to the fifth floor. Della was still sleeping soundly. The lights above her chamber were still blinking like the others. Now that Tim had verified that she was okay, he started to relax. In the shower the thought had occurred to him, *what if my dream was her saying good-bye.* He gently touched the glass in front of her.

"I love you, Mom. I'll find a way to wake you up. I

71

promise."

Turning away, he headed down to the doctor's apartment again.

Seeing the filth and the awful state of the kitchen again, Tim began to have second thoughts about finding anything of use in there. The first cupboard was nearly empty, just a few glasses and plates. The second cupboard was better. A few foil pouches of vegetables and ready-to-heat meals. He put them into his messenger bag. In the next cupboard he struck gold, a stash of unopened, one pound packages of ground coffee. He put all six into his bag. The messenger bag bulged and the strap dug into Tim's neck and shoulder but he didn't care. Thoughts of sipping fresh, hot coffee sustained him.

While he was there, Tim decided to have a look at the other apartment. After making sure the lock engaged on Dr. Anderson's door, he headed down the hall. Dr. Dever's apartment was on the opposite side of the floor. When he reached the corner he heard the elevator across from Dr. Dever's apartment ding. He flattened himself against the wall and listened. Around the corner ahead of him, he heard voices. Male voices. *Two, no three, no four of them.*

"Check those doors!" one of them ordered. His voice was deep and guff with a heavy Hispanic accent.

"It's locked," a younger voice said.

"Kick it in!" the first guy ordered.

Tim heard loud bangs that sounded like the younger guy was throwing himself at the steel door. The sound became louder as he was apparently joined by others.

"Forget it and try the next!"

"Hey, it's unlocked! It's someone's office." Tim realized they must have found Dr. Dever's office. They were moving away from him, along the south hall. Tim started to breathe again.

"See if there are any keys," someone yelled.

It sounded as though they were tearing the room apart. Tim could hear loud banging and draws slamming. This was his chance. He headed for the stairwell in the corner, back the way he'd come. Right before he reached it, the noise stopped and he heard them at the end of the hall. He stopped just in time, flattening himself against the wall again. He listened. The loud thumps from the men trying to break through locked doors drew nearer.

Tim turned around and ran for Dr. Dever's apartment.

"Did you hear that?" Tim heard one of them say when he reached her door.

"What?"

"Silencio!"

Oh my god, they heard me.

Tim fumbled with the keycards, his hands shaking. Quickly he pressed the card against the reader. It clicked.

"It sounded like it was this way."

The door opened and he slipped inside. The lock engaged when the metal door shut. Tim's pulse throbbed loudly in his ears while his hands continued to tremble. He pressed his back against the door and slid down until he sat on the floor.

"Try those doors again!"

The sound of the men banging against the doors drew nearer and nearer. Tim's heart thumped louder and faster. He tried to calm himself with a couple slow, deep breaths but it didn't work. They were headed for his door. He braced himself. The doorknob rattled. *Thank heaven it's fake, just for show.* The first thump shook the door.

"Try it again!" one of the men ordered.

"I think I dislocated my shoulder," a voice groaned.

"You little sissy, get out of the way!"

Thud! The door reverberated.

"Knock it off. You guys are just hearing things. There's no one and nothing here. Let's go," snapped the gruff man.

Tim listened while the sound of footsteps faded in the distance. The elevator ding was faint but he still heard it. *They left. I can relax.*

Once Tim's shaking subsided and his pulse returned to normal, he climbed to his feet and switched on the lights. To his surprise, the apartment was neat and, despite the layer of dust covering everything, fairly clean.

"Thank you, Dr. Dever," he whispered.

The floorplan was the same as Dr. Anderson's apartment: to the left of the front door was a modest-sized kitchen with pass-through into the dining room/living room in the back. The master bedroom suite was through two glass paned French doors to the right off the living room.

Tim searched the bookcases in the living room to see if she had a Binder Fourteen among her books. There was nothing, just fiction novels and photo albums, no blue binders anywhere. *Guess she didn't bring her work home with her.*

He went into her bedroom. A brass bed sat with the headboard against the wall opposite the doors, just like Dr. Anderson's bed. A dresser with a large mirror sat to the right of the doors at an angle. The position and the wasted space behind the dresser woke up Tim's OCD. He suppressed it and began to quickly check the drawers.

"I'm sorry," I apologized to her, "but I have to."

On one of her nightstands Tim noticed a framed photograph of a man in a soccer uniform with a soccer ball under his arm. He was smiling at the camera. There was something about him that looked familiar but Tim didn't have time to dwell on it.

He made a thorough of her apartment before heading back to the kitchen. Finding a canvas shopping bag in a drawer, he filled it with the contents of her food cabinet. Finally, he was ready to leave.

When he walked into the foyer, it came to him. The man in the photograph was Isaac Dever, the captain of the Portland Timbers. He was shot and killed by a member of a rival team after the Timbers won the MLS Cup. They tried to make it look like a random drive-by shooting but witnesses were able to identify the man responsible. *Isaac must have been the doctor's husband.*

Tim put his ear near the door and listened for any sound of the men outside before switching off the light and slipping into the hall.

He wasted no time and headed for the garage. The stairs would be too risky and so would the elevator. There was no telling where the intruders were or if they left the SAC. The man door in the garage was the nearest, quickest and most unexpected way out of the building.

Moments later Tim was outside, running south down First Avenue toward Baseline.

He didn't stop until he reached Dennis Avenue. A bit winded, he continued at a brisk pace. When he reached the Bjorges', he noticed John was standing on the porch watching George and Godfrey try to start an odd-looking lawn mower. It looked as though they had taken an old, gas-powered mower and attached a power cell and solar tiles to it.

"Better give it up, boys," John called out. "It's not going to work. Better grab my old scythe and cut the grass."

"Hey, Mr. Bjorge!" Tim greeted and waved.

"Hi, Tim. Where have ya' been?" John answered and

walked down the steps. "I thought you were stopping by this morning."

Godfrey and George, looking dejected, waved at Tim while they pushed their contraption back to the barn.

"I got an early start so I walked into town. I needed to check on my mom and do some more looking around. I've got something for you." He pulled up the flap on his messenger bag and pulled out three bags of coffee. "Here. I found these in Dr. Anderson's apartment. I figure he isn't going to use them." He also handed John some of the other packages of food he'd found.

"Oh my, thank you, Tim. I never thought we'd see this again. Anna and the boys will be so pleased. We've all been missing our morning coffee. And thank you for all this other stuff too." John looked at the foil bags in his arms and smiled.

"No problem. I just hope it's all still good," Tim said and gathered up his bags.

"They should be. As long as the seal isn't broken," he said and then his eyes lit up. "Say, you haven't run across anything that tells where the government's food storage facility is around here, have you?"

"No, but I wasn't looking for that. I was looking for the missing binder."

"Well, before we can wake everyone up, we should find it. We're going to need a lot of food."

"I see what you mean. Oh, when I was checking out the doc's apartment, a bunch of thugs, I'm guessing inmates, came snooping around."

"Did they see you?"

"No. I hid in Dr. Dever's apartment but I could hear them trying to break through several doors. They finally gave up and left."

John nodded but appeared concerned.

"There's something else I want you to see. Think you might be up for a trip to town tomorrow?"

"Sure," he said and nodded. "We can even try out your Bug. The power cell seems to be charging up."

"Great!"

Tim left the Bjorges' and practically ran to his parents' house. He couldn't wait to show Lily what he'd found and to tell her about his car. Philip was asleep in his chair in the front room. Tim looked in on him before heading to the kitchen. Lily wasn't there. *She must still be out back trying to catch those chickens.* Tim took out a packet of coffee and opened it. He inhaled a deep breath. It still smelled fresh. He pulled out the coffee maker and threw a new filter in the basket. He carefully measured out the grounds and then pressed the power button. While he stood watching, the coffee maker began its cycle. In no time, the kitchen was filled with the scent of fresh brewed coffee. Tim took a deep breath and closed his eyes.

"Smells good."

Tim jumped and turned around at the sound of his dad's voice.

"Hi, Dad!"

"I think I'll have a cup," he said, oblivious to Tim's reaction to him speaking.

"Sure, I'll get it." Tim said and grabbed his dad's favorite coffee mug from the cupboard and filled it.

Philip sat down at the table in his usual spot, facing the back door.

"It's hot, Dad," Tim warned out of habit, sounding as if he were talking to a child. He hated when he did that.

He watched his dad carefully sip his drink, waiting for his reaction. There was none. He just sat and looked around the kitchen as if it were just another day. Tim poured himself a cup and took a sip. It was a bit weak but it tasted good.

Lily still hadn't come in by the time they finished their first cup of coffee and Tim didn't hear anything outside. He was beginning to get worried.

"Let's go for a walk outside," he suggested to his dad.

Philip grabbed his walking stick and stood up.

The afternoon sun was descending. Tim guessed that it was about three. The two men walked around to the back where Della kept her chicken pen. Tim was shocked at the sight. Lily had done a fine job patching the holes in the coop and fixing the wire enclosure. Sadly, however, he didn't see any chickens occupying the pen. What's more, Lily was nowhere in sight.

Suddenly there was the sound of a chicken frantically squawking. Then the triumphant yell, "I caught you!" It was Lily's voice. She came running around the corner of the barn with a large white hen in her hands, its wings flapping and head bobbing. Tim rushed to open the door of the pen for her. Lily tossed the chicken inside and he shut the wire door.

"I got one!" she announced proudly.

"I see that. Good job!"

"Now, I just need to get the other three and that pesky rooster."

"Need some help?"

"Sure," Lily said and led the way.

By the time the sun went down, the three had rounded up the other chickens and even the rooster. Philip had stunned it with his walking stick when it charged at him. That made getting the large bird into the enclosure a cinch.

"Now we need to figure out what to feed them," Lily said.

"Over on First Avenue by the railroad tracks, there used

to be a feed and grain place," Tim recalled.

"Are you suggesting breaking in and taking whatever?" Lily asked.

Tim wasn't expecting her hesitation and felt guilty about saying anything.

"I suppose I could leave my name and an IOU. Given the circumstances I'm pretty sure they'd understand."

"You could take that wheelbarrow in the barn so you wouldn't have to carry it all?" Lily suggested.

"Better yet, Mr. Bjorge thinks my Bug will be ready to drive tomorrow."

"Really? Great!"

"How would you like a cup of coffee?"

"What? Are you serious?"

"Yep, come on."

The three headed back into the house.

That night Tim found it hard to sleep. He felt like a kid on Christmas Eve thinking about driving his car. He finally fell asleep only to be awakened a short time later by the crowing of that blasted rooster. He lay in bed, counting the number of times the bird crowed and hoped he wouldn't wake his father. Finally, Tim climbed out of bed and dressed.

Lily was awake. She was in the kitchen looking at the ready-to-heat meal packets.

"These are great," she said. "Do they have any more?"

"I don't know. I can check."

"I liked the beef stew we had last night it tasted great."

"It did, didn't it?" Tim smiled. "Well, I'm gonna get going."

"No coffee?"

"Nah, I'll save it for when I get back. I'm too excited

about my car. I'll see you later."

Tim ran all the way to the Bjorges's, hoping they were awake.

"Morning, Mr. Bjorge." Tim said spotting his neighbor heading toward the barn.

John stopped and turned around. "Hey, Tim, you're up early. Thanks for the coffee," he said and raised his mug in the air.

"No problem. Glad you like it."

"Well, ready to give your Volkswagen a try?"

"Sure am," Tim answered scarcely able to contain his excitement.

"What have you there?" he asked and looked at the laptop in Tim's hands.

"Oh, I found this in Dr. Anderson's apartment. I think it's his laptop."

"It looks like a laptop to me," John said with a slight laugh.

"Ha, ha," Tim teased back. "I was hoping George would take a look at it and see if he can find anything that might help us wake the others."

John turned back toward the house. "George!" he shouted.

George stuck his head out of his upstairs bedroom window. "What is it, Dad?"

"Tim, here, has a computer he wants you to look at. So, get down here."

"Sure thing," George answered. "Be right down, Tim."

George was always the geek in school. He loved computers and anything electronic. He was always working on ideas for new programs and apps. After high school he went to Oregon State and earned a Computer Science Degree.

Tim was closer friends with Godfrey back then. George was too much of a brainiac. Whereas Godfrey was a bit more like Tim, an average student. They graduated in the middle of their class and didn't let it bother them. Godfrey worked in his father's garage. George opened a computer repair shop on Main Street.

As for Tim, after graduating from Lewis and Clark, he got a job working for a law firm in Portland as a paralegal. After four years on the job, he saved up enough to put a down payment on a condo in Orenco and moved out. George and Godfrey still lived with their parents.

All through school and even after, people had trouble telling the George and Godfrey apart. It didn't bother Godfrey but George hated it. Tim could always tell which was which, though. George's chin was slightly more rounded than Godfrey's.

The back door of the farmhouse opened. George emerged. He looked a lot like his father, dark hair and blue eyes, but he definitely worked in an office. Tim never thought about it before but none of them married. Tim had come close once but she ended up marrying some other guy because, as she told Tim, "he asked." He didn't think either George or Godfrey ever had a serious relationship.

"So, where's this computer you want me to look at?" George asked.

"Here," Tim answered and held it out.

George took a look at it and frowned. "Where did you find this?"

"It was in Dr. Anderson's apartment at the SAC."

He turned it over and then opened it up. "What did he do to it?"

"I have no idea. His whole apartment looked like a

disaster area. You wouldn't believe a doctor could live in such a pig sty. Think you can get anything off it?"

"As long as the hard drive is still intact, I should be able to get something. Anything in particular you're looking for?"

"Yeah, anything that will tell me how to wake up the others."

George looked at Tim. Tim couldn't tell what he was thinking. Then George started to nod his head.

"I'll see what I can find." He turned around and headed back into the house.

Tim looked at John. "Guess I'm ready. Oh, I need to check out the feed and grain store on First. Lily caught some chickens yesterday."

"No problem," he answered.

John disconnected the charger cable, wound it up and hung it on a nearby support post. "The power cell is holding its charge, but I don't know how long it'll last," he said. "Climb in and give her a try."

Tim sat down in the driver's seat. It felt good to be behind the wheel again. He closed his eyes and turned the key in the ignition. The engine turned on and started making a strange puttering sound.

John gave a victory yell and raised his fists over his head.

Tim leaned out of the door, "What's that sound?"

"The boys wanted to surprise you," John answered. "George installed a recording of an old Model T engine."

George and Godfrey came running into the garage. Both were laughing.

"Whaddaya think?" Godfrey asked.

Tim smiled. "I love it. Thanks guys."

The twins gave each other a high five.

"We better get going," John said.

"Great, you should drive," Tim said. "After all, you're the one who got it running again."

John didn't object. He closed the hood and climbed behind the wheel. Tim took his seat on the passenger side.

"See you later," Tim shouted at the twins.

"I'll take it nice and slow," John said. "I want to feel how the engine runs."

He backed the car out of the barn and turned it toward the road. Anna, George and Godfrey stood on the back steps of the house with smiles on their faces. They waved at John and Tim as they drove away.

John turned north on 331st Avenue and headed toward the Tualatin Valley Highway.

"Feels good so far," he reported.

They headed east back into Hillsboro, however, when they reached First Avenue instead of turning left, John turned south, toward the feed store.

The three-story grain and feed warehouse was right across the railroad tracks. Back in the day it was an ideal location because the men could unload the grain out of the rail cars right into the big silos in back. Then the workers would bag it and stack it in the warehouse until it was eventually sold at the store in front. However, after sitting idle for so long, the building's roof had collapsed and the corrugated metal walls had buckled and rusted in more than a few places.

"Doesn't look promising," John said while they sat parked in front of the old store.

"Yeah," Tim agreed. "Let's take a look anyway."

The damage outside was nothing compared to what they found inside. When the roof collapsed, it sent heavy beams through the second floor and into the store shelves on the first. There was evidence of rats and mice on the floor everywhere.

Tim shuddered as his OCD reared its head. He focused on finding the grain.

Carefully they made their way to the back of the building where the warehouse was located. The heavy plastic curtain that hung in the doorway had been reduced to tattered strips, most of which lay on the floor. Tim stopped and stared in awe at the rows of large metal storage containers, stacked two high. He vaguely remembered hearing something about grain storage but couldn't recall the details.

The pair slowly walked down one aisle and then another.

"Any idea which one would have chicken feed in it?" John asked.

Tim shook his head. "Not a clue. Guess we'll just have to start opening them up."

"These don't appear to be ordinary storage containers," John said.

Tim had to agree after looking at the electronic display on the door and the sign below warning that the contents were under pressure. Another sign advised following the proper opening procedures to avoid injury.

"Avoid injury?" John said out loud. "I don't like the sound of that. Any guess where we'd find the instructions?"

"Your guess is as good as mine," Tim answered. He took a closer look at the display and noticed a menu icon. He tapped it and the display listed off several options, one of them being a list of contents and another, the opening procedure. "Bingo! Found them."

After checking the list on several containers they found the one they wanted. Tim carefully keyed in the codes according to the instructions and jumped back. The door opened with a loud hiss. They each took a large, heavy foil, sack of chicken feed and put in the back of the Bug. After following the instructions again the storage container was resealed and the two were on their way again. This time John insisted that Tim drive.

With the windows down a bit, Tim listened to the puttering sound effects. The faster he drove, the louder it seemed to get.

"Think it's okay if we take a short drive around town?" Tim asked.

"As long as it's not too long," John answered.

"Great." Tim turned right on Oak Street and headed east toward Tenth Avenue. He ignored the traffic lights and pressed on the accelerator.

"Okay, speedy, that's fast enough," John said in a fatherly tone.

Tim looked at his speed and eased off the pedal. The Bug slowed to within the posted limit. He turned left on Tenth and drove up to Main Street. Another left and the SAC came into view at the opposite end of town.

Tim pulled up to the curb in front of the SAC and parked on the wrong side of the street. Still wary of the gang, he looked around to be sure no one was lurking. After locking the car the two headed inside.

"What I want to show you is on Lower Level Two," Tim told John when they stepped into the elevator. He pressed the button and the car moved downward.

The doors opened. "This way," Tim directed and led the way toward the southwest corner. "You're going to love this. Are you ready?" Tim held the ID badge up to the sensor. The steel door clicked and unlocked. He opened the door and stepped inside. The motion sensor activated and the lights came on.

"You weren't kidding!" John gasped. He walked into the

garage and looked at all of the parts and tires that lined the walls. Then he walked over to the Hummers. "Have you tried to start them?"

"Yes. No good."

"Well, let me have a look at them. I'll see if I can't get them going."

"Sure. Hey, I'd like to run up and see my mom, do you mind?"

"Not at all; you go ahead."

"Oh, before I forget, if anyone knocks on the door, don't open it. I have a keycard and will let myself in when I come back. Those thugs could still be out there somewhere."

"No worries," John said already eyeing the boxes of power cells.

Tim slipped out the door and took the elevator up to the fifth floor. He went straight to his mother's chamber. She was still sleeping soundly. The lights above her tube were still blinking in their normal rhythm.

"Hi, Mom," he greeted her. "Dad's doing okay. He finally spoke again yesterday. He didn't say much but at least he can still talk. He helped Lily and I catch some chickens, three hens and a rooster. So maybe we'll have some fresh eggs again." Tim looked down the aisle. He turned back to his mother.

"Not much longer, Mom, I promise," he said and pressed his palm gently against the glass that encased her.

Tim made a quick walk around the floor and checked the other tubes; no one else had awakened. He headed downstairs. When the elevator stopped on the first floor, his breath caught. He stepped to the side opposite the keypad, ready to jump out should the need be. The doors opened. To his relief, no one was waiting. He decided to check on his Bug.

Just when he rounded the front desk in the lobby, he

heard shouting outside. *They're back!* Without thinking, he ran to the front doors but stopped before he tripped the sensor.

Five men surrounded his Bug. Three were dressed in jeans, t-shirts and jackets and looked like any casual group of men. The other two were dressed in the orange jumpsuits worn by residents of the Washington County Jail.

"Come on, hurry up! What's taking jou so long?" the taller and heavier of the group with a definite Hispanic accent ordered. He stood back on the bottom step and judging by the way he ordered the others around, Tim pegged him as the leader.

"I'm working on it!"

Tim recognized the voice from the other day.

"I thought you said you knew how to jimmy a lock," the man standing beside the smaller one sneered. They both had their backs toward the SAC while they were tried to open the driver's side door. The larger man gave the small one a hard shove, knocking him to the sidewalk. "Let me do it!"

"Hey!" Tim heard himself shout. The SAC's doors opened and he rushed down the steps, stopping midway. "Get away from my car!"

What was I thinking?

As one, all five of the men turned and looked at him. Tim backed up a step. The two men closest to Tim charged him. Tim turned and started to run for the doors but they grabbed his arms and drug him backward down the steps. They forced him to his knees in front of their leader.

Tim looked up at the bald Hispanic man standing over him. Tattoos covered his arms, neck and half of his face and head. He sneered and pulled a pistol from the back of his jeans. He scratched his scruffy cheek with the barrel.

"Your car?" he asked while he nodded his head. "I think

you are mistaken, senor. This is *my* car. So hand over *my* keys."

Tim tightened his jaw and didn't say a word.

"I'm going to get them one way or another," he said then aimed the pistol at Tim's head.

Tim felt his strength melt away. His hands trembled. One of the thugs let go of his arm. Nervously, Tim dug in the pocket of his jeans and pulled out the key. One of the men beside him grabbed it and handed it to the bald man.

"That's better," he said but didn't lower the gun. "Too bad you was a minute too late."

Just then the youngest of the pack jumped between them with his back to Tim.

"No!" he said firmly and held out his hands to stop the leader. "You've got the keys. Leave him be."

"Oh-ho," the leader chuckled. "You sweet on him, mi pequeno?"

"No!" the boy answered. Tim could hear the repulsion in his tone.

"Oh too bad for him then," he said and took aim at Tim again.

"Stop! Okay, yes. Yes, I'm sweet on him. So please, leave him alone."

The leader laughed again, showing his rotted teeth. "Buscar hombres, coño joven se encontró un papi!"

"Aw," the others responded in a sarcastic tone that needed no translation.

"Okay, okay, you can have him. Come on!" The leader lowered his gun. Walking over to the Bug, he unlocked the doors. He pulled out the wire that the young rescuer was using in his attempt to jimmy the lock. He threw it aside before climbing behind the wheel.

The other four ran for the car. Two men climbed in the backseat. The other man grabbed the younger one and pushed him aside. He then took his place in the passenger seat and slammed the door.

"Hey, what about me?" the boy screamed and pounded on the hood of the Bug.

"Ir a la mierda!" the passenger shouted through the window.

"But you promised. I let you—"

"Adiós maricón," the leader shouted.

The leader put the key in the ignition and turned it. The puttering sound effects seemed to make the four go wild. They made high pitched sounds that sounded like bird calls.

The driver made a U-turn and stopped. Sticking his hand out of the window, he fired a shot into the air and let out another yell. The car sped off. The puttering sound grew louder and then started to fade.

"Wait! Come back!" the one left behind shouted and ran into the street.

The car turned the corner several blocks away and headed south, toward Oak Street, the main drag out of town.

"No!" the boy shouted, this time sounding as if he were crying.

"Hey," Tim called to him. The young man turned around. "Don't I know you?" Tim asked.

The young man's eyes widened and he looked scared.

"It's okay," Tim tried to reassure him. "I'm not going to harm you. You saved my life. Why?"

"Forget it," he said with a bitter tone.

"No, I can't. Thank you."

"Don't go thinkin' you're special 'cause you're not. I just didn't want to see any more killing. That's all."

"Any more? You mean they've killed others? Who?"

"Those people in the basement. You buried them. I saw you."

"The Mayor, Police Chief and Sheriff?"

"Yeah," he answered still standing in the middle of the street.

"But why?"

"Because Pedro said they were the ones who locked him and the others up."

"But why their families, their children?"

"I don't know. You saw him. You figure it out."

He turned and looked down Main Street toward the east. Tim had the feeling if he continued to question him about the murders, he'd run.

"Where are they taking my car?"

"Why do you care? You'll never see it again."

There it was that familiar belligerent attitude.

"I know. Just curious, I guess."

He glanced at Tim and then back down the street. "They're going to Mexico," he muttered. "Pedro has family there and says the law can't touch them there."

"I see. So, what about you?"

"I don't know."

"Well, you have that money you stole from the bank?"

"What? I didn't steal no money!" he snapped.

"Oh? Then what was in that bag you took from the bank?"

"My stuff, pictures of my parents and my clothes." His tone seemed to soften.

"You have family?"

"Yeah, doesn't everybody?"

"Are they awake?"

He shook his head. "They're still stuck in that building." He looked up toward the top floors of the SAC.

Tim glanced over his shoulder. "Mine too. I mean my mother is still inside. My name is Tim, what's yours?"

The young man eyed Tim as though he were debating on whether or not to answer.

"Henry," he answered quickly which let Tim know he wasn't about to repeat it.

"Nice to meet you," Tim said and sat down on the steps. "How old are you, Henry?"

"You writing a book or something?" he snapped.

"No. I was just wanting to get to know you."

"Hey, I only said I was sweet on you so Pedro wouldn't blast your brains all over the sidewalk. I didn't mean it. I'm no homo."

"No, I didn't think you were."

"I only did that stuff with them because they said they would take me with them," he said and turned away. "But they lied!" he shouted.

"I'm sorry," Tim said.

Henry turned and looked at Tim. His brown eyes appeared to study him as if he could read Tim's mind.

"Eighteen," he answered with a bit of pride.

"Eighteen? Why were you in jail?"

"I don't want to talk about it."

"It's okay." Tim could see Henry was becoming uncomfortable, so he let him off the hook and didn't pursue it. "You have a place to stay?"

"Yeah."

"Food?"

"Some."

"What are you going to do now?"

"I told you already, I dunno."

"Those guys you were with, were they trying to break into the rooms in the basement yesterday?"

Henry's eyes widened with shock. "How'd you know about that?"

Now Tim felt anxious, he didn't want to let on that he was in the apartment. Even though Henry had just saved Tim's life, Tim wasn't ready to trust him that much. "I noticed some of the doors were dented. I was just inside searching for a binder that might have the instructions on how to wake everyone up."

"Oh," he said. "Yeah, it was them."

"Did they take anything? A book?"

"No," he answered shaking his head and backing away which made Tim not believe him.

"Henry, are you sure, because without it your family may never wake up."

He really started to fidget. "I've gotta go."

Before Tim could stop him, Henry took off running north on Second Avenue, heading for the same part of town as the last time their paths crossed. Tim turned around and headed back inside.

After that last bit of conversation, Tim knew that searching for the book here was pointless. If those thugs had it, it was on its way to Mexico. The only hope of waking everyone was to find another copy either by sorting through the papers in Dr. Anderson's apartment or finding one at another SAC. According to Dr. Dever's log, the SAC in Forest Grove was destroyed by fire. The next nearest SAC was in Aloha.

When Tim opened the door to the garage John was waiting for him with a big grin on his face.

"They're running like a top," he announced.

"They are? How?"

"They're a hybrid of sorts like your Bug," he answered. "Hidden in the roof of each one are solar tiles. I just had to switch out the power cells and they started right up. They have the Never Flat, solid rubber tires, so they're good to go."

"Good, we'll be needing them."

"Why? Is there something wrong with the Volkswagen?" John asked giving Tim a confused look.

"No. It's on its way to Mexico."

"What?"

"It's been carjacked by that gang of inmates. I also found out they're responsible for murdering the mayor and the rest of the town officials."

John began to laugh.

"What's so funny?"

"They won't make it to Mexico," he answered.

"What do you mean?"

"When I connected the charger to the power cell, I had to disconnect the solar tiles. The power cell doesn't have a full charge and with going through the passes, they'll be lucky if they make it as far as Sacramento?"

"How sure are you about that? I mean, are we rid of them?"

"I'm sure they won't be back," John said. The confidence in his voice calmed Tim's frayed nerves. "What do you say we take these and head back to the feed store before going home?" he suggested.

"That sounds good to me. I've always wanted to drive one of these."

Tim climbed behind the wheel and found a garage door opener clipped to the visor. He pressed it and waited while the steel door rattled and rose. The he followed John up the ramp to First Avenue, closing the garage door behind them. *It's nice having a secure entrance into the building, not to mention a parking spot.*

After a quick stop at the feed store for more chicken feed, Tim followed John back to his farm. He wanted to check on George's progress with the computer. When they drove up the driveway, George, Godfrey and Anna came rushing out of the house. The twins' eyes were wide and their mouths agape.

"Where on earth did you get that?" Anna asked sounding less than pleased. "John, you didn't steal it did you?"

"No, Anna. They were in the garage at the Center. We're only *borrowing* them for a while since Tim's Volkswagen was stolen."

"Stolen?" Anna shrieked and looked at Tim. He nodded. Her expression softened. "Well, as long as you're only borrowing them." She walked over to John's Hummer and peered inside. She shook her head as if she didn't approve. "I have supper on the stove," she said and went back into the house.

"Hey, Dad, can I drive it?" Godfrey asked.

"Sure, park it in the barn. I don't think it's a good idea to leave it out in the open." John tossed the key to his son.

"Hey, Tim," George called. "Got a second?"

"Sure." Tim followed George over to the front porch. He leaned against the rail while George picked up the laptop and sat down on one of the wooden patio chairs.

"Where did you say you found this laptop?"

"I found it in Dr. Anderson's bedroom. It was buried under a bunch of papers and clothes. Why?"

George scratched his head. "It doesn't appear to be his. I mean, I was able to access the hard drive and there was nothing on it related to the Center. The saved files have the author name of Stephen O'Rourke."

"The sheriff's son?"

"One and the same."

"Are you sure?"

"Positive. I found a file titled 'Family' with pictures of the sheriff so I'm a hundred percent. I wonder if his dad knew his son was into gay porn?"

"Are you kidding me?"

"Nope," George shook his head. "Ol' Stevie boy had quite the collection of videos and pictures. He was into older dudes from the look of it."

"You looked at them?"

"Not intentionally. When I opened the file I couldn't help seeing the photos. Quite kinky stuff. Anyway, it wasn't the doctor's. Sorry."

"That's okay. I appreciate your help. Funny, now I wonder how Dr. Anderson came to have it."

"Good question. Oh! One other thing," George said in a thoughtful tone. "I don't know if it's accurate but when I started up the computer, the date showed August 1, 2095."

Tim suddenly felt numb. "2095? If that's true, we were asleep for nearly fifty-three years."

"Or longer. The only way to know for certain is to check the date on another computer."

"What does yours say?"

He shook his head. "Mine is fried. There must have been a power surge or something."

"Oh."

"Here, you want this?" he held out the laptop to Tim.

"No, you keep it. You could probably use it more than me. Thanks for checking. I guess I best be getting home."

That night, Tim couldn't sleep. Every time he closed his

eyes giant numbers flashed in his head, 2-0-9-5.

It can't be true. I couldn't have slept that long. That would make me eighty-one years old. No way. It must be a mistake.

Day Eighteen. At breakfast, Lily reminded Tim about checking for more meal pouches. With everything that happened the day before, he had completely spaced it. She said she understood but Tim could tell she was disappointed and it tugged at his heart. She's such a sweet girl, the last thing he wanted to do was disappoint her. He assured her he wouldn't forget this time and meant it.

Tim pulled the Hummer into the Bjorges's driveway right when the sun peeked over the top of Mt. Hood. He knew it was early but he also knew that they would all be awake. Sure enough, John came out of the house, coffee mug in hand.

"Morning, Tim."

"Good morning, Mr. Bjorge. Can I talk to George?"

"Sure," he answered and then turned his head to the side. "George, you have company!" he shouted. "You want to come in?"

"No, I'd like to talk to him outside, if that's all right?"

"Sure."

While John continued to the barn, George came out of the house.

"Hey, Tim. What's up?"

"I was wondering if you would like to go on a little road trip with me. I'm going to Aloha. I want to see what happened to the SAC there. Dr. Dever's journal said they lost contact with them after seven years. I want to see why and if I can find someone or something to help me wake everyone up. I'd like it if you would go with me since you know computers."

George was hesitant. He didn't appear as though he wanted to join Tim.

"Sure, we'll go with you," Godfrey answered and opened the screen door. He had been listening the whole time. "I'll grab our coats and let mom know." He rushed back into the house.

"You in?" Tim asked George.

"What if there isn't anyone?"

"In that case I thought about heading over to the West Beaverton SAC. Maybe even drive into Portland. One of these places has to have the manual still."

"What if we run into those thugs and they steal the Hummer?"

"We won't. Your dad said they would make it as far as Sacramento. They should be there by now. So, no worries; besides, we'll be careful. I promise."

George appeared to be thinking it over when Godfrey came out of the house still putting on his jacket.

"Okay, let's go," he said.

"Fine," George agreed. "I get shotgun."

Shotgun. Tim laughed inside. He hadn't heard that term in—who knew how long. He climbed into the driver's seat.

The Aloha SAC was built south of the high school on 185th Avenue. Tim was thankful that Godfrey came along. Another set of eyes looking around for any sign of trouble was a good thing.

When they reached Kinnaman Road and the SAC came into view Tim slammed on the brakes. No one said a word. All three quietly stared at what was left of the SAC building in disbelief. Twisted metal fingers reached toward the sky. The rubble reminded Tim of the old photographs of Germany after the Second World War. Slowly Tim let the Hummer inch closer.

"What are you doing?" George asked in a panic.

"I want to see what happened."

"You have your answer. They're all dead. There's nothing more to see."

Tim heard the fear in his voice. To be honest, he was afraid too but he had to see if there was something salvageable that could be of help to them, to him.

"We'll just take a quick look and then be out of here. I promise."

The closer they came the more apparent it was that there was nothing left. The building and everything inside had been reduced to rubble a long time ago. So long that wild trees and shrubs had already laid claim to the land. Something else caught Tim's attention and sent a surge of fear throughout him. The outside shell of the concrete building was riddled with what looked like bullets holes. Tim knew by their silence that Godfrey and George saw them too. Tim threw the Hummer in reverse and quickly turned it around. He headed back up 185th toward T.V. Highway.

"Now what?" George asked.

"We check out West Beaverton," Tim answered.

"Are you insane? Did you see that? People did that which means some people didn't go into suspended animation. That could have been us in there."

"But it wasn't. Doesn't that seem a little strange to you?"

"What? That we weren't killed in our sleep? No, not really," George answered shaking his head. "Have you lost your freaking mind?"

"No, I haven't."

"I think we should go back to Hillsboro. We can figure out another way."

"Tim, stop!" Godfrey shouted from the backseat.

Tim slammed on the brakes causing everyone to lurch forward.

"What?" Tim asked.

"Look! Over there. I saw someone."

Tim glanced in the mirror to see which way Godfrey was pointing. He looked ahead in the distance. *How could I have missed that?* Arguing with George had distracted Tim more than he realized. Coming toward them, about a block and a half away, waving a cane in the air was an old man.

"Turn down there!" George shouted and pointed up the side street. "Hurry!"

Tim heard the fear in George's voice. It took every bit of Tim's strength not do as he suggested.

"No," Tim said. "Let's see who he is and what he wants."

"It's a trap, I tell you." George's voice raised an octave. "Drive!"

"I don't think so, George. Look at him. He's old and all alone."

"But there could be others lurking in the shadows or he could have a grenade in his pocket."

"A grenade, George?" Tim looked at his friend. Part of him wanted to laugh but the other part was also frightened by the possibility.

"I think he's alone," Godfrey said. "Besides, if there were others, they'd have to be as old as him, wouldn't they?"

There was a bit of logic in what Godfrey said, however small a bit. Tim held onto it and put the Hummer in park. "Godfrey, climb up here and take the wheel. I'm going to go see who he is and what he wants. First sign of trouble get out of here."

"Leave you?" he asked.

Tim hadn't really thought of that part. "Just wait for me," he answered and opened the door.

"That's far enough!" Tim shouted to the old man when he was still about thirty-or-so feet away.

The old man stopped.

"What's your name?" Tim asked.

"William Smith," the man answered. Tim heard the tentativeness in his voice. He was definitely hiding something. "Where are you from?" he asked.

"Portland," Tim lied.

"Portland? Where'd you get that Hummer?"

"From our SAC."

"Your SAC?" He sounded surprised which made Tim feel even more ill at ease. "What's your name?"

"Tim Stone."

"You a doctor?"

"No."

William took a step back. At that moment Tim realized the old man as afraid of *him*.

"Wait!" Tim shouted. "I woke up."

"You woke up? You mean your SAC wasn't destroyed?"

"No. What about you, where are you from?"

"There," he said and pointed at the rubble in the distance. "My partner and I escaped before they blew it up."

"Your partner? You mean you were in charge of that SAC?"

"Yes, I'm Dr. William Smith."

Tim felt excited. He looked over his shoulder at Godfrey and George. They were listening intently. Tim couldn't believe their luck. They didn't need a manual anymore. They had something much better, someone who knew how to wake everyone up.

After a bit more shouting back and forth, both Tim and William began to feel at ease and that neither posed a threat to the other. After George patted Dr. Smith down, he allowed the doctor to climb into the back seat of the Hummer beside Tim. Godfrey headed back to T.V. Highway and following Tim's unspoken prompting in the mirror, turned toward Portland to keep up their ruse. When they reached Murray Boulevard, Godfrey turned right and crossed the tracks. He pulled into the overgrown field that was once the front lawn of the Sisters of Saint Mary convent. In the open area, they could see if anyone was coming.

"So, Dr. Smith," George said turning around in his seat and facing their guest. "Mind telling us what happened?"

"It was a long time ago, I'm not sure I can remember," he answered.

"Just how long ago?" Tim asked, hoping he could confirm what year it was.

"I can't say exactly. I lost track of the years."

"Back to what happened at the SAC, try harder to remember," George snapped. The hostility in his voice even made Tim jump. William recoiled seemingly bracing himself to be struck. Tim glared at George, hoping he would ease up.

"Please, Dr. Smith," Tim spoke up in a calmer tone. "If you could tell us anything, that would be great."

While he waited for the old man to begin, Tim looked at him. His hair was white and thin. His face was pale and weathered. He clutched the ball at the top of his cane with his right hand and placed his left hand over it. His skin was thin, making his hands look bony and his knuckles large. *He's no threat to us.*

"After everyone in our center was asleep, Victor and I settled into our job of monitoring the computers and checking on everyone. We made regular check-ins with the other centers in our district, Forest Grove, Hillsboro, Beaverton. But after about several years we lost contact with the Beaverton centers. We tried raising Portland, Seattle, Sacramento, Boise and even D.C. but had no success. We were cut off.

"Then late one day while making rounds, we heard a loud rumble outside. At first we thought it might be an earthquake. When the building didn't move, we went to the windows and looked out. That's when we saw them."

"Them?" George interrupted.

"About fifty people dressed in camo, armed with weapons and a rocket launcher. We realized then what was about to happen. Victor and I had no choice but abandon everyone and make a run for it.

"When we reached the interior hallway we heard gunfire and breaking glass on all sides. We knew they had the SAC surrounded. We made for the one exit that we were sure wouldn't be covered. It was in the floor of the basement and led to the sewers."

Tim looked at Godfrey and George. Both seemed engrossed in the story. Tim glanced outside but there was no one coming. He turned back to the doctor.

"We crawled out of the sewer about five blocks away right when they launched a rocket at the building. It was horrible. All of those helpless people were gone in a massive fireball. When the cowards went to fire a second rocket it blew up in the launcher, wiping themselves out. Sort of poetic justice, wouldn't you say?"

No one answered.

"Then what happened? I mean, with you and this Victor guy?" Godfrey asked.

The old man seemed to hesitate. Tim noticed his hands

shook a little while they held onto his cane.

"Neither of us was sure what to do, where to go. We thought for certain that this wasn't the only group of rebels and that others may come, so we got as far away from the Center as we could. We headed toward Hillsboro at first but then decided against it. So we found a house away from the main streets and took up living there, about a mile away from the Center. We avoided using any lights at night or making any fires. We didn't want to attract any attention. As the years passed and we heard no one, we started to relax. The realization that we could be the only and last two people on Earth was a bit overwhelming. We tried not to think about it and kept ourselves busy. We planted a garden and did all those normal things. "

"Didn't you try contact any of the other SAC's in the area to warn them?" George asked.

"How? All our means of communication were destroyed in that building. Besides, we figured what happened to us must have happened to the others."

"So, where's this Victor guy now?" Godfrey interjected.

William's eyes teared. He looked extremely uncomfortable. He looked down. "He passed away a few months ago."

"This sounds like a bunch of crap." George snapped.

"George!" Tim said and gave him a stern look. He turned around. "I'm sorry for that, Dr. Smith. About the bombing, do you have any idea who those people were?"

"They were part of a movement called Naturalists started by a Reverend Jesse Davison in Georgia. They opposed the plan to put people into suspended animation believing it was an affront to God. You see, man needed to deal with the consequences of not taking care of the Earth and either make things right or face extinction like so many other species had done in the past. Putting people in suspended animation was like cheating, a coward's way out."

"Funny, I don't remember hearing about them," Godfrey said.

"Well, it was an underground movement and very hush-hush. The government kept it out of the press but they warned us."

"So, how did they end up here in Aloha, Oregon of all places?" Tim asked.

"In order to escape being captured and forced into suspended animation, they scattered throughout the country and were told to avoid the major cities. They were to wait until the heathens were asleep and then they were to destroy the Centers."

The more Tim listened to his story, the more he became confused. Back on the street, he'd shown them an ID badge with a picture of a young man on it. Tim had no way of knowing if it was really this man's. He assumed it was because he had the badge. Tim remembered the two badges in his own pocket and started to wonder. William's story sounded plausible but how did he know so much about this group of rebels? How did he know about their instructions? Something didn't feel right. Even though Tim wanted to believe William was telling the truth, he was having serious doubts.

"Well, I guess we should get you back home," Tim said.

William looked at him. "Home? I thought you would take me to your Center in Portland?"

"Yeah, Tim. He could help us wake everyone up," Godfrey said looking in the rearview mirror.

Tim tried to signal him without letting the doctor see.

"What? You mean that there are people still in suspended

animation?" Dr. Smith perked up.

"Yes. Only a handful of us woke up somehow on our own." Godfrey continued, ignoring Tim's cringing in the mirror. "The rest of the town is still asleep."

"Town? I thought you said you were from Portland."

"It's getting late," Tim spoke up putting his hand on Godfrey's left shoulder and giving it a hard squeeze. "We will take you home and come back tomorrow," he said to William.

Godfrey finally took the hint and turned back around.

"Yeah, Doc. We should be getting back," he said and started the engine. "So, just tell us where you live—"

"Godfrey…" George interrupted, sounding frightened.

Tim looked beside him at William. The old man was holding the barrel of a small pistol against the back of George's head.

"Where'd that come from?" Tim gasped before he realized what he had said.

"Your buddy here really shouldn't be such a homophobe when he's trying to frisk a man. I had the gun stuck down the front of my jeans," he laughed and shoved the barrel of the pistol into the back of George's head causing George to nod.

"What do you want?" Tim asked.

"For one thing, I'm not going to let you dump me off somewhere. You're going to take me to your Center where all those heathens are. I'm going to finish what should have been done decades ago and then I'm going to kill you."

"So, you're not Dr. Smith?" Tim said already knowing the answer.

The old man laughed.

"And all that talk about the exploding rocket launcher was just a lie."

"No, that was true. It was also true that Dr. Smith and his

partner escaped. Pastor Victor and I went after them right before the launcher jammed and blew. We apprehended Smith and his partner and carried out the sentence for their crime."

"You mean you killed them in cold blood," Godfrey snapped.

"We carried out God's Will."

"What do you know—"

"Enough!" the old man shouted, silencing Godfrey. "Now, you will drive me to your Center and don't try to fool me by taking me to Portland. My squad destroyed all the Centers in the Portland-Vancouver area. So, I knew you were lying."

Tim glanced at Godfrey in the mirror. Godfrey was looking back. Tim nodded.

"Okay, let's head back to Sherwood," Tim said hoping the old man wouldn't know anything about the SAC there and that somehow he would figure a way out of this mess before they arrived.

The old man kept his pistol aimed at George's head. Godfrey turned west back onto the Tualatin Valley Highway. He drove slowly, continually glancing in the mirror at the old man. Tim could tell he was worried for his brother.

Godfrey turned south on 170th Avenue. The Hummer rocked when it went over the railroad tracks. The old man's extended hand bobbed in the air.

"Hurry up!" he snarled. "You drive like an old woman!"

Godfrey stepped harder on the accelerator but still kept the Hummer's speed lower than the posted limit.

At Rigert Road he turned west again; then south on 175th Avenue. It was an almost straight shot into Sherwood from there. They would be there in no time and Tim still didn't have a plan. He glanced at the old man.

"So, since William Smith isn't your real name, do you mind telling us what is?" he asked their captor.

"I see no harm in telling you, since you're all going to die anyway," he snarled. "It's Leonard Bowers."

"Bowers," Tim repeated with a nod, not that it meant anything special. "So, how do you plan on destroying the SAC?"

"It's really quite simple. I'll just destroy the main computer."

"How will you get in without a key?"

He held up the pistol, finally pointing it away from the back of George's head. That was Tim's chance. While the barrel pointed toward the roof, Tim grabbed the old man's wrist and twisted his arm toward the back of the Hummer. Leonard was surprisingly strong for an old man but for the first time in his life, Tim was stronger. Leonard let out a groan and dropped the gun. It fell to the floor in the back. Still, Tim held onto Leonard's wrist with all his might. Leonard quit struggling and grimaced, letting out a gasp. That's when Tim knew something was wrong. He let go of the man. Leonard fell back against the door. His forehead was covered in sweat. He wasn't breathing.

"What's wrong?" Tim asked.

No response.

Godfrey slammed on the brakes. The Hummer skidded to a stop. George jumped out and threw the door open beside Leonard. The old man started to fall. Tim grabbed him. He unbuckled the seatbelt. George pulled him out onto the ground and began to kick him.

"George! Stop it!" Tim shouted.

"That bastard held a gun to my head!"

"George, something's wrong with him," Tim said and

stood between them and pushed George away.

"You think?" George snapped with sarcasm.

"I'm serious. He's sick or something."

"I don't care. Let him hold a gun to your head and see how sympathetic you'd be."

George was not letting go of his anger and quite honestly, Tim didn't blame him. It wasn't all that long ago Tim had a gun pointed at him. He knew the feeling, the helplessness, the fear.

Godfrey rounded the front of the Hummer and rushed to Leonard. "Guys," he said sounding as if he'd seen a ghost. "I think our problem is solved."

"What?" Tim turned around and looked down at their abductor lying on the ground, eyes starring blindly at the sky. He wasn't breathing. Tim bent down and carefully felt Leonard's bruised wrist for a pulse. There was none. Tim dropped the man's arm and stood up, backing away. "He's dead?"

Godfrey knelt down and felt Leonard's neck for a pulse. "As the proverbial doornail," he answered. "He's an old man. He probably had a heart attack or something."

"A heart attack? Are you sure?" George asked. There was a touch of remorse in his voice.

"Yeah, pretty sure," Godfrey answered.

Whether he was telling the truth or not, Tim wasn't sure, but judging by the way Leonard acted, it sounded plausible.

"Let's get out of here," George said and started back for the Hummer.

"Wait! We can't just leave him here like this."

"Tim, why not? He's dead. We can't do anything for him now."

Tim knew George was right but at the same time, it didn't

108

feel like the thing to do. "Shouldn't we bury him?"

"With what? We didn't bring any shovels. Are you going to dig a grave with your bare hands?"

Tim didn't answer. He looked at the fields on both sides of the road hoping for an idea to come. Nothing did. Maybe George was right. Maybe their only option was to just leave him here alongside the road like a dead animal. *No. It's not right.*

"Can we at least take his body into the field and put him to rest there? Maybe cover him with rocks or something."

"Fine!" George snapped.

Tim could tell that George wasn't pleased with the idea but he also knew George would cave in and help, if for no other reason than to get out of there faster.

They dragged the Leonard's lifeless body across the small ditch and into the field.

"Okay, this is as far as I go," George said when they were about twenty feet from the road.

"Now rocks," Tim said.

Like a child who didn't want to do what he was told, George threw his hands up and stood in place while he looked from side to side. "There's none," he announced. "We've done all we could, he's on his own. Let's get going."

This time Tim had no more strength to argue. He followed the twins back to the Hummer.

"Give me the keys, I'm driving," George said.

Neither Godfrey nor Tim protested.

They reached the Bjorges' home right as the sun was beginning to set. John and Anna came rushing out to greet them. They sat on the front porch and over a cup of coffee, recounted their failed mission.

"I wouldn't write it off as a total failure, boys," John said.

"We now know that help is not coming from the East. Maybe we need to look to the West or the South."

"True," Tim agreed. "I should be getting home. Lily will be worried. Oh crap! I did it again."

"What?" Godfrey asked.

"I forgot to stop at the SAC and check for more food."

Tim closed the barn doors, hiding the Hummer from any curious eyes and headed into the house. Lily met him at the back door. She threw her arms around his neck and gave him a hug. Tim hugged her back.

"I was worried," she whispered in his ear.

"Me too," Tim said.

Lily let go and stepped back. "So, did you find any more . . ." She looked at his empty hands. "You forgot?"

Tim gave Lily what he called the Reader's Digest version of the day's trip. She listened quietly. When he reached the part where the old man had his heart attack, she didn't say anything. He told her after that happened, they all just wanted to get home. She said she understood, but Tim still felt a tug on his heart. He had disappointed her again.

That night he lay awake in bed and stared at the dark ceiling in his bedroom. He couldn't stop thinking about Leonard. How could he claim to be a religious man and yet kill all those people? Tim turned over and closed his eyes.

EPISODE III:
LIGHTS OUT

Tim watched the dark velvet sky fade into pinks, yellows and blue as once again the sun rose over Mt. Hood in the east. *Another night and only a few hours of fitful sleep, when is this going to end?* He pulled the blanket around his shoulders and nestled himself deeper into the padded loveseat on the front porch of his parents' farmhouse. He sipped his coffee and watched the world wake up.

Inside the house he heard a stirring. *It's Lily. Dad doesn't get up until closer to noon.* Philip seemed to sleep more and was quieter since coming out of suspended animation. He still dragged one foot a bit when he walked which worried Tim a lot.

"Morning," Lily greeted Tim through the screen door.

"Hey, sleep well?" he answered back and moved the blanket, making room for her to sit down beside him if she wanted.

"I slept okay, but it looks like you didn't. Did you spend the night out here again?" she asked and walked out onto the porch, careful not to let the screen door slam behind her. She didn't sit down beside him. Instead she leaned against one of the porch support posts and wrapped her arms around herself.

"Guilty," Tim answered.

"More bad dreams?"

"Yeah."

"You know, my mom used to say if you tell someone your bad dream, it will stop."

"Oh?" Tim said and cocked his head to the side. "I don't think it'll work."

"Well, you don't know unless you try. Why don't you tell me? Maybe that will make it stop?"

Tim eyed her; she seemed so mature and insightful for being eighteen. He didn't know why he felt as though he needed to protect her from the truth. She obviously could handle it, probably better than him.

"I don't know, Lily."

"What have you got to lose?"

Tim looked into her golden brown eyes and his uncertainty eased. "Okay," he said, "I keep dreaming that I'm searching through a mountain of papers. In the background I hear my mother's voice urging me on. 'You can do it. You can do it.' I'm digging and looking fast as I can. But, then I hear a man's voice. 'Time's up,' he says. Then I hear my mother again. 'You're too late.' I turn around and I'm standing outside her chamber. She's dead, just a skeleton. Then I wake up."

"That's dreadful," Lily said and gave Tim a sympathetic look.

Tim wanted to wrap his arms around her but he didn't move.

Lily suddenly grimaced and tightened her hold on her stomach.

"Still not feeling well?" Tim asked.

"I think I'm coming down with the flu or something," she answered and clenched her teeth. After a moment whatever it was passed and she smiled again. "You hungry? I can make you some eggs if you like?"

"No, I think I'll take a shower and then head into town if you don't mind?"

"No, not at all."

Tim went up the stairs to his bedroom and tossed the blanket back on the bed. When he turned around, he caught a glimpse of the box on the corner of his old desk. For the past couple weeks, he had purposely ignored it. Learning about the Naturalists and what they planned from that crazy old man was too much. Tim just wanted to forget about him and about his lunatic friends and focus on finding the binder, but the box wouldn't let him. The box was a constant reminder. It was their radio. At least when he glanced at the papers inside, it said as much. *No, I'm not ready to look at it*. He reached to turn off his desk lamp just when the light flickered, giving him a start. He quickly shut it off and stared at it for a moment before heading downstairs to take a shower.

After his shower, he dressed and then headed back into town. Hillsboro had changed a lot since his father's childhood days, no doubt about it. No longer was it a farming town. High tech industries and manufacturing plants had taken over the farmlands to the north and east. The population changed, not only in number but in personality. It was no longer a population of country folk. It was a town of geeks and computer nerds. Toward the west, between Hillsboro and Cornelius, only a handful of farms remained and even some of those had sold portions of their land to housing developers.

However, downtown Hillsboro still held some of its

original charm. Even though a few of the older buildings had been replaced with newer ones, there were still enough of the historic buildings lining Main Street to remind Tim of the past. The U.S. Bank building on the corner of 2nd Avenue and Main Street was still there, though its name had changed several times. Across the street, the building that once housed Jacobsen's Bookstore still stood, when everyone went to sleep it was an internet café. Down the street the old Venetian Theater Bistro sign still hung above its entrance. It was a bit weathered.

After driving around the block a couple times to be sure that no one was around, Tim slipped into the parking garage beneath the Suspended Animation Center across from the Courthouse. The metal door rattled shut. Tim turned off the Hummer's engine and sat for a moment, gripping the steering wheel and resting his forehead against his hands.

How did this happen. How did I, a simple paralegal at Taylor, Thomas and Young Law Firm in Portland, end up holding the keys to a SAC? I wasn't the first person to wake up from suspended animation, why didn't one of them take the keys? For that matter, why didn't the escaped inmates grab them when they killed the mayor and police? Why was it my responsibility to wake everyone up? Why do I care so much?

The elevator doors opened on the fifth floor. Tim walked around the reception desk and into the sleep chamber room that was nearly the size of an entire square block. Everything was quiet, not a sound. The blinking lights above each sleep chamber let him know that they were still working and that the people in them were still safe and asleep.

Tim walked straight to his mother's chamber. She stood, leaning against the padded back of the tube. The tube itself, as with all the tubes, was slightly tilted back about ten degrees.

The video he saw before going to sleep claimed it was for comfort. *Who would know?*

Gently he touched the glass tube that imprisoned her like Snow White in her glass coffin. *I wish I knew how to open it, how to wake her from this cursed sleep.*

"Hi, Mom," Tim said out loud and sat down in the bottom of the empty chamber across from her. *Does she hear me when I talk to her? Does she even know I'm here?*

"It's me, Tim. I'm still trying to find a way to wake you up. Dad is doing fine but he needs you. I need you. I can't take care of him by myself. I don't know how. I don't know him like you do."

Tim looked at the floor. Silence engulfed him. "I'm still having that nightmare, Mom. Lily said if I told someone about the dream, the nightmares would stop. She insisted I tell her. So, I did. Oh Mom, I know she's ten years younger than me but she's so smart. I know you'll like her."

The one-sided conversation lagged. Tim sat in silence again. After a while, he stood up, kissed his fingers and pressed them against the glass. "I'll come back again later."

Tim took the elevator to the fifteenth floor and began his rounds. It had been nearly eight weeks since anyone else woke up. Still, he felt the need to check. Methodically he surveyed each room and each floor, working his way down.

On the thirteenth floor he heard someone talking. The sound filled him instantly with fear but the more he listened, the fear faded away. Quietly he made his way along the end of the rows of sleep chambers. The sound of Henry's voice grew louder and clearer. Tim stopped and peered down the ninth aisle. About halfway down he spotted Henry talking to someone still asleep in a chamber.

Tim stepped out from behind the end chamber. "Hi,

Henry."

Henry jumped and took a step back. He looked like a frightened, trapped animal. His eyes darted left and right as though looking for a way to escape but the only way out was behind Tim.

"What are you doing here?" he demanded, trying to sound tough but sounding more like he had been caught doing something he shouldn't.

"The same thing you are, I guess. I'm visiting my mother."

He looked around again but this time he appeared to be looking at the people in the tubes on either side of the aisle.

"She's on this floor?" he asked.

"No," Tim answered. Instinctively he decided not to tell him where. Even though Henry had saved him from the inmates, Tim still wasn't sure he could trust him. "Do you come here often?"

"Once or twice a day," he answered.

"Me, too." Tim slowly walked closer. Henry appeared nervous, but didn't run.

"How have you been?" Tim tried again at a conversation.

"Okay," Henry gave his one-word answer.

When Tim stopped he turned and glanced at the chamber in front of Henry. The woman appeared young. Her face showed no sign of wrinkles. Her dark, almost black, hair hung loosely in curls about her shoulders. Her head was tilted up against the back of the tube. Her hands were clasped in front of her.

"She's very pretty," Tim said.

"Thank you," Henry answered for her.

Tim glanced at the tube to her right. A young girl about ten years old, he guessed, slept soundly. Next to her was a man who resembled Henry but looked grim. His face was creased and weathered. His hands were thick and calloused.

"Is that your sister and father?"

Henry looked at the girl and smiled.

"Yes," he answered. Tim noticed Henry's smile disappeared when he looked at his father.

"I'm still trying to find a way to wake everyone up. Are you sure those guys didn't have a blue binder with them when they left?"

He shook his head but his eyes and expression didn't appear convincing.

"I've gotta go," he said and backed away, inching himself past Tim.

"No, please, don't go. I wanted you to know, if you're tired of being alone, you could always come and stay with my father, Lily and me."

"With that bitch?" he said and stopped. "No way! I'm not looking to get slapped around by her again."

"She won't," Tim tried to assure him but Henry started moving away again. "Please, think about it. If you want to stay with us, wait for me in front of the SAC."

"No way!" he shouted before he ran for the door.

Day Sixty. Tim managed a few hours of restful sleep before he woke up in time to see the sun rise. It had been several weeks since he had his nightmare. *Maybe talking about my dream to Lily worked after all.* After he dressed, he decided to bite the bullet and look in the box.

He set the painted, khaki green, wooden box on his bed and opened it. Tucked into the hinged lid was a log book and a laminated card with, what he assumed were call letters. In the box was the radio, complete with microphone and a rubber antenna that screwed into the corner. The power cord was missing but he tried turning it on anyway, hoping it had a power cell backup. If it did, it was dead. He turned his attention to the log book.

The book was medium sized, about five inches by seven inches. It was bound in leather and embossed with a Celtic Knot design. Tim carefully opened it. The paper was a bit yellowed with age but seemed to be in good shape. *The doctor wasn't going to win any awards for penmanship*, Tim laughed to himself. The handwriting was more of a scribble, but it was still slightly legible. The first page was a list of codenames.

Dove = HQ

Raven = West

Sparrow = Central

Hawk = North

Pigeon = East

Eagle = South

Tim noticed that Raven was circled. *That must be Dr. Anderson's codename.* He flipped a few pages ahead and began reading.

August 29th, 9:20p.m. Checked in with Dove. The nest is feathered. All chicks are gathered and sleeping soundly.

September 29th, 10:30a.m. Fledgling is beginning to have second thoughts. Informed Dove. Dove says to relax and wait. No need to rush the mission. He will inform us when to proceed.

January 17th, 3:30p.m. It's been months since any word from Dove. The radio has been silent.

June 18th, 2:10p.m. It's been nearly a year and still no word on our mission.

He flipped a few more pages.

January 17th, 4:40p.m. Year 7. A strong thunderstorm is battering the building. Hail about the size of quarters is pounding the air system vents on the roof and the windows. I don't know how much longer they will hold. Fledgling is growing anxious for the mission to be over.

April 17th, 10:00a.m. Dove gives the go ahead to proceed with the mission but not to tell Fledgling. Will take the radio and laptop outside to the safe zone before setting the bomb.

"Bomb?" Tim jumped ahead. The handwriting was different.

December 17th, Found a radio and laptop. Forest Grove SAC destroyed. Read Chuck's notes. Still can't believe it. How could he?

December 18th, Spent the night in the Hummer trying to figure out the password to

Chuck's laptop. No success. At dawn decided to walk through the rubble, not sure what I'm looking for but just seems like the thing to do. Found nothing. Not sure what to do. Don't feel like going back to the SAC just yet. Decide to take a drive and check out McMinnville and Newberg first.

December 19th, Spent the night in McMinnville. The SAC is still standing and all looks normal. Decided not to make my presence known for fear one or both of them could be involved. Instead, parked two blocks away and just watched for a while. Heading to Newberg.

Newberg SAC appears fine. Want to look around some more. Will head to Sherwood and then north to Aloha before heading back to Hillsboro. Not sure what I will tell Michelle.

OH MY GOD! Aloha SAC is destroyed. The building looks like it was under attack from the outside. I can't linger too long to check it out. I gotta get out of here.

What is going on? Who are they and why

are they doing this? I don't understand.

December 20th, I returned "home". Michelle wants to know where I've been. I'm no longer sure I can trust her, so I tell her the Forest Grove SAC was destroyed by what appeared to be an explosion in the ventilation system. She wanted to know how I figured that out. I told her I looked through the rubble. She gave me a look that made me uncomfortable. Could she be in on it? I have to be careful.

"Oh my god, he wasn't nuts!"

There was a knock on the bedroom door that nearly sent Tim jumping through the ceiling.

"Tim?" Lily called through the door.

"Yes?" he answered while scrambling to put the papers and log book back into the box.

"Who are you talking to?"

"Uh, no one, just myself." He stuffed the radio under his bed and opened the door.

She stepped back in the open landing and smiled at him.

"Well, I was wondering how you slept? You haven't been sleeping on the front porch lately."

"I'm good. I think I'm going to be fine."

"Great," she said and smiled. "Would you like some coffee?"

"Sounds good."

Moments later, while Tim sat at the kitchen table and sipped the weak coffee, the kitchen light blinked.

Lily jumped and turned around, staring up at the light in the ceiling. "What was that?"

"I don't know. Maybe the bulb is about to go out? After all, it's old too." Tim smiled but he was just as worried. He remembered what John said about the drain on the power system and couldn't help but wonder if that was the problem.

When he finished his coffee he told Lily he needed to go see George about something. She was her usual accommodating self and Tim promised her he wouldn't be long.

When he arrived at the Bjorges' farm, he found George and Godfrey in the barn tinkering with old Bessie. They had already fixed her engine and started her up but now they were replacing some of the boards that made up her floor. Seeing them working on Bessie reminded Tim of when they were all kids. John had started working on Bessie when George, Godfrey and Tim were still in grade school. When they got older, George and Godfrey started helping him. It was their father-son time John would say which was Tim's cue to go home.

"Hey guys," Tim greeted them.

Godfrey looked over his shoulder and smiled but George kept his head down, focused on tightening the bolt that held the new board in place.

"Hi, Tim."

"Say, did your lights flicker a little bit ago?"

Godfrey looked at George. They both shook their heads.

"Not that I noticed," Godfrey answered. "Why?"

"No reason. Say, where's your dad?"

"He's in the kitchen with Mom."

"You guys have a second, I have some news I think you'll find interesting."

"Sure," George looked up and set the socket wrench down. "I'm finished anyway."

They headed into the house. John was seated at the table in the kitchen while Anna washed the dishes by hand. Even though she had a dishwasher, Godfrey said, she preferred to do the dishes the old-fashioned way. He even said his mother stored plastic grocery bags in the dishwasher. Tim didn't have the nerve to check to see if Godfrey was telling the truth.

The three joined John at the table. John put his book aside. Anna continued to clean her kitchen but paused from time to time to listen while Tim filled them in on what he'd found.

"So, where's the laptop?" John asked.

"I don't know. The only one I found was in his apartment. That was the one I gave George."

"Well, I don't think Dr. Anderson would have left it lying around; not if he suspected Dr. Dever was involved. How thoroughly did you search his place?"

"Not much really. His apartment is a mess with books papers and trash all over the place. I've mainly been focused on his bedroom where I found the empty binder. I've been sorting through a ton of papers but still haven't found the ones to the missing binder.

"Well, maybe you boys should all take another look," John suggested.

John didn't have to say it twice. Godfrey was always itching for any excuse to drive the Hummer. They both grabbed their jackets and before long the three were headed into Hillsboro.

Hillsboro was still as quiet as a ghost town. Tim couldn't

understand with the number of empty chambers where all the people had gone. With his daily trips into town, he was sure he should have seen someone by now. They arrived at the SAC and quickly shut the garage door. The last thing they needed was for someone to carjack the Hummer.

"Before we get started, I need to check on something," Tim told Godfrey and George.

"That's fine. We'll go with you," Godfrey said.

Tim checked in on his mother. The lights above her sleep chamber were still blinking, letting him know she was safe. He skipped his normal rounds and the three headed to the lower level where the apartments were.

"Brace yourselves, guys," Tim warned while he held the keycard against the reader. The lock clicked.

"Oh my god! It's a total disaster." George gasped in a sarcastic tone.

"Are you making fun of me?" Tim asked and glared at him.

"A little, maybe," he admitted with a smirk. "But you were right, this is a mess." Even though George agreed with Tim, his tone still said it was no big deal.

Searching the apartment took hours. George and Godfrey gathered up the papers in the apartment and stacked them on the floor by the bed while Tim sorted through them as fast as he could. Still, when the twins were finished, Tim was nowhere near done. George and Godfrey set to work gathering up the clothes. They piled them in a heap in an empty corner of the bedroom.

"Still haven't found a laptop," George announced.

"Does he have a safe?" Godfrey asked.

"A safe?" George scoffed. "Why would he need a safe? There's no one around to break in. Everyone's asleep."

"I don't know, but they always have them in the movies," Godfrey snipped.

"Not a bad idea. Why don't one of you check out there and the other in the back rooms while I finish sorting these papers?" Tim suggested.

"Fine," George answered sounding a kid again.

"Don't forget to look behind pictures on the walls and for hidden doors," Godfrey called out to George.

"You watched too much T.V.," George shouted back.

Tim quietly laughed.

By the time Tim had finished sorting the papers, his eyes had had enough of reading the fine print. He decided to have a look around the bedroom. He took an armful of hanging clothes out of the closet and piled them on the chair in the corner. Returning to the closet he felt the back wall. *Nothing*. The shelf above revealed nothing as well.

Tim headed into the living room and found George stretched out and leaning back in the strange chair. His feet were resting on the cleared off coffee table.

"Any luck?"

"No," George answered and shrugged.

"Nothing in here," Godfrey called out and returned to the living room. "George!" he snapped.

"What? I looked" George responded. "So now where?"

"I don't know."

"What about his office?" Godfrey asked.

Tim couldn't believe he hadn't thought of that sooner. Of course, Dr. Anderson had an office. It was on the north hall.

They left the apartment, the door locked behind them, and headed around the corner to the door with "Doctor Anderson" painted on the glass window. Tim held the keycard to the sensor and the lock clicked open. Godfrey grabbed the doorknob and pulled it open.

"What the hell?" he said looking into the closet. The sign on the window had just been a decoration, an empty façade. "Now where?" Godfrey groaned.

"There's a computer room on Lower Level Four," Tim suggested. "One of them had to have known how to run them. Maybe Dr. Anderson was the one and his office was down there. Let's go check it out."

"Sounds reasonable," George said.

They took the elevator down two flights to Lower Level Four and emerged into the lobby. The room seemed darker than Tim remembered. The LED lights in the ceiling weren't as bright. *Perhaps the computers also monitored the lights, putting them in energy saving mode or something to make them last.* They walked over to the door to the computer room. Either the lights had become brighter or Tim's eyes had adjusted to the dimness. He ignored the "Authorized Personnel Only" sign and held Dr. Anderson's badge against the electronic sensor. The lock clicked. They were in.

When George opened the door, all three were surprised by what they saw. It was a viewing room of sorts. A glass wall directly opposite the entry door separated the moderately-sized room from the rows of cables, wires and computer equipment the size of refrigerators on the other side. George walked up to the glass and seemed to be keenly interested in what he saw.

"Hey, over here," Godfrey called out. "I think this is it."

Tim looked away from the window. Godfrey was standing in front of a door to the left. He gave the doorknob a try. "Locked," he announced.

Tim noticed a strip of metal on the floor by Godfrey's feet. He picked it up and turned it over. It was a nameplate with Dr. Robert Anderson and a bunch of letters engraved after his name.

"Good job, Godfrey," Tim said and held the card up to the sensor.

Click.

He opened the door and walked into the office. The lights automatically came on. To his surprise, Dr. Anderson's office was neat. After seeing his apartment Tim had expected to find a similar scene. Instead, a large, oak desk sat symmetrically in the center of the room. Three computer monitors sat side by side in the center of the desktop, a desk lamp stood in one corner, and a framed photograph, the other. Behind the desk a floor-to-ceiling bookcase covered the wall. A series of burgundy binders labeled from A to Z filled the first set of shelves along with some fake plants and a variety of knick-knacks. Another series of tan binders with similar labeling filled the rest. Tim noticed a few of the tan binders had been pulled out and were lying in a heap on the floor. Turning around he saw a bank of computer monitors built into the wall above the entrance door. Each monitor screen was divided into four smaller squares. There was a crawling script in each. He moved closer to get a better look.

The images in the small panes were the different sleep chamber rooms on the upper floors. At seemingly random times the scene in each switched to another view. There was a number in the upper left corner identifying the floor. Tim quickly looked for number 13, to see if he could spot Henry visiting his family.

"Hey, take a look at this," George practically shouted, holding up an old photo frame he had taken off a side table by a lounge area. "Seems the good doctor was batting for the other team," he laughed.

Tim turned to see what George was talking about. George

handed him the framed photograph. Even though it was slightly faded with age, Tim recognized the man on the right. It was Robert, the man who had helped him and his parents when they came to the center. He was dressed in a black tux and standing with his arm around a blonde man with a short, neatly trimmed beard who was also dressed in a black tux.

"Here's another," George said while he continued to snoop around. He handed it to Godfrey.

"Wait a minute," Godfrey said, looking at the photo and then holding out so Tim could see it. "I've seen that guy."

"Are you sure?" Tim asked. "When?"

"Yes, I'm sure. He was in the elevator when I woke up. The reason I remember him is because he stayed behind when we reached the first floor."

Tim hesitated for a moment and stared at the picture. *I wonder if he knows the doctor is dead.*

"Let's just stay focused on finding that laptop," Tim said and shook off his thoughts. He set the photo back on the side table and glanced at the others. One of a park scene caught his eye. He recognized it.

"Hey, look here," Godfrey called out.

Tim turned around. Godfrey was standing beside the bookcase with one of the burgundy binders in his hand.

"These list all of the people in the SAC, with their birth dates, addresses, family connections, occupations. It even tells what chamber they're in." He continued to flip the pages.

"Let me see," George said and took the binder from him. "This is just the T's," he said and handed it back to his brother. "Where are the B's?"

"Guys, really?" Tim sighed. "We need to find that laptop. George, why don't you check out his computer?"

"We will, just give us a sec," Godfrey said, brushing Tim

off. He looked over his brother's shoulder while George flipped through the pages of another binder.

Disgusted, Tim walked over to the half-empty shelf at the opposite end of the bookcase. Careful not to step on any of the binders on the floor, He looked at the back of the bookcase.

"Guys!" he announced. "Found it."

"The laptop?"

"No, a safe."

"Cool!" Godfrey said and left his brother who was still flipping through pages of the binder. "Is it open?" he asked and crowded in front of Tim to take a look. "Oh," he said sounding disappointed. "It's empty." He reached into it and moved his hand around, inspecting every inch of the interior. "Damn!" he cursed and pulled his hand out. "You don't think his friend beat us to it?"

"I don't know, but I wouldn't be surprised." Tim looked at the door to the safe when Godfrey moved out of the way. "It doesn't appear to have been pried open or anything. George, see if you can find his home address on this computer," Tim asked, trying not to sound too impatient.

"Better yet," George said closing the binder and grabbing another marked on the spine with a large "A". He flipped through the pages, running his index finger down the list of names.

"Nothing," he reported. "No Robert Anderson."

"That's probably because he didn't go to sleep," Tim said, this time not caring if sounded a bit upset that George didn't check the computer.

Tim walked back over to the side table and took a closer look at the many framed photographs for a clue. He picked up one that was a selfie of the doctor and his partner standing in front of a house. The house number was clearly visible on the wall beside the front door.

"Hey, I know where this house is!"

"You do?" Godfrey asked.

"Yes, this is near my condo in Orenco Station. Come on, let's go!"

"Go?"

"Yes, go. I want to find this guy. Maybe he can help us."

"You guys go ahead. I'll stay here, if you don't mind," George said, picking up another binder. "I want to look through these. Maybe I can find something."

"Okay. Keep the door locked and don't open it for anyone. We'll be back to pick you up."

Tim didn't wait for George to answer. He rushed back to the elevator leaving Godfrey to secure the door behind them. They rode up two floors to the garage. The prospect of going back to his neighborhood had Tim excited. He was anxious to see how his condo had faired, especially after learning of the fire that destroyed Lily's home.

Cornell Road didn't weather well. The pavement was cracked and weeds had begun to reclaim the land beneath it, especially along the section between the airport and fair grounds. *My Bug would never have been able to navigate this part of the road,* Tim thought. The Hummer had no problem.

When they passed Brookwood Parkway the road improved. It wasn't as cracked or torn up. The wooden fence to the left that once provided a barrier between a housing development and the road had rotted away in places, leaving huge gaps. The parking lot of the old Intel complex on the south side of the road was a field of overgrown grass.

Tim turned left onto NE Orenco Station Parkway. It felt so normal. The buildings still looked the same, except for the trim around the windows and doors which needed a good coat of paint. It was strange not seeing the sidewalks filled with window shoppers and people on their coffee breaks.

When he reached Brighton Drive, Tim stopped.

"Now where?" Godfrey asked.

Tim looked at the photograph again and then looked around. The park, directly in front of them, looked so different. Ivy had overtaken the gazebo. All that remained of the wooden benches to the left were the rusted metal frames. Some of the glass globes on the street lamps were broken, their decorative brass bands lay on the ground like fallen halos.

"This way," he said and turned right and then left, heading north on Orenco Station Parkway again.

"How can you be sure which house it is?" Godfrey asked.

"We'll just have to see. I've lived in this neighborhood for nearly three years before...well, you know. I recognized the house and if I'm not totally mistaken it's up here on the right, the second house before we get to Rosebay Drive. And there it is!"

Tim parked by the curb, ignoring the No Parking sign. The sign seemed so pointless, like many of the old world's rules. Even when the rest of the people wake up, Tim couldn't imagine life would ever go back to the way it was. How could it? Entire cities and towns were gone thanks to the Naturalists, how many survived, he didn't know. He just knew Hillsboro had to survive and it was up to him to wake everyone up.

The old craftsman style, two-story house looked a little weathered like all the other houses but it appeared to be in good shape. The lawn and flowerbeds were overgrown but the concrete walkway still looked solid. Tim and Godfrey walked up the steps of the front porch. Tim took a deep breath and knocked.

"Well, there's no turning back now," he said and drew a

nervous breath.

There was no answer.

He knocked again.

"Who is it?" came a man's voice from inside.

"My name is Tim Stone. I'm a neighbor."

There was the sound of a security chain being latched and then the door opened, only to be stopped when the chain reached its full, six inch extension. The blonde man from the photograph peeked out at them. From what Tim could see, he hadn't aged a bit. His hair and his beard were still neatly trimmed. The only difference was his eyes were red and puffy as though he'd been crying. "What do you want?" he asked in a raspy voice.

"I was wondering if we could talk to you for a moment."

He eyed the two suspiciously.

"About what?"

"About Dr. Anderson and the SAC."

There seemed to be a flash of recognition in his eyes.

"What makes you think I know anything about him?" he asked and eyed Godfrey warily.

"Because of this," Tim answered and held up the picture.

The man behind the door instantly reached through the small opening and grabbed at the photo, his thin fingers clawing the air. Instinctively Tim pulled it back.

"Where did you get that?" he demanded and continued to reach for the picture. This time Tim let him take it.

"From Dr. Anderson's office, it was on his table."

"I know," he snapped. "How did you get in there?"

"I have his keycard," Tim answered. "May we come in and talk?"

He eyed them again.

"No. Go away!" he snapped and slammed the door.

"That went well, I'd say," Godfrey quipped. He turned and headed for the Hummer.

Tim hesitated at the door and listened, for what, he wasn't sure. Faint sounds of sobbing seeped out through the cracks around the door. Tim imagined the man hugging the photo of his partner while he crumpled to the floor, leaning his back against the door. Then again, maybe he'd seen too many movies. In any event, Tim couldn't help but ache for the man's pain. He walked away.

"Now what?" Godfrey asked when Tim climbed in the passenger seat.

"Let's swing by my place before we head back to the SAC."

Tim's condo was only a few blocks away. It appeared to have survived his absence well. Everything inside still looked the way it did when he left except for a coat of dust that covered everything. The air inside smelled musty and stale. Tim resisted the urge to open a window. Instead he quickly grabbed some clothes and they were on their way again.

They found George where they left him in Dr. Anderson's office. He was sitting in the doctor's chair behind the desk going through one of the binders. The binders that were on the floor were now put neatly back on their shelf.

"It's about time!" he snapped.

"Sorry, we hurried as fast as we could." Tim answered.

"Yeah, you wouldn't want us to get a speeding ticket would you?" Godfrey teased and laughed at his own joke.

George frowned and then put the binder he was looking at on the desk. "Look what I've found."

Godfrey and Tim stood behind him and looked over his shoulders.

"When I was looking through these binders, I noticed

several of the names were in red. I tried to find a key or something that would explain what it means but I couldn't find anything."

"So," Godfrey said, "Big deal."

"It *is* a big deal," George snapped. "Look!" He picked up a binder from the stack on the corner of the desk. Flipping it open, he pointed. "Mom, Dad, you and I are red." He grabbed another open binder.

Godfrey leaned forward and looked.

"What's more," he continued. "Tim, your parents are red, too, but you're not."

"Give me that," Tim said taking the book and looking at the red type for himself. "You didn't find anything in these binders that said what this means?"

"No," George answered.

"What about in his computer?"

"I'm not touching it," George finally admitted. He pushed the chair back, away from the desk. Godfrey and Tim jumped out of the way. He stood up and walked around the desk to the center of the office and stared at the monitors on the wall. "Those displays are monitoring the vital signs of everyone still asleep. The computers are regulating temperatures, air flow and God knows what else. There's no way I'm going to touch any computer in here."

Tim moved closer to the monitors, this time looking for his mother's name. There were no names, only numbers. He turned around and faced the twins.

"Okay, I guess we're done here for now. Let's go home."

Minutes later, Tim said his good-byes to George and Godfrey at their house and headed down the road to his parents' farmhouse. He couldn't get the image of Dr. Anderson's partner out of his mind. He looked so sad. It was obvious he knew the doctor was dead.

After dinner, while Philip dozed in his chair in the front room with the television playing nothing but static, Tim filled Lily in on what they found and about Dr. Anderson's partner.

"That poor man," she frowned.

"I want to go back to see him tomorrow; alone this time. Maybe he will talk if it's only me."

"You should take him some food. He's probably starved. I'll put together a small basket."

"That's so nice of you," Tim said. He couldn't wait for his mother to meet her.

Day Sixty-one. The sky was dark with thunder clouds. The morning air felt cold. Tim sat in the Hummer and stared at the house on Orenco Parkway. He thought about what he would say but then began to wonder if the man inside was watching him from the front window or even an upstairs window. He would probably be wondering what Tim was doing. The more Tim thought, the more nervous he grew. He grabbed the basket Lily had prepared and headed up the walk.

"Who is it?" came the answer to his knock.

"It's me, Tim Stone. We met yesterday."

"Go away!"

"I have something for you," Tim called through the door.

"What?"

"Won't you open the door?"

The door opened the length of the security chain. The man peeked out.

"I have some food for you, some fresh eggs and some vegetables, meal packets . . ."

The man eyed the basket and then closed the door. Tim heard the sound of the security chain being removed and then the door opened wide.

"Okay," he said as though giving up. "You can come in if you must."

The man was Tim's height, about six foot. He was thinner than Tim, perhaps from not eating for days. He shut the front door and replaced the security chain before showing Tim to the living room to the left of the entry. Tim set the basket down on the large, round, oak coffee table in the center of the room.

"Thank you," his host said. "I'm—I'm sorry about yesterday."

"No," Tim interrupted. "You have nothing to apologize for."

He nodded and motioned for Tim to sit down. Tim sat down on one of the overstuffed chairs while his host sat down on the sofa beneath a large, picture window. He took the small, decorative sofa pillow from behind him and sat back. Wrapping his arms around the pillow, he hugged it as a child would a Teddy Bear. He stared at the basket on the coffee table.

The room felt very comfortable, not at all what Tim expected from two guys living together. The sofa was dark green, Tim's favorite color. It still looked new despite being over fifty-three years old. The two overstuffed chairs were upholstered in a green, yellow and purple plaid pattern that made Tim think of a Scottish tartan. A flickering light caught Tim's eye. Beside him, to his right, was a fireplace with a very ornate, antique, wooden mantle. Instead of a warm fire, a fat candle burned inside. The room could have come straight out of a magazine, Tim suspected.

"I'm Derrick," the man introduced himself. His voice was a bit hoarse and he didn't look at Tim.

"Hi, Derrick," Tim said, wondering how to bring up the

subject he wanted to talk to him about.

The room fell silent. Derrick continued to stare at the basket.

"Lily," Tim finally spoke, "caught some chickens at my parents' farm on the other side of Hillsboro. They're good layers. She thought you might like some eggs."

Derrick only nodded and the room went silent again.

"How are you doing?" Tim asked.

Derrick's head jerked sharply and he looked at Tim. His eyes teared up. He shook his head. "Not good. I didn't want to go to sleep. I begged him to let me stay awake with him," he answered and went back to staring at the basket. "Robbie said he didn't like it either but I had to; that Dever woman would never go for it. The rule was only two were to remain awake. We didn't have a choice. The last thing Robbie said to me before he put me under was, 'It's not so bad. You always did like the daddy types.' I told him he wasn't funny. At least I think I told him." He looked at the fireplace. "We were supposed to grow old *together*." Tears escaped from the corners of his blue, bloodshot eyes. He quickly wiped them away and regained his composure.

"Secretly Robbie planned that once everyone was asleep and the bitch was preoccupied with whatever she was supposed to do, he would wake me. I was supposed to hide out in his apartment. But when I woke up and he wasn't there, I knew something went wrong. I went looking for him and that's when I saw your friend in the elevator. He wasn't supposed to be awake. When he got out on the first floor he asked me if I needed help. I shook my head and let the doors close.

"When I saw Robbie's apartment a mess I began to panic. It wasn't like him. He obsesses about being neat. I thought I would check out that bitch's office before heading to Robbie's and that's when I found them." Tears flowed freely down Derrick's cheeks and he began to rock back and forth. "It wasn't supposed to be like this," he groaned and squeezed he pillow tighter.

Hearing Derrick sob, Tim could feel how deep his pain was and how much he must have loved the doctor. It felt so foreign. Tim had girlfriends before and one of them made him think about getting married, but the relationship ended before he ever got around to asking her. Thinking about it now, Tim wasn't sure he was really in love, not the kind that Derrick and Dr. Anderson seemed to have. "I'm so sorry," Tim said.

"I don't know what I'm supposed to do," Derrick cried and looked at Tim. "Won't someone please tell me, what am I supposed to do, now?"

"Do you have family around here?" Tim asked and immediately felt guilty. Derrick was asking for him help and here he was trying to push him onto someone else.

"Not around here," he answered. "They're all back in Chicago. I tried to call them but the phones aren't working. I don't even know if they're still . . ."

The room fell silent except for Derrick's sobbing but even those seemed to have softened. Tim tried desperately to find a way to comfort him and yet at the same time felt slightly embarrassed and uneasy. Tim had seen only one grown man cry before, his dad. The first time was when he learned that Sarah died. Then next was when his parents died. But this was different. Tim thought of what his mother said to comfort him when his sister died, "Everything's going to be okay, Timmy." Somehow, he didn't think that would work for this man.

Suddenly, Derrick threw the pillow aside and stood up. He wiped the tears from his cheeks. "No!" he reprimanded himself.

"It's okay," Tim said. "I can't imagine what you must be going through."

Derrick ignored him and looked blindly around the room. "I've got to get out of here. I need some air."

Tim jumped to his feet but Derrick was at the front door first. He opened it and went out onto the porch. Tim followed. After shutting the door Derrick headed down the walk and crossed the street. He started walking south toward the shops. Tim had to quicken his pace to keep up.

"So, how long were you and the doctor together?" Tim asked trying to find out more about them and hoping Derrick wouldn't crumple into another bought of grief.

"Five years. We met while we were both working at Kaiser Hospital. I'm—was a nurse there. Who knows now?" He stopped and turned around to face Tim. "Why are you here?"

"I was hoping you could help me."

"Help you? With what?"

"How much do you know about what happened to us?"

"Nothing except what Robbie wrote in his journal and a letter to me. I found it in his safe with some of our other things."

"A journal?"

"Yes."

"Did it say how to wake everyone up?"

Derrick gave Tim a strange look. "What do you mean?"

"In a word, we all over slept. Instead of being awakened after twenty years, we slept for nearly fifty-three years."

Derrick's eyes widened and he staggered back slightly as if he lost his balance for a moment. He looked around at the park and then back at Tim. "Are you sure?"

"Yes. The date on the computer in Dr. Anderson's office

and on another I found confirmed it."

"That means he's been dead for over forty-four years."

Tim sensed by the remote tone in Derrick's voice that he was beginning to slip away into his grief again.

"Did the journal say anything else? I mean, why this happened?" Tim asked not wanting to give him the chance.

"Not exactly," Derrick answered and was back. He wiped his eyes and took a deep breath. He looked around and then walked over to a raised flowerbed surrounded by a brick retaining wall and sat down.

Tim followed him but stood with his arms folded over his chest. The looked at the ground for a moment and then looked at Derrick. "Do you know how to wake everyone up?"

Derrick looked confused. "I thought you said everyone overslept. Why does that matter now?"

"Because not everyone woke up. There are floors of people still asleep back at the SAC."

Derrick's back straightened while Tim's words appeared to sink in. He looked at Tim. His eyes appeared cold and unfeeling. "Maybe it's for the best," he answered. "Let them sleep."

"I can't," Tim snapped. "My mother is still asleep. My father has Alzheimer's and he's awake. He needs her."

Derrick's eyebrows pinched and he looked confused. He looked around and then shrugged. "Well, you should just be glad your father woke up at all."

"What?" Tim nearly shrieked. "What's that supposed to mean?"

"According to what Robbie wrote in his journal, the government had a secret plan. Once everyone was in suspended animation the people in charge of the Centers were to dispose of the 'undesirables.' They were to clean up the human race. Anyone over sixty was considered too old to wake up. Of those under sixty, all those who were in jails and prisons, along with ones who have a mental or physical disability were next." He looked at Tim with a contemptuous expression. "Did you know the government, after all its outward support of equal rights and gay marriage, secretly considered being gay a mental illness?"

Tim shook his head.

"Yeah," he continued. "All those of the LGBTQ Community were to be 'culled.' That's the word they used to pretty it up but what it really is, is murder."

"The red," Tim said out loud as Derrick's words finally registered.

"What?" Derrick asked.

"George, that's Godfrey's twin brother, he noticed in the binders behind Dr. Anderson's desk that some of the names were in red. His parents' names and my parents' names were in red. It must mean they weren't supposed to wake up."

"Well, Robbie wouldn't do it." Derrick said confidently. "He said in his letter that the Dever woman was planning on following instructions. He said he put her off for seven years but she was tired of waiting and wanted to get it over with, with or without his help. He wrote that he was going to stop her."

"Did he say how?"

Derrick shook his head. "No. That was where the letter stopped. There was nothing more in his journal either."

Tim stared at a crack in the sidewalk. This was all too much to process. His mind was reeling. He thought about when he found the two bodies. There was only one gun and it was by Dr. Anderson's remains. He had assumed that Dr. Anderson had shot Dr. Dever and then himself. This wasn't making any sense. *The gun Pedro held to my head! It must have been hers. He found the gun,* a voice in his head said. It started to come together. Perhaps she caught him going through her desk and she shot him first but he was able to get a round off of his own. *But what about the note? What did he mean, Oh God, what have I done?*

"Are you okay?" Derrick asked Tim, interrupting his thoughts and snapping him back into the moment.

"I don't know," Tim answered him. "I guess I should be going. Are you going to be okay?"

"What choice do I have?"

"Mind if I drop by again sometime?"

"I guess," he said. Tim started for the Hummer. "Hey, if I find out anything more from his journal how can I let you know?" Derrick asked.

Tim stopped and turned back. "I'll give you my parents' address. I'm staying there until I figure out how to wake my mother up. I've got a pen and paper in the Hummer."

After giving him the information, Tim started back toward town. He made a quick stop at the SAC to check on his mom before heading for home. He was tired of thinking about Dr. Anderson, Dr. Dever and the government's plan. Part of him wished Derrick had never said a word. It was just too much. It reaffirmed Tim's distrust of the leaders of this country. While they put forth the pretense that they were there to serve the good of the people, they were really serving only themselves. Tim wondered where they fit into their own plans since most of them were past the sixty year mark. Were they to be culled? Or, had they even gone to sleep? Tim's head hurt. He just wanted to get home and see his dad and Lily. *I want my normal back.*

Walking up the front steps to the porch, Tim froze. Music

poured from inside the house. He rushed inside, into the front room. Philip was sitting in his chair smiling and rocking to the beat of an old Country Western song that Tim hadn't heard since he was a kid.

"You're back," Lily announced. "I found some of your father's old records in a closet and thought we'd try them out. Your dad showed me how to work the record player." She nodded toward the old stereo console that was used as a side table between his dad's and his mom's chairs. Originally it had been his Grandpa's, along with the old albums. Philip inherited them.

"It's nice to hear music again," Tim said and sat down on the arm of the sofa and closed his eyes. The music began to wash away the stresses of the day.

Day Sixty-two. Tim awoke again to the sounds of Lily throwing up. He gagged and fought the urge to join her. He had always had a low tolerance for that sound, or was it just a weak stomach? *Damn these thin walls!* He rolled over, pulling his pillow over his ears to muffle the sound and waited for her to finish.

Minutes later they met in the hallway right when she stepped out of the bathroom. Her face was damp with sweat and pale; her eyes, bloodshot. Tim smiled sympathetically at her.

"You okay?"

"It'll pass," she answered.

"Too bad I don't know if any of the doctors in town woke up but then again, we'd need a pharmacist and then there's no telling if the meds would do any good this far after their expiration dates." Tim knew he was rambling and could tell she was not in the mood to listen. "I'm sorry. Can I get you anything?" he asked following her back to her room.

"I'll be fine," she answered.

"Well, I'll go make some coffee. I know it's not tea but it may as well be."

"Whatever." She closed the bedroom door and ended his feeble attempt at conversation.

Tim went back to his bedroom and after a few moments emerged dressed for the day. He avoided the bathroom upstairs, trying to silence the memory of Lily puking. Downstairs he headed into the kitchen and grabbed the coffee pot. He stood in front of the sink with the pot under the running faucet. While it filled, he looked up through the window at the back yard. Above him he heard Lily moving around, then her footsteps on the stairs, followed by the creaking of the front door being opened. She had gone outside to sit in the morning air and watch the sun come up, their normal routine.

It didn't take long for the coffee to finish brewing. It was so weak, Tim could see through it. *I really need to find some more.* He poured two cups and went to join her. When he reached his father's bedroom, he put his ear to the door. The restful sound of his father's snoring slipped faintly around the door. Tim listened for a moment, letting it wrap around him like a warm hug before he continued to the front porch.

Lily was sitting on the small wicker loveseat. She had her feet pulled up with her arms wrapped around her legs and her chin resting on her knees. She was staring at the field across the street. Tim handed her a steaming cup.

"Here you go."

She took the cup but didn't take her eyes off the field.

"What are you looking at?" Tim turned around and nearly dropped his cup. "How long have they been there?"

"Don't know," she whispered. "They were there when I came outside. Whose field is that?"

"It's my dad's," Tim answered, matching her volume. His heart pounded faster with excitement. "We need a rope."

"For what?"

"To tie them up."

"Tie them up? What kind of farmers were you?" she asked. Tim could hear the smirk in her tone.

"We were dirt farmers. Dad grew stuff," Tim answered and didn't care if he sounded patronizing.

"That explains everything," Lily laughed. "You can't just tie a rope around them like you do a dog. They're cows. They need to be able to graze in a field like that." She gestured toward the field.

"How do you know?"

"Because my uncle owned a dairy. I used to help him during the summer. What we need is a fenced pasture. Did your dad fence his land?"

"Yeah, but that was to keep animals out not in."

"What about a barn?"

"I'd be afraid to put them in ours."

"What about the Bjorges'?"

Tim felt a jolt inside. "I don't think so."

"Well, before we go and try catching them we should make sure we have a place for them."

"I still think we should catch them. We could fix a pen for them after."

"I'll look around," Lily insisted. "For now, we should let them be."

Much as Tim hated the thought of them wandering off, he didn't have the slightest clue when it came to taking care of them. So, reluctantly he deferred to Lily. He sat down on the porch rail and leaned against the post.

"You know what you said last night," Lily spoke slowly, thoughtfully, "about the government's plan to do away with people over sixty."

"Yes." Tim nodded.

"My parents wouldn't have made it. My dad was sixty-two and my mom had just turned sixty. They would have died anyway."

Tim looked at her. She was still staring at the field, her eyes dry and tearless. "I'm sorry," was all he could think to say.

"I'm glad Dr. Anderson stopped her. At least you still have your parents and friends. Do you think in other parts of the state and world they went ahead with it?"

Instantly the image of Leonard's weathered old face popped into Tim's head. Leonard's haughty voice rang in his ears, "My squad destroyed all the Centers in the Portland-Vancouver area." Tim shivered and folded his arms over his chest.

"I don't know," he answered. "But it could explain why there isn't any television or radio. I mean, if people in other centers woke up we'd have that stuff, right?"

Lily nodded her head. "I guess so."

They fell into silent thought while they watched the sun continue to rise over Mt. Hood. Tim's mind kept flashing with more and more unanswered questions. He pushed them aside and tried to stay focused on the most important matter at hand, waking up his mom and the rest of the town.

"Tim," Lily jolted him out of his thoughts. "I think I'd like to take a trip into town today, if that's okay?"

"Sure," he answered trying not to sound surprised. "Want me to drive you? We could take Dad with us."

"No, I want to walk around by myself."

"Okay." Tim couldn't help but think about what she said when he found her. How a gang of hoodlums had abducted her and used her for their entertainment. The gang that stole his Bug was gone but he couldn't be sure there weren't others.

Suddenly the realization that he was worried about her hit him. He looked at her. "Are you sure you'll be okay?"

"I'll be careful."

While Lily was away, Tim took his dad for a walk around the field behind the barn. They walked the fence line. Every time they came to a place where the barbed wire had come loose from the iron fence post, Philip would stop and fix it without saying a word.

"Dad, be careful," Tim warned when he saw his father's bare hands. The thought of him poking himself with the rusty old wire and not knowing if there were any doctors around worried Tim. If Philip heard his son, he didn't show it. He kept twisting the wire and clipping it back into place as he had done thousands of times before.

When they reached the northeast corner of the field where Philip's land bordered the Bjorges', John called out to them and waved. Tim waved back.

"'Morning, Mr. Bjorge," he yelled.

"Wait a sec, Tim," John returned while he hurried across his field toward them.

Suddenly Tim felt nervous. Did John see the cow and its calf this morning too? Was he going to try to claim them for his family? With three men they would surely be better able to catch them than just Lily and him. Tim decided to play dumb if John mentioned them.

"Good to see you out, Phil," John greeted. "How are you doing?"

"Everyone I can and the easy ones twice," came Philip's standard answer followed by a little chuckle.

John smiled and nodded. "Well, good for you," he said then looked Tim. "What brings you two out this morning?"

"We're just out for a walk around the property. A bit of fresh air and exercise," Tim answered trying his best to be vague.

"The boys and I were wondering how your visit with that man went yesterday?" John asked. "Any luck with finding out where the government's food bank is or how to wake everyone up?"

"Oh," Tim groaned. "No, I completely spaced it; but, I did find out something interesting." He gave John a brief recount of what he learned about the government's plan. John listened and every once in a while shook his head in disgust.

"That's incredible," he kept repeating.

Anna called for John from the back door of their house. John waved her off and turned back to us.

"Anna wanted me to ask if you have any more eggs. She's dried some fruit if you'd like to make an exchange?"

"Sure. I'll get some and drop them by when Lily gets back from town."

"I thought that was her. What's she doing in town?"

"I don't know. I think she may be visiting her parents' graves. She asked me about them before she left. I think the news about the government's plan may have upset her."

"Poor girl," he said and started to turn away. "You three need to come to dinner sometime. There isn't much but we can still have a good meal. Good to see you, Phil. Take care of yourself and those two."

Philip smiled and nodded.

"Sounds like a plan. I'll be by this afternoon," Tim said

nearly shouting it at the end.

Tim turned back to the fence and gave a quiet sigh. John hadn't mentioned the cows. They were safe. Along with a rising feeling of relief came another feeling that pulled Tim down, guilt. *Was I being greedy by not mentioning the cows to him? Was I being selfish, wanting to keep them for my family? What was I afraid of? That they suddenly wouldn't share with us anymore? The cows didn't belong to me, or them, or anyone for that matter. Surely the five of us stand a better chance in corralling them than just Lily and me alone.* Tim felt ashamed for not telling John about the cows.

Before he realized it Tim and his dad had reached the northwest corner of the property. Philip had successfully reattached the downed wire to the poles on two sides of the field. *Guess it's true what they say about old habits.*

"We should probably go back to the house," Tim said.

"Okay," Philip responded.

When they reached the house, Tim helped his father wash the rust from his hands in the kitchen sink. While Philip dried his hands, Tim washed his.

"How about I fix us something to eat?" Tim said.

His father didn't respond. He headed off to the front room and sat down in his chair. The walk had worn him out. He was asleep when Tim brought him a bowl of soup and one of Mrs. Bjorge' biscuits. Tim set the tray down on the coffee table and tucked the afghan from the sofa around his dad and went outside.

He settled into one of the wicker chairs and looked out at the field across the street. The cow was in the farthest corner away from the road. He couldn't see the calf in the tall grass and assumed it was napping while its mother grazed. Birds chirped on the branches of the trees in the front yard, breaking the silence of the summer afternoon. Tim closed his eyes for a moment.

"Tim?"

He heard someone call his name and jumped, wide awake.

"Oh, sorry," Derrick said and took a step back. "I didn't mean to startle you."

"Derrick?" Tim said, confused. "How did you—" He spotted a bicycle on the front lawn.

"After you left yesterday, I took another look at the stuff from the safe. I thought this was Robbie's laptop but it's not." He held out the computer to Tim. "I don't know why it was in the safe."

"I do," Tim admitted. "Would you care to sit down? Would you like some water?"

"Sure, thank you," he said and sat down on the loveseat.

Tim put the laptop in his chair and went inside for the water. When he came back out he noticed an overstuffed backpack at the foot of the steps.

"Here you go," he said and handed Derrick the glass.

"Thank you," he said and drank it quickly. He set the empty glass on the porch beside the loveseat.

"This laptop belonged to one of the heads of the Forest Grove SAC," Tim explained. "Its owner took it outside along with a radio and then went back inside to set a bomb. I'm guessing something went wrong and he didn't make it out before the bomb went off. The SAC was destroyed and the entire population was wiped out, no survivors."

"What? You're making that up."

"I wish I were. Along with the radio, I found a log book. Dr. Anderson wrote in it after he found it. He said after seeing the rubble, he took a trip to McMinnville and Newberg to check on them. They were still intact but he didn't go inside because he wasn't sure he could trust anyone. He found Aloha just as I had, destroyed."

"I don't understand," Derrick said shaking his head. "Who? Why?"

"From what I've found out, a group who called themselves Naturalists opposed the whole suspended animation plan saying it was against God's plan for man. Evidently some of them managed to infiltrate the program and get assigned to various SACs around Portland. I imagine it was the same in other cities. The rest of the Naturalist hid out and avoided being put to sleep. How they did that, I don't know for sure. Anyway after everyone was asleep they surfaced and began destroying the SACs, killing everyone inside."

"How do you know all of this?" Derrick asked, eyeing Tim suspiciously.

"Godfrey, George and I ran into an old man in Aloha. He tried to pass himself off as the lone survivor and one of the heads of the Aloha SAC but he turned out to be one of the Naturalists. He told us that his group had destroyed the centers in Portland and were working their way west when their rocket launcher malfunctioned, exploding and wiping them all out except for him and his buddy."

"That's crazy. Why would they do that?"

"He said it was because we had cheated God and time. Man has a set lifespan and what we had done was unnatural."

"But weren't they themselves playing God? What a bunch of hypocrites."

"I agree but that doesn't change what they did. Besides, history is filled with religious fanatics killing people in the name of God."

"And this was all documented in that notebook?"

"It's supported in part."

"What happened to the rest of their kind?"

"I have no idea. The fact that we are all still here means they didn't make it to Hillsboro."

"I guess."

Derrick looked shaken by the news. He stared at the field across the way. Tim suddenly remembered his cows. He glanced at the field and saw they were gone. Again, guilt began to churn in his gut. *They weren't my cows. Why was I being so possessive, greedy?*

"What do you suppose is on that laptop?" Derrick asked.

"I had hoped that it would tell us how to wake everyone up, but now that I think about it, I'm not so sure."

"Interesting. On a different subject, who is that up the road?"

"That's John and Anna Bjorge's place," Tim answered. "You met their son, Godfrey in the elevator when you woke up. I've known them nearly all my life."

"Oh," Derrick responded and looked up the road.

"Why do you ask?"

"No reason. I just noticed an older man watching me when I rode past the house. He looks vaguely familiar for some reason."

"Well, Mr. Bjorge owns a mechanic shop on the corner of First and Baseline. Maybe that's why?"

"Yeah." Derrick nodded. "Say, do you think he could fix my car? It won't start."

"He might. Want me to ask him?"

"Would you?"

"Sure."

The conversation fell silent. Derrick looked around as though something was on his mind. Tim tried not to stare at him.

"That's quite a long bike ride from Orenco," Tim broke the silence. "About six miles?"

"Yes, but it was fairly easy. No traffic." Derrick smiled.

"True. If you want to go, I can take you home when Lily gets back?"

He looked in the direction of his backpack. Tim could tell by the expression on his face that there was something he wanted to ask.

"Or, you're always welcome to stay here. We don't have a lot of room but I could fix up a cot or something for you."

"Are you sure you wouldn't mind?" Derrick asked. Tim could tell by the way his body relaxed that he was relieved by the offer.

"Of course not."

"It's just I don't want to be alone and there's no one in our neighborhood."

"I understand." Tim nodded. "I have to admit, I have an ulterior motive. You being a nurse and all, you might be able to help me with my dad. And I think Lily is coming down with something. She's been throwing up lately."

Derrick smiled. He seemed to be pleased that he was needed. "I'd be happy to help."

"Dad's napping right now but I'll show you around."

It was nearly sundown by the time Lily returned. Tim was beginning to worry and found himself walking to the front door and looking out at the road for her every few minutes.

"Whose bike is that on the front lawn?" she asked when she walked into the kitchen.

"Oh, that's mine," Derrick answered.

Lily just stood in the doorway and stared at the stranger, her mouth slightly agape.

"Lily, this is Derrick, the man I went to see yesterday."

"Thank you for the food," he said to her.

"Nice to meet you," she answered but still looked wary.

"I see you've been shopping," Tim said nodding at the bags in her arms.

She looked a bit embarrassed, like a young child being caught with her hand in the cookie jar.

"Sort of," she answered and set the bags on the counter by the sink. "I would have paid for this stuff but there wasn't anyone around and I didn't have any money anyway."

"Well, it's the thought that counts," Derrick spoke up with a bit of levity in his voice. It seemed to work, Lily relaxed.

"So, where's your dad?"

"He went to bed. I think I wore him out today. We walked the fence line out back. I wanted to see how much repair work needs to be done. I didn't expect Dad to repair the fence while we walked but he did."

"That's great," she said eyeing Derrick.

Tim recognized that look. It was a mixture of fear, paranoia and shame. The same feelings he'd been having all day after seeing the cows.

"It's okay, Lily," Tim said. "If we're able to catch the cows, we'll share the milk the same as we're sharing the eggs. So, what did you find?"

Lily pulled leaned against the counter. "The stores are a disaster," she began. "I went to that store on Sixth and Baseline. Someone had smashed the glass in the doors and ransacked the place. There wasn't much left. I managed to find a couple cans of coffee and some canned fruit in the back. Then I went to the store on Tenth by the cop shop. It was the same. Even the little stores were picked over. People must be hoarding the stuff. They couldn't possibly be using it all. The only stuff they didn't seem to touch was the cleaning supplies and paper goods."

"Oh that reminds me, Mr. Bjorge wanted me to ask if you know where the government's food facility is?" Tim asked Derrick.

"No. I don't."

"Do you think it would be in any of Dr. Anderson's stuff?"

"I doubt it. He would have told me."

"Dang!" Tim said and tried to think. "Maybe it's in one of the binders in Dr. Dever's office."

"It's possible," Derrick agreed. "Had things gone according to what the government presented to us, everyone would have awakened and gone back to work as though it were the next day. This looting would never have happened."

"True," Tim agreed. He looked at Lily. "Sorry. So, what else did you find?"

"I needed some clothes. I can't keep wearing your mom's old stuff," she said then quickly covered her mouth and looked worried. "She's going to need them when she wakes up."

Tim laughed. "Don't worry about that. I'm sure when my mom wakes up; she won't mind that you wore some of her clothes."

"Hang on a second," Derrick interrupted. "I don't mean to be a downer but what's the plan after you wake everyone up?"

Tim shrugged his shoulders. "They go home and we all settle into a new normal."

"That's all well and good but how are you going to feed them? Winter's coming you know, what then?" Derrick asked.

"I don't know."

"Well, we need a better plan before you wake everyone

up only to have them starve to death."

"But what if the power goes out?" Tim asked.

"There are backup systems at the SAC to keep things running. I vote that we let everyone sleep until we find enough food to keep everyone alive."

"But—"

"We have no choice," Derrick said with a note of finality in his tone. "If you wake them up without anything to sustain them, you'd be no better than those people you talked about."

Tim tried not to show it but he began to regret inviting Derrick to stay. He resented Derrick's questioning his determination to wake everyone up. *Who was he to tell me what to do?*

Tim took a deep breath.

"If we find the government's food stash, we can go forward," Derrick assured him. "I'll even help look."

"Okay, as much as it pains me to say it because I'd really like to have everyone awake again and life to return to normal, if we can't the facility before we find a way to wake them up, we'll let the them sleep, but my mom wakes up."

Day Sixty-three. The sound of Lily vomiting loudly woke Tim from a sound sleep. His stomach muscles tightened. A lump rose in his throat. He buried his head under his pillow to block out the sound and calm his agitated stomach.

When calm was restored, Tim dressed and went downstairs. He expected to see Lily since he had heard her on the stairs but instead he found Derrick in the kitchen. A fresh pot of dark coffee sat warming by the stove. A platter of steaming scrambled eggs and diced potatoes was set in the middle of the table. Philip continued eating and didn't look up.

"You're up early," Tim said to his dad.

Philip gave him a confused look. "What do you mean early? I'm always up with the sun."

Tim caught himself before he tried correcting his dad.

Derrick handed Tim a cup of coffee and gave him a look that told him, he knew what he was about to say.

"Thanks," Tim said, "for the coffee and the look." Derrick smiled and went back for his coffee. Tim pulled out a chair and sat down.

"So, what's the story with Lily?" Derrick asked.

"What do you mean?"

"Who is she? How'd she wake up?"

"I don't know. I found her here after I woke up. She said she lived by the airport with her parents. While we were all asleep there was a storm and a fire that wiped out her neighborhood. She stumbled around town for a few days and ended up here. That's all I know." Tim purposely didn't tell him everything. Derrick didn't need to know about the gang and what they did to her.

Derrick nodded. "How long has she been throwing up?"

"Maybe a few days, a week at most, I'm not really sure. I try not to listen." *I try not to think about it, too. Just thinking about it now makes my stomach feel queasy.* "Why?"

"Just trying to figure out what's causing it."

"Think she ate something bad?"

"That's a possibility but food poisoning normally doesn't last that long."

Tim looked at his dad. Philip was staring at Derrick, the kind of stare Tim had come to read as his father asking himself, do I know you? Philip used to ask it out loud. *That's odd; I can't remember when he stopped.*

Tim took a bite of the eggs. "These are really good, Derrick."

"Thanks."

"You're not going to eat?" Tim asked noticing Derrick still standing by sink.

"I had some earlier. Besides, I think Lily will be hungry."

"Oh, she's never hungry in the morning. She's usually sick—" *It's morning sickness. She's pregnant.*

"What?" Derrick asked.

"Nothing," Tim answered and shook his head. "Just thinking about stuff." He took a sip of coffee and hoped the conversation would die.

Without a word, Philip picked up his coffee cup and headed for his chair in the front room. Derrick poured a cup of coffee for Lily. Tim grabbed his cup and followed Derrick out to the front porch.

Lily was in her usual morning spot, sitting on the end of the wicker loveseat with her knees tucked under her chin. She was staring at the field across the street again.

"They're back," she said taking the cup that Derrick offered her. "And they brought a couple friends."

Tim looked across the way to the field. Sure enough, there were three cows and the calf.

"Damn! I still need to check the west fence out back and then run some new fence across the south end of the field to close it in."

"Well, let's go have a look!" Derrick volunteered. Tim could hear the excitement in his voice. He set his coffee cup down on the porch rail. "Lily, you okay enough to keep an eye on our friends?"

Tim felt a flash of resentment go through him at the sound of Derrick's *our*, or was it jealousy?

Heading out back, the two stopped at the barn and gathered up as many iron posts and spools of barbed wire they both could carry. The fence along the west side of the field was in decent shape. Only a handful of places needed patching. After running back to the barn for the forgotten sledgehammer, they began the task of fencing off the south end of the one by two acre pasture.

The noise from driving the posts into the ground brought George and Godfrey running. When they spotted Derrick, they stopped.

"Hey, you're the guy—"

"Yes, I'm Derrick," he answered and held out his hand to Godfrey. "I'm sorry for being so rude the other day."

"It's okay," Godfrey answered but his tone sounded less certain.

Derrick introduced himself and George.

"So what are you guys doing?" George asked.

"We're building a fence," Tim answered not intentionally trying to be vague.

"Duh," Godfrey said.

"Duh? No one uses, duh, anymore," George teased and laughed.

They all laughed. It seemed like it had been forever since Tim had heard that word.

"What are you going to put in here?" Godfrey looked around at the tall grass and weeds.

"There are some cows across the street. I'm hoping to be able to herd them over here. Wanna help?"

"What's in it for us?" George asked eyeing Tim suspiciously.

"Well, milk, for starters. They'll be all of our cows—your family's and mine. We'll share everything."

"Sure," Godfrey was quick to answer for them. "I'll grab our sledgehammer and be right back."

With the Bjorges' help, the men finished the south fence in no time. Herding the three cows and calf was a different story. The only person with any experience was Lily. Even with her guidance it took them into the early evening to finally get the last of the cows inside the fenced pasture.

"Are you still heading into town to check out the SAC?" Godfrey asked while they walked back to the house.

"Always," Tim answered. "I won't be able to rest until I make sure my mom's okay."

"I'll go with you, if you like," Derrick volunteered.

"Sure."

An hour later, Derrick helped Tim make the rounds, checking to be sure everyone was still safely asleep. Tim checked on his mom while Derrick waited for him by the elevators. She was still resting peacefully. Tim didn't linger too long. He promised Lily they would be quick.

"I love you," he said kissing his fingertips and pressing them against the glass that separated them.

When he turned to leave the lights flickered, or at least he thought they did. He quickened his pace.

"Did you see that?" he asked when he reached the elevators.

"See what?"

"The lights. Did they blink just now?"

"No," Derrick answered shaking his head. "Don't worry. I told you. Even if the power does go out, this building has a back-up system that will kick on. Robbie told me all about the safety features when he was trying to convince me to go under."

"Let's get home."

The drive back to the house was easy. Being the only car on the road meant not having to obey the traffic signs. *You best not get too used to this,* Tim warned myself.

Lily was sitting in the front room. Dad had already gone to bed.

"Everything okay?" she asked as she always did when Tim came home.

"Yep, all safe and sound. How was it with Dad?"

Derrick sat down in Tim's mom's chair in front of the window. Lily moved her feet and Tim sat beside her on the sofa.

"Tim, who's Sarah?" she asked.

Tim felt his body stiffen as if a jolt of electricity suddenly shot through him. He looked at her and tried not to appear shaken.

"Why?"

"No reason," Lily shrugged. "Just when I was helping your father to bed, he called me by that name."

Tim looked away, avoiding her eyes. He glanced at Derrick but he appeared to be waiting to hear the answer.

"Sarah was my older sister."

"Was? What happened to her?" Lily asked.

"She died when I was ten. She got mixed up with an older boy she met at a school dance. He was from Portland, I think. One night she lied and said she was going to a friend's house but when Mom and Dad checked they found out she wasn't there. That's when they knew she had snuck out to see that guy. So, they waited up for her. When she got home, I remember hearing them. They had a huge argument. Dad forbade her to ever see that boy again. Sarah told them they couldn't stop her, that she was seventeen, practically an adult, and old enough to make up her own mind and choose her own friends. They sent her to her room.

"The next morning, when Mom went to check on her,

Sarah was gone. When she didn't come home by dinnertime, Dad called the police and reported her missing. The policeman told Dad and Mom, with runaways, when they're no longer having fun or the person they ran off with tired of them, they usually come home on their own. He told them to try not to worry that they would do everything they could to find her in the meantime. After a year passed, it seemed as though the cop's idea wasn't working.

"Then one night, the police came to the house. They told my parents they found Sarah when they did a sting. She had been working as a prostitute in Northeast Portland. They arrested her pimp. When Mom asked where Sarah was and when could they see her, the cop told her that Sarah had been beaten up pretty bad. She was taken to Providence Hospital.

"When Mom and Dad arrived, they found out that Sarah was pregnant. Her pimp was the one who had beaten her up because she got pregnant. The doctor said he didn't think she would pull through. She died a few hours later. I didn't get to see her."

"Oh my," Lily gasped and wrapped her arms around her stomach. "That's horrible!"

"Turned out that older guy she met was a pimp. The police said he would go to high school parties and recruit vulnerable girls. He would get them to fall for him and then he'd reel them in and put them to work.

"I remember a friend of Sarah's told Mom after the funeral that Sarah had called her a couple nights before she the raid and said she wanted to come home. After Sarah's funeral, neither Mom nor Dad ever talked about her again. That is, until today, I guess." Tim looked at Lily.

"I'm so sorry."

"It's okay. I'm over it. What bothers me is if Dad thought

you were Sarah, then he's forgotten about her being dead and he's becoming worse."

"Not necessarily," Derrick spoke up. "Studies have shown that Alzheimer's patients live in the moment. The part of their brain that sorts things into the past, present and future is misfiring. Their sense of time has become muddled for them. It's not that they have forgotten something; their memories are all still there. It's they are having trouble with the *when* it happened. Something may trigger a memory and having no concept of time, they don't know if it just happened or if it's from the distant past. It's not that they have regressed and are living in a past time as some used to think."

Just then the lights flickered and the stereo wavered giving everyone a start. Once they recovered, Tim turned the stereo off.

"Guess it's time for bed," Lily said. "Night, all." To Tim's surprise she gave him a hug and kissed his cheek before heading upstairs.

"You look worried," Derrick said.

"I am. I know you told me that the SAC has solar power and back-up power cells and all but what if the power goes out and the generators don't kick on?"

"Don't worry. Robbie said there are battery back-ups for the computers so if by some reason the power should go out and the generators don't fire up, the computers that run the SAC will stay on, doing their job. The government thought of everything."

"That's what worries me. I've never trusted the government and the one time I did, I find out I shouldn't have."

Derrick nodded. "Well, let's get some sleep. Worrying isn't going to change anything."

"True." Tim walked over to Dad's chair and picked up the television remote. With the stereo turned off, he realized that his dad and Lily had left the television turned on. He aimed the remote at the screen.

Suddenly an image of a man standing in front of a news desk holding a microphone replaced the blank screen and static.

"Are we on?" he asked some unseen person.

Tim jumped, nearly dropping the remote. Derrick stopped in the doorway and came back into the room. He stared at the television.

"We are?" the man in the TV continued talking. "Good. If anyone out there is watching—"

The lights flickered again. The picture on the television disappeared for a moment and then started to come back. Suddenly the lights went out.

EPISODE IV:
THE UNDESIRABLES

Darkness surrounded Tim, squeezing him in its grasp like a giant hand and making it hard for him to breathe. He struggled within himself to remain calm but it was a battle he was quickly losing. At age twenty-eight, soon to be twenty-nine, he hated to admit that he was still afraid of the dark or rather, not being able to see. Scotomaphobia, his therapist called it. Either way, it was a paralyzing fear.

Tim stood frozen, unable to remember where things were in his parents' front room. With each breath, he could feel the panic in his chest begin to swell and overtake him.

Mom! He heard a voice in his head scream.

Stay calm. Derrick said the SAC has a battery back-up. She will be okay. Besides, it could be just a tripped circuit. Just because there's no power here, doesn't mean the whole town is out, a calmer voice reasoned.

Slowly Tim's eyes began to adjust to the darkness. He began to make out shadows. He could see the window to his right, a lighter shade of grey than the wall. He could make out Derrick's form still standing in the doorway where he was when the lights went out.

Slowly Tim inched his way across the floor, sliding his feet so as not to bump into some unseen piece of furniture. With every step he drew nearer to the only other person in the room. Tim grabbed Derrick's arm. He felt his strength return and a sense of calm replace his fear.

"I think my mom has some candles in the dining room buffet," Tim said.

"Okay," Derrick answered. His voice was steady and unwavering and it worked to keep Tim's anxiety from returning.

With blind confidence, Tim walked into the dining room, around the table to the front of the buffet which stood against the opposite wall from the foyer door. He slid the top drawer open and felt its contents of linen table cloths and napkins. Then he found what he was searching for.

"Aha!" he announced and picked up a taper, holding it up for no one to see.

Just then there was a thud and the table shook. Derrick grunted in pain.

"You okay?" Tim asked.

"Yeah, I didn't want children anyway," he moaned.

"I'm sorry," Tim apologized and grimaced. "I found the candles."

"Great," Derrick said sounding less than enthused. "So how are we going to light it?"

"My mom keeps matches in an old matchstick holder on the wall by the stove in the kitchen."

Tim walked to the end of the table. Derrick put his hand on Tim's shoulder to guide him. Tim slowly made his way into the kitchen and left Derrick by the breakfast table. Still sliding his feet he made his way to the stove. The matchstick holder was where he remembered. He took out one wooden stick and struck it on the side of the holder. The tip flared up and instantly the darkness retreated. Tim lit the candle.

The kitchen became a bit brighter but Tim could still see the darkness lurking a few feet away. It felt like a cat, poised and ready to pounce the instant the flame was extinguished. That was something Tim wasn't about to let happen.

With renewed confidence and determination, Tim walked back into the dining room. He took one of the candle holders from the top of the buffet and dripped a bit of the melted wax into the cup before sticking the bottom of the taper into it. He then took out another candle and did the same in the matching candle holder. The darkness fled the dining room completely.

Feeling more like usual self, Tim's thoughts returned to his mother.

"Derrick, I need to get to the SAC and make sure my mom's okay."

"I'll go with you," he volunteered for which Tim was quietly grateful.

After waking Lily and telling her what happened, Tim and Derrick made their way outside. The night sky was blanketed by a thick layer of clouds that blocked any light from the moon and stars. Darkness once again rushed at Tim and pressed against him but he held fast to Derrick's shoulder. At least knowing that someone was with him gave Tim enough strength to keep moving.

They found the Hummer in the driveway where Tim had parked it. Slipping behind the wheel, Tim immediately turned the headlights on and chased the darkness back to a safe distance. It crouched behind the corners of the barn and waited.

"We need to stop at the Bjorges'," Tim told Derrick then

turned the ignition key.

The darkness was like nothing he had ever experienced before. Even with the headlights on it felt as though he couldn't see. Tim drove slowly, practically at walking speed, up the road and turned into the Bjorges' driveway. From the look of the dim, flickering light in their kitchen window, Tim knew their power was out too. He knocked on the back door.

"Timothy?" Mrs. Bjorge greeted me. Her long, grey hair was in a braid and draped over her left shoulder. She pulled the collar of her bathrobe tighter around her neck.

"I'm sorry to disturb you. Are Godfrey and George still up?"

"Yes," Godfrey answered from behind his mother.

"And we're right with you," George added seemingly anticipating Tim's next question.

They each kissed their mom on the cheek and moments later the four were off to the SAC.

When Tim reached the highway, he turned east toward town. At the top of the hill overlooking Hillsboro, he stopped suddenly.

Even with the headlights on, he couldn't see a thing. It was as if the whole town had been swallowed up by some ungodly creature. He could feel it all around them, pressing against the outsides of the car and trying to get in. Tim sat, his hands gripping the steering wheel tighter, frozen and unable to breathe.

"What's the matter?" he heard Godfrey behind him.

"What are we doing?" George asked.

Tim couldn't answer. His eyes were fixed on the darkness in front of them.

"Tim," Derrick said and touched his arm. "Are you okay?"

Tim forced himself to look down at his arm, at Derrick's hand. He took a deep breath and switched the headlights to high beams. The darkness backed away.

"Yes," he answered and stepped on the accelerator.

Ignoring the One Way signs, Tim drove east on Baseline, taking the shortest route to First Avenue where he turned north. He drove straight to the Suspended Animation Center; no driving around to be sure there wasn't anyone watching. Forgoing the garage, he parked in front of the SAC across from the Washington County Courthouse complex on Main Street. He turned the Hummer so that the headlights shone on the front steps and doors.

Together the four rushed up the concrete steps but as Tim feared, the automatic doors didn't open before them. Immediately he began to try to pry the doors open. Godfrey stepped up and began to try to help.

"Stop it!" Derrick shouted.

When neither of them obeyed, he grabbed Godfrey and pulled him away. Turning to Tim he gave him a shove. "I said, stop it!"

"But I need to get in to check on my mother."

"I know that. These doors are made to swing open like a normal door if there was ever a power failure. That was, as long as they are completely closed. If you even move them a fraction of an inch they seize up and won't open."

"I didn't know."

"Of course you didn't," Derrick answered and began to pull on the door. With a bit of protest, the door swung open.

"Godfrey, turn off the Hummer's headlights and lock it. We don't need it getting stolen." Derrick ordered.

While Godfrey rushed back down the steps, the rest of them made their way inside.

"Hey, the emergency lights are working. That must mean the generators are on." Tim said when he saw the flood lights by the elevators and the ceiling above the reception desk.

"Not necessarily," Derrick answered.

"What? But—"

"Those lights work independently from the generators. They run off small power cells attached beneath them. See those boxes?"

Tim did. He couldn't believe he hadn't noticed them before. He felt as though his heart had sunk into his stomach.

"I need to check on my mom," he repeated sounding a little less hopeful.

"Wait," Derrick snapped and grabbed his arm again to stop him from leaving. "If you really want to help her, we have to stick together. We need to go down to Robbie's office and check the computers, first. They'll tell us not only about your mother but everyone else as well."

"But—"

"If you want to help her, it has to be done from his office."

Tim looked at Derrick. Derrick knew the center better than he did, so he relented. The computers that monitored Tim's mother, keeping her and everyone else in suspended animation alive in this building were controlled from Dr. Anderson's office in the basement, Lower Level Four. Tim never felt so helpless. He knew nothing about the suspended animation process, let alone the computer system. His anxiety began to make him feel nauseous.

They took the stairs down four. The elevators were not running. Derrick explained that everything that ran on electricity was rated in level of priority. During a power outage, things of a lesser priority, like the elevators, were shut down while other things like the ventilation system and computers, given a higher priority, remained on. Even the lights in the stairwell, while they were on, appeared to be running at half power.

When they reached Lower Level Four, the LED lights in the reception room were out. Only the emergency lights with their small cells were on, and even they were dim. The four quickly made their way to Dr. Anderson's office door. Tim started to pull out the keycard but Derrick took one from his own pocket. He held against the sensor beside the door knob.

The lock clicked. They were in.

Derrick and George rushed into Dr. Anderson's desk. Godfrey and Tim followed. With every step Tim's fear grew which made his feet feel heavy and his legs, weak.

He walked into the office but didn't turn around. He didn't want to see the monitors on the wall above the door. Instead he focused on Derrick who pulled out the doctor's chair and sat down behind the computer monitors. His hands moved quickly over the keyboard while he stared at the center monitor.

"We've got power!" he announced. "The generators are online."

Tim didn't realize that he had been holding his breath. When he heard the news, he heaved a sigh and gasped for air. His fear began to subside.

Derrick continued typing.

"I didn't know you knew about the computer system," George commented looking over Derrick's shoulder, watching every keystroke and application that flashed up on the monitor.

"Yeah," Derrick answered. "Robbie trained me on it. He said if I knew how to use it, he could make a case for my being awakened early if that bitch doctor discovered me." His hands slowed their typing for a moment. He seemed distracted by his thoughts. Then just as quickly he went back to typing at lightning speed.

"So does that mean you know how to wake everyone up?" Tim asked.

Derrick shook his head. "No, Robbie was going to show me that part after he woke me up. Uh-oh." Derrick stopped typing, his eyes fixed on the monitor in front of him.

"What?" Tim nearly shrieked.

"Derrick, what's that mean?" George leaned over Derrick's shoulder and pointed at the monitor.

"Not good," he answered. "I'll be right back."

"What is it? What's wrong?"

Derrick ignored Tim's questions and headed for the door to the right of the desk, the one that led into the computer server room. Tim followed him.

The room was warm from the rows of refrigerator-sized computer servers. There was a humming sound, not too loud but enough to be annoying to the ear if anyone stayed in the room too long. Tim tried to block it out.

It was obvious that Derrick had been in there before and knew where he was headed. He walked quickly, turning down one aisle and then another.

"What's wrong?" Tim repeated over the humming.

"I need to check the batteries."

He stopped when he reached the back wall. A single door with a narrow glass window stood before them. There wasn't a doorknob or lock. Derrick gave it a shove and the door swung open without hesitation. A single row of LED lights that ran from the door to the back of the room came on.

The room was large, about thirty feet square. Thick twisted cables came out of the ceiling and connected to the rows of coffin-sized metal boxes. Derrick started down the aisle but stopped.

"No!"

"What?" Tim looked at the floor. "What's that?"

"It's acid," Derrick answered.

Tim looked at the large metal boxes nearby and noticed it was cracked and corroded.

"What's it mean?"

"It means that whatever floor or floors this power cell was supporting is now off-line."

"Off line?" Tim repeated and felt his anxiety returning. "Does that mean . . . Look, there's another one!" Tim pointed across the room at another corroded box.

Derrick didn't acknowledge him. He continued around the room, avoiding the acid on the floor. Tim followed. Of the many power cells, three had ruptured and were no good. There was no way of telling what floors the cells supported by looking at them. Tim felt tears pushing against his eyes while his fear rose.

Derrick rushed to the tall metal cabinet against the back wall. He opened it and began unplugging and plugging in cords quickly. Closing the cabinet, he brushed past Tim and back into the outer room.

When they returned to the office, George jumped up from sitting at the computer. Godfrey stepped back from the desk to let Derrick pass.

"What did you find out?" Godfrey asked.

Derrick didn't say a word. He took his seat in front of the computer again and began typing frantically.

"What's going on?" George asked and looked at Tim.

"Three of the backup power cells are no good. They burst and there's acid everywhere."

"Is that bad?" George asked his gaze moving between Derrick and Tim.

"I'd say it is," Derrick told him. "It means that three floors, possibly more, have no computer support. Without it…"

Godfrey looked at his twin brother and then back at Derrick. He didn't say another word.

"Well, I've identified the floors," Derrick said still typing on the keyboard and staring at the monitor. "The good news is, there were only three affected, Lower Level Three, Lower Level One and the Thirteenth Floor."

"No!" Tim gasped.

Everyone stared at Tim. Derrick stopped typing for moment but quickly resumed.

"What's the matter?" George asked.

"Derrick, you have to do something. The thirteenth floor is still full of people. Henry's family is on that floor."

"Henry?" Godfrey asked.

"The boy who saved me from those thugs who stole my Bug," Tim blurted. "Can you save them?"

"I'm trying," Derrick answered. "They still have power supporting their chambers. I have no way of knowing how long they didn't have the computers monitoring them, so I don't know if they were in any real danger."

While Derrick continued to type, Tim began to pace. He felt antsy and helpless at the same time. He wanted to run up the sixteen flights to check on Henry's family but knew there was nothing he could do. *This can't be happening.*

After what felt like hours, but was really only minutes, Derrick stopped typing. He sat back in his chair and looked up.

"Okay, I've been able to reactivate the computers that monitor the three floors," he announced.

"You can do that from here?" George asked.

"Yes. It's a bit technical but Robbie showed me what to do. I just hope that it wasn't too late."

"How can we know?" Tim asked, leaning on the desk as much for support as trying to see what the monitor said.

"Well, do you have a name of someone on that floor?"

Tim thought for a moment. He tried to remember what was on the nameplate beside Henry's mother but came up empty.

"I can't remember."

"A last name?" he asked.

Tim shook his head. At that moment he realized that he didn't even know Henry's last name.

"Then you need to take a walk."

"What good would knowing a name do?" George asked.

"A lot," Derrick said and began typing again. "What's your mom's name, Tim?"

"Della Stone." Tim walked around the desk. He stood beside George and looked over Derrick's shoulder.

Derrick typed her name and then pressed the enter key.

"Well," he said. "That's odd."

"What?" Tim asked.

"It says here, she's awake!"

Tim's heart jumped. He lunged forward.

"Where?" he nearly shouted in Derrick's ear.

"Right there." Derrick pointed at the screen.

Sure enough, where he pointed said, "Revived".

"I don't understand. When?"

"That it doesn't say," Derrick answered. He pulled open the top desk drawer and took out a notepad. He wrote on it and tore off the top page. "Let's go find out."

"Mind if I take a look at this search feature?" George

asked.

"No," Derrick answered. "You can't hurt anything as long as you don't go off that application."

Tim followed Derrick out of the office and into the hallway. He couldn't believe it. His mother was awake! How or when, it didn't matter. She was finally coming home.

"I want to check out Level Three on our way up," Derrick said.

"There's no one left on that floor or Level One for that matter."

Derrick suddenly stopped and spun around to face Tim.

"Are you sure?" The tone of his voice made Tim's anxiety return.

"Quite. The Bjorges' and I buried everyone from Level Three. Seems the thugs who stole my car didn't like the government or police. They took a pipe to the glass chambers."

"All of them?"

Tim could hear the disbelief in Derrick's tone.

"Yes. Even the children."

"Oh dear, God," he gasped and leaned against the rail. "What about Level One?"

"All those chambers were empty."

His expression changed from puzzlement and shock to worry. He turned without a word and continued up the stairs.

"What's wrong? What's the matter?"

Derrick seemed to ignore Tim's questions and kept climbing the stairs. Tim followed but remained confused and in the dark.

They bypassed Lower Level One and continued to the fifth floor. The muscles in Tim's legs burned and ached. He was winded and struggled to catch his breath. Walking up these stairs was a lot different than walking around town. He was definitely getting a workout.

Derrick walked past the reception desk and into the sleep chamber room. He seemed to know right where to go. He glanced at the paper in his hand.

Tim's excitement grew with every step. He couldn't believe he was going to be able to really hug his mother and take her home. When they turned up his mother's aisle, Tim's excitement vanished.

"I thought you said she was awake?"

"I did. Well, that's what the computer said. See."

He showed Tim the slip of paper on which he had written some numbers.

"It says right here—" Derrick stopped and looked at the paper and then up at the flashing lights. Below the lights was a row of numbers Tim didn't remember seeing before. "That's not right."

Derrick turned around and looked at the chamber across the aisle, the chamber that Tim had been in.

"This is the chamber she was supposed to be in."

"That was mine."

"Yours? Did you two switch places?"

"No."

"Then someone must have messed up somewhere because it shows that she was supposed to be in this chamber."

Tim's heart sank.

"I'm so sorry," Derrick apologized and put his hand on Tim's shoulder. "Come on. Let's check out the thirteenth floor."

Walking up the next eight flights of stairs was a lot harder than the previous eight. The excitement that motivated Tim up to the fifth floor was gone. He felt himself sink deeper and deeper into depression with every step upward while the voices in his head became louder and argued.

It's your fault she's still asleep. If it weren't for you, she would be awake and taking care of your father but you took her chamber.

But I didn't know it was hers. I just did what I was told.

That's the problem! You always do what you're told and never question anything. You are such a fool. You knew you couldn't trust them and yet you led your parents into their hands.

I had no choice! It wasn't my fault!

Then whose is it?

I don't know! I don't know!

"Do you remember where this Henry's family is?" Derrick asked silencing the voices in Tim's head.

"The ninth row, about halfway down or so."

While they walked Tim glanced at the lights above the chambers. They were blinking. He took it to mean that all was okay and began to relax.

Just then he saw it. The lights above the seventh row were all out. The eighth row's were out as well. His legs felt like they were made of rubber, his knees were weak. Tim steadied himself against the wall and continued to inch his way toward the ninth row. He struggled for air. His head felt strange. The room was beginning to spin. He could see Derrick before him, looking at him. Everything went dark.

"Tim! Tim! Wake up!" he heard Derrick's voice call.

Tim opened his eyes and found that he was on the floor.

"What happened?"

"You passed out. Take a few deep breaths."

Tim did as he was told.

"Feeling better?"

"Yes," he nodded.

"Think you could stand up?"

"I'll try."

With Derrick's help Tim was able to get back on his feet. He leaned against the wall for added support.

"Guess I'm a bit out of shape." Tim tried to make light of what happened.

"Don't worry about it. Walking up sixteen flights of stairs is bound to get to the best of us." Derrick said and flashed Tim a sympathetic smile. "You were saying that this kid's mother is about half way down this aisle?"

"Yes, on the right."

"You steady enough to come with me?"

"Sure," Tim said and reached for Derrick's arm. Derrick graciously obliged.

Slowly the two started down the aisle. Tim glanced up at the dark lights above the chambers.

Please, God, not Henry's family, he whispered to himself.

With every step he took, he felt tears pushing against his eyes, his throat tightened. He stopped.

"Here."

Tim looked at the woman behind the curved glass. She still looked the same as when he saw her before. Her head was tilted back, resting against the padding on the back of the tube. Her wavy, black hair hung loosely about her shoulders. Her light brown skin looked soft and supple.

"No! No! No!" he heard himself groan. He pressed his palms against the glass between us. "I'm so sorry. I'm so sorry."

"Hey, it's not your fault," Derrick said in a sympathetic yet cold sort of tone.

Tim heard Derrick's voice and felt his hand on his shoulder. He knew what Derrick was trying to do but it wasn't any use.

"But I promised him. I promised Henry I'd find a way to wake his family up."

"You can't blame yourself—"

"You don't understand." Tim snapped. He turned and started back for the hallway. He had to get out of there. He had seen enough and it was too much.

"Tim," Derrick said while he followed him. "You're right, I don't understand. Why is it your responsibility to wake everyone up?"

"It just is."

Tim swung the door open with such anger and force it hit the wall with a bang loud enough to wake the dead, but it didn't.

"Says who?"

"Says me." Tim stopped in front of the reception desk and turned around to face Derrick. "If I don't do it, who will? I mean, I don't see anyone else stepping up to bat here. Do you?"

"No," Derrick admitted, shaking his head. "But that doesn't mean you are responsible when things out of your control don't go right."

"I know that. I mean, my head knows that but my heart doesn't agree. Those aren't just *things* in there. They're people. They're someone's sisters and brothers, daughters and sons, mothers, fathers. I know what it feels like to lose someone. I also know what it feels like to not be able to help the ones you love. I don't want anyone else to have to feel that way."

"Tim, one important fact I learned in my years as a nurse is that death is inevitable. At some time or another, everyone will have to face it; and, sometimes all we can do is try to make them as comfortable as possible until it happens."

"No, I can't give up on them."

"Tim, you're not God. You can't protect or save everyone. Some things are out of your control—"

"But I still have to try."

Derrick looked at Tim for what felt like a long time. Finally he nodded his head. "Okay, I give."

They headed back down the stairs to Lower Level Four and to Dr. Anderson's office. Neither spoke. The sound of their footfalls echoed up and down the stairwell. Even the voices in Tim's head were silent.

"Hi guys," George said looking up from behind the computer monitor when Tim and Derrick entered the office. "So, where's your mom?"

Tim noticed the questioning expressions on George's and Godfrey's faces. He didn't answer.

"She's still asleep," Derrick said for Tim.

"What? But I thought—"

"Somehow Tim ended up in the chamber she was assigned to and she's in his."

"So, that means she was supposed to wake up and you were supposed to still be asleep," Godfrey said as though thinking out loud.

"Thanks for pointing that out, Godfrey. It really helps a lot," Tim said, not caring that he sounded annoyed.

"I'm sorry," Godfrey apologized and looked confused.

Tim was too tired both physically and emotionally to care. The last thing he wanted to do was to think. Sleep sounded good to him. Slipping into a mindless world of dreams and away from this nightmare would be a welcome blessing.

"Come on," Derrick said. "We can't do anymore here

tonight. What's done is done. Let's go home and get some rest."

Tim let Derrick drive back to the farmhouse. Even though the sun was starting to come up behind Mt. Hood, and the world seemed brighter, Tim felt himself slip deeper and deeper into a dark depression. They dropped the twins off at their home.

"Are you going to be okay?" Godfrey asked sounding sincerely concerned.

"Nothing a little sleep won't cure," Tim answered but inside he knew that was a lie. There was nothing short of a miracle that would make him feel better. "I'm sorry for snapping at you guys."

Day Sixty-four. Try as he might, Tim couldn't sleep. He did manage an hour or two but images of Henry's mother and little sister crowded his mind. *What am I going to tell him?* He looked at his alarm clock out of habit. The display was flashing.

Flashing!

He jumped out of bed. *The power is back on!* He quickly threw on some clothes. When he reached the top of the stairs he became aware of voices below, in the kitchen.

"Well, look who's finally up," Godfrey greeted.

Tim looked around the room. Lily had made coffee and passed it around to their guests John, Godfrey and George Bjorge. Tim's dad sat in his usual chair at the table and Derrick sat across from him.

"The power's back?"

John smiled and shook his head. "No."

"Dad got your old generator in the barn going with one of the power cells from the SAC's garage," Godfrey explained.

"Oh." Tim heard the disappointment in his tone before he felt it. "Thank you, Mr. Bjorge."

"Coffee?" Lily asked and held out a steaming cup to him.

"Thank you."

"George told me about the problem at the SAC," John said. "Maybe I could take a look at those generators. They haven't had to work in over fifty years. They may need a bit of a tune up."

"Sure," Tim shrugged and looked at Derrick.

"That would be great, John," he said. "The last thing we need is for any of them to quit working."

"Great. Let's go." Godfrey set his coffee mug down beside the sink and rubbed his hands together, obviously anxious to leave.

"Hang on," John said. "Let Tim finish his coffee and wake up."

Tim took a sip of his coffee and set the mug on the table. He was eager to get back to the SAC, but not for the same reason. He wanted to see if he could catch Henry before he discovered the fate of his family.

"I'm ready, Mr. Bjorge," he said. "Lily, are you okay here with Dad?"

"Of course." She smiled at Philip. "We'll be fine."

"Derrick?"

Derrick nodded and pushed his chair back from the table. "Let's do this."

Minutes later they were all standing in the lobby of Hillsboro's Suspended Animation Center. The afternoon sun shone through the wall of windows and illuminated their surroundings. It looked quite different from the day Tim first arrived there with his parents. Dust covered everything. Shards of broken glass from the shattered windows lay scattered across the floor and glistened like fallen stars.

"I'll show you where the generators are," Derrick said to John.

The five headed to the stairs.

"Hey, I'm going to go check on something. I'll catch up with you later."

"Do you want us to come with you?" Godfrey offered.

Tim glanced at George who elbowed his twin. It was obvious to Tim, Godfrey spoke only for himself.

"No, I want to look around by myself. You guys go with Derrick and your dad."

"Okay." Godfrey agreed and nodded.

"What's the matter with you? I don't want to run around this old building. I want to do some more looking at the computer," George tried to lower his voice but Tim still heard him. The stairwell seemed to amplify even a whisper.

"Sorry," Godfrey apologized.

"I'll meet you in Dr. Anderson's office in a few," Tim said and started up the stairs.

Tim was relieved that neither of the Bjorge twins pressed him about coming along. If he were to find Henry, he wanted to do it alone. Neither of them held out any positive hope for him. *Juvenile Delinquents grow up to be Adult Delinquents,* George muttered whenever Tim suggested Henry could change.

But neither of them saw how selfless Henry was when he stood up for Tim against his fellow thugs and saved Tim's life. Henry didn't know him. Even when they made fun of him and called him a queer, Henry took their verbal abuse and didn't back down. *No, George was wrong. Henry could become something better.* Tim just needed to help Henry see it for himself.

Tim passed the fifth floor without stopping. He had to get to Henry. With each passing floor, Tim's Nikes felt like concrete blocks.

The light in the stairwell seemed dimmer than it had the night before. *The batteries must be running down*, he reasoned.

The muscles in his legs complained about the number of flights of stairs they'd climbed. They ached for him to stop and give them a rest but Tim ignored them and pressed on.

Suddenly he stopped. His feet refused to take another step. Tim stared at the darkness above him and then looked back at the dimming light behind. The urge to turn around was strong and rang loud in his ears.

There was only one more flight left to reach the thirteenth floor. *You can't turn back now*, he told himself, but his feet still wouldn't budge.

What if the power is out on the entire floor now?

It won't be. The other lights are powered by the generators. There will be light just twenty more steps to go.

With every bit of strength he could muster, Tim gripped the handrail. Pulling himself forward he forced his feet to continue. His pulse was already racing due to the exertion of climbing eleven flights. His lungs burned from exhaustion.

You can do this, he kept telling himself over and over.

He gripped the handrail tighter and continued to pull himself upward, stair step by stair step. Darkness surrounded him and began to press against him. He hesitated and looked down, over the center handrail. Through the narrow space between the stairs he could see light below. Darkness eased its hold slightly and allowed him to take a deep breath. He turned back and with renewed strength made it up the last five steps. Tim swung the fire door open and light from the hallway immediately chased the darkness away, freeing him.

Safely in the light of the thirteenth floor, Tim leaned against the wall and took a moment to rest from his climb. He looked around for a chair but saw none.

This wasn't meant to be a waiting room.

After a brief rest he pushed off and headed into the large room that housed the suspended animation chambers. Anxiety began to pull him down from the inside.

What am I going to say to him? I'm sorry but your mom, sister and dad didn't make it? I know I promised I'd find a way to wake them up, but such are the promises adults make to children.

"When you are eight, then you can have a pet rabbit. In fact we will raise rabbits!" Della's voice echoed.

"This summer after the harvest, we'll go to Disneyland," Philip promised.

"When you graduate from high school, we'll get you a car of your own," his father said.

Tim remembered every word. None of those things happened.

What if Henry blames me?

Why shouldn't he? He saved your life and this is how you reward him? I'd blame you too!

Again Tim stopped. "No. I can't do this," he said out loud. He turned to leave and froze. "Henry!"

"What are you doing here?"

Tim could hear the suspicion in Henry's tone and see it in his dark brown eyes.

"I came to see how you're doing."

"I'm fine. I don't need you spying on me. Just leave me alone."

He started to charge past but Tim grabbed his arm to stop him. Henry pulled himself away and now stood between Tim and Aisle Nine.

"Henry, please, I need to talk to you."

He glared at Tim with the typical expression of youthful disdain for adults.

"Why?"

"Henry, last night the power went out."

He looked at the lights in the ceiling.

"Really?" he said with an unconcerned shrug. "They seem to be working fine."

"Henry—"

"Look man, you don't need to keep saying my name. You're beginning to creep me out."

"Sorry. What I'm trying to say is, your mom—"

"What about my mom?" His tone changed and Tim could hear the anxiousness in his voice. Without warning Henry turned around and ran for his mother's chamber.

"Wait!" Tim called while he feebly chased after Henry. His legs wobbled like those of a man more than twice his age.

"Henry, I'm so sorry," he panted when he caught up with him.

"For what?" he snapped back.

Tim looked at Henry's mother. She still looked the same; her light brown skin looked fresh. Her cheeks still rosy. Not at all what Tim expected of someone nearly twelve hours dead.

Tim looked at the lights at the top of the chamber. They were still not blinking.

"I—" Tim didn't know what to say.

"Just leave me alone," he snapped. "Why don't you visit your own mom and stop stalking me."

Tim sheepishly backed away.

Walking into Dr. Anderson's office Tim found Derrick in front of the computer. George and Godfrey were standing behind him, looking over his shoulders.

"So, how's your mom?" Godfrey asked.

"Ah, she's fine," Tim answered and stifled his feeling of guilt before they had a chance to overwhelm him. "I didn't go to see her. I know it's totally illogical and probably crazy, but I feel guilty that I'm awake when it should have been her."

"That is crazy," George said.

"You don't have to agree with me, George," Tim interrupted. "Thanks."

"What I mean is; you didn't choose your chamber did you?"

"No, Dr. Anderson did."

Derrick looked up sharply. "He did?"

"Yes. The guy in blue scrubs was going to have my mother go first but we insisted he have my dad go instead. So, he did. Then Dr. Anderson had my mom step into the tube next to my dad."

"Oh, that's what happened," Derrick said.

"What?" Tim asked.

"Robbie didn't put her in the right chamber. He probably thought she belonged beside your dad like the other married couples."

"See, it wasn't your fault," Godfrey said and slapped Tim on the back.

"Ow! So, where's your dad?" Tim asked and changed the subject.

"He's still down looking at the generators."

"Are you ready for some good news?" Derrick asked and peered over the computer screen at the three of them.

"Sure."

"Well, you know how the indicator lights on the thirteenth floor aren't working?"

"Yeah," Tim answered.

"It appears there must be a problem with the circuit that operates them. The computer says everyone is still safe and sound."

"They're alive?" Tim gasped.

"Yes. So you don't have to worry about giving Henry the bad news, because there isn't any. His mom and family are fine."

Tim grabbed a chair and sat down before he fell down again.

"What's the matter?" Derrick asked.

Tim didn't answer him.

"You didn't run into him and tell him—"

"No—I mean, yes—I mean, I ran into him but I didn't say anything. He wouldn't give me a chance."

"Well, good for him," Godfrey spoke up.

"Whose side are you on? One minute you don't like Henry and the next—oh never mind." Tim said sounding defeated even in his own ears.

"You have to see this," George spoke up. "Pull up that kid again."

"You mean, Henry?" Derrick asked.

"Yeah. Show Tim what it says about him. Come here and see."

Tim pulled himself to his feet and walked around behind the desk. He stood beside George and looked over Derrick's shoulder.

On the monitor was Henry's mugshot. Derrick scrolled down through a list of what appeared to be his convictions. There was one for larceny, breaking and entry, being in possession of stolen goods.

"So what, big deal," Tim said.

"There's more," George said.

"I don't care. I already knew he was in jail. Let's see what it says about you. Derrick, pull up George."

Derrick typed quickly and in a second a photo of George flashed up on the screen.

"Now let's see what they say about you."

As Derrick scrolled down Tim noticed a red dot after George's name.

"What's that mean?"

"It means that he's marked for termination."

"What?" George gasped and pushed Tim aside to get a closer look.

While Derrick continued to scroll down the page, Tim read quietly and quickly. He looked at George. They must have seen it at the same time because George straightened up and started shaking his head.

"What?" Godfrey asked trying to look over Tim's shoulder and Derrick's.

"Don't give it a second thought, George. They don't know you," Tim said trying to comfort him. "Anyone who knows you knows it's not true."

"What? What's it say?" Godfrey asked.

Derrick looked over his shoulder at George. George nodded.

"It says that your brother is a homosexual and possible child molester. He was marked as an undesirable and slated for termination."

"What?" Godfrey gasped. "That's crazy! What's it say about me?"

Again Derrick typed on the keyboard. The screen blinked and Godfrey's image appeared. Next to his name was the same blinking red icon.

Derrick began to scroll and Tim began to read again.

"What?" Godfrey gasped. "Who wrote this? Where did they get their information? This is slander!"

"Actually, it's libel. Slander is verbal defamation. Libel is written." Tim heard himself correct Godfrey.

"I don't care, it's not true."

"What?" George asked.

"You tell him," Godfrey snapped. Folding his arms over his chest, he turned away in a huff and walked over to the wall of windows that looked into the server room.

"It says that Godfrey is an unemployed, homeless, drug user," Tim reluctantly answered.

"Is that all?" George scoffed and joined his brother at the windows. He put his arm around Godfrey's shoulders. "That's nothing, Godfrey. At least you're not a pedophile."

"I don't care about that. What bothers me is *they* thought it and they were going to kill us for it. It's not right. Who died and made them God?"

"Obviously, no one, God," George teased and smiled. He gave his brother a one-armed hug. "We're still here thanks to Dr. Anderson."

"True." Godfrey nodded.

George gave Godfrey a real hug.

"So, let me see if I have this right," Tim said to Derrick. "I'm awake because of a mistake when I was put into the wrong sleep chamber. My dad, Mr. and Mrs. Bjorge are awake because they are over sixty. You, George and Godfrey are awake because you were all tagged as *undesirables*."

"True," Derrick answered with a nod.

"Then who was on Lower Level One and what about Lily?"

"Just to clarify," Derrick said and turned his chair around

so he could look at Tim and the twins. "The label of Undesirable was applied to more than just bums and gay people. It applied to convicts, inmates, physically and mentally challenged people, the elderly and people over sixty as well. The people on Lower Level One were inmates, the people being housed in the county and city jails."

"That still doesn't explain why Lily was awakened."

"Well, let's take a look at her."

Derrick's fingers quickly typed out her name and hit the enter key.

"That's odd," he said. "There's no record with that name."

"What do you mean, there's nothing. She told me her name is Lily Evers. Her parents were Curtis and Melinda Evers. We buried them."

Derrick typed in Curtis Evers. Moments later the photo of a middle-aged man appeared. Derrick scrolled down to the bio.

"That's odd. It does mention they have a daughter, Serena, but no mention of a Lily or Lillian."

"Impossible! She said she had brothers. Where are they?"

"There's no mention of any sons in his bio. Maybe you have their names wrong. Where did you get them?"

"She gave them to me and they were on the name plates beside their chambers."

"I see," he said. "Let me try this another way."

Again he typed quickly and hit the enter key. This time, however, when the screen changed it brought up a list of twenty-some names. Slowly he scrolled down.

"Here," he said and stopped. He clicked on a name and seconds later Lily's image appeared on the screen.

"That's her! See—"

Tim froze when he read the name in the basic information

to the right of the photograph. "No! That can't be right. It's wrong!"

"Lavinia Lillian Fisher," Derrick read aloud. "Address, unknown. Age, eighteen. Marital status, single." He continued to scroll down to her bio. "Here's the answer," he announced. "She woke up because she was incarcerated."

"No! I'm telling you that is impossible! I know about that case. There is no way this could be Lily. It has to be another mistake," Tim snapped.

"What's wrong? Who is she?" Godfrey asked, turning away from the window and looking at Tim.

"What was she in there for?" George asked.

Both of the twins came back over to the desk and stood in front of it, while Tim continued to look over Derrick's shoulder at the image of the girl he knew as Lily.

"It says she was convicted of Robbery 2 and received a five year and ten month sentence," Derrick read.

"I remember reading the transcripts from that trial," Tim spoke up. "Miss Fisher' boyfriend was supposed to drive her home from her summer job as a cook's helper at a restaurant on the edge of Astoria. They got in an argument and she insisted he stop the car and let her out. After walking off her anger she realized she was tired and a long way from home, so she decided to hitchhike. Two young men picked her up and promised to take her to her door but they had to make one stop first. They pulled into a gas station market. Miss Fisher said she stayed in the car and after the two men went inside, she heard what she thought were shots and saw the men run from the store and down the street. Not knowing what to do, and afraid of what might have happened she stayed in the car. The police found her there, hiding in the back seat." Tim stopped and looked at the picture again. He shook his head. *This is not her.*

"What she'd heard had indeed been gun shots," Tim recounted. "The men who picked her up had tried to rob the store. When the clerk refused to give them the money they shot, not at her, but at the wall behind her. They claimed they only meant to scare her. Unfortunately one of the shots ricocheted and struck the clerk's child, who had been sitting on the floor behind the counter working on a coloring book. The clerk often took the child to work with her for a short time until her sitter could pick her up for the rest of the evening shift.

"The child died. Because a deadly weapon was used and a person was harmed it became robbery in the first degree. The jury didn't believe that Miss Fisher was unaware of what the two men were doing. She denied smoking marijuana with them, even though blood tests showed she had THC in her blood and marijuana was found in the car.

"The belief was that these three were friends. That they had driven around getting high and that they planned the robbery together. Because Miss Fisher had not entered the store they did knock her charge down to Robbery 2 and under Measure 11 she was given a five year and ten month sentence."

Tim shook his head and continued to stare at the image on the monitor. "This can't be my Lily."

"What do you mean? That's her picture. It is her."

"She was railroaded," Tim said and shrugged.

"What? You couldn't possibly be falling for the idea that she didn't have anything to do with that. How long have you known her? A couple months at most?"

"Sixty-four days," Tim answered and looked at the picture again. "No! I don't want to believe it."

"Well, regardless, the fact remains that she lied about her name and she was in with the other inmates, probably waiting to be transferred to one of the state prisons.," Derrick spoke up. "And the people you buried were not her parents."

Tim had seen and heard enough. He walked away from the desk and sat down in one of the chairs in the sitting area by the door.

"So, Derrick, if I understand you correctly, the people who woke up were the ones the government labeled as Undesirables?" George asked, changing the subject.

"That's the way it looks." Derrick agreed.

"So, instead of programing the computer to terminate us, Dr. Anderson changed it to wake us up."

"Okay. It sounds possible." Derrick nodded.

"But why so late? I mean, everyone was supposed to sleep for twenty years. From what we have found out, we slept for nearly fifty-three years. Why so long?"

"I don't know."

"Well shouldn't the others have awakened by now?"

"One would think," Derrick answered.

"Is there a way the computer will tell you when the others are supposed to wake up?"

From across the room Tim watched as Derrick began typing again. Derrick paused, looked at the monitor and then typed some more. After what seemed like several minutes he stopped.

"That's odd, the Sleep Duration Date is blank for everyone still under." He sat back in his chair and frowned while he appeared to think. "My guess is Robbie must have been trying to change the S. D. Date for the Undesirables and that Dever bitch caught him in the act. Since he was an Undesirable, she shot him and he returned fire. He was wounded, instead of typing 2062, his fingers slipped and he typed 2095 instead. As for everyone else, I have no idea unless she was part of that radical group and planned on killing everyone. I don't know. That's just my theory." He shrugged and shook his head.

"That sounds plausible enough," Tim spoke up. "And that would explain this SAC, but what about the other SAC's? Why haven't we seen people passing through town or heard of others being awake?"

"You saw that news guy on TV before the lights went out, remember?" Derrick answered.

"True."

"You what?" George gasped and glared at Tim. "Why didn't you tell us?"

"It's not like we didn't have more important things to worry about last night. Besides, it was only for a brief second and then the power went off. I didn't even get a good look at the guy to be able to tell who or where he was."

"Forget about that, you guys," Godfrey interrupted. "Derrick, can't you just enter a date and wake everyone else up?" Godfrey asked.

"I don't know how," he answered. "If I do it wrong—"

Before he could finish his thought, John appeared in the doorway. His shirt had smudges of black grime and dust. He continued to wipe his hands on a rag like those Tim saw him use in his mechanic shop.

"Sorry to keep you, boys," he greeted them. "I've taken a look at the generators and we have a problem."

"What sort of problem?" Derrick asked.

"Two of the ten are dead and beyond repairing. Another one is limping along but it's only a matter of time before it shuts down."

"Can you fix it?" Godfrey asked.

"If I had the parts, I could."

"What about at the shop? Are there any—"

"No, these are too large. I don't have anything that would work on them."

"What if we could get the parts from another SAC?" Tim asked, remembering the journal and that the SACs in Newberg and McMinnville were standing.

"That could work," John said and nodded.

"Then I think we should take a trip to Newberg first thing in the morning. Do you think the generator will last that long?"

"I imagine so."

"Good. I think we've done enough for one day. We should head back home."

It was already dark when they left the SAC. Tim let Derrick drive while he sat in the backseat with the twins. Even with having one of them on either side of him, he could feel the cold fingers of darkness outside the Hummer reaching for him. He closed his eyes and tried to ignore them.

Derrick dropped John and his sons off at their farmhouse and they all said their good nights before turning the Hummer toward home. Thoughts of Lily, no, make that Lavinia flooded Tim's mind.

"Have you thought about what you are going to say to her?" Derrick asked almost as if he could hear Tim's thoughts.

"No."

"Well, if it would help, I would be willing to be there when you talk with her."

"Thanks."

"I think we should do it tonight since we will be gone most of the day tomorrow."

Tim suddenly felt sick. *Tonight?* He knew Derrick was

right. He wasn't going to be able to sleep until he got to the bottom of it anyway.

Tim's dad was already in bed when they arrived at the house. Lily was sitting on the front porch. An old Coleman lantern, Tim recognized from the barn, hung from a nail in the rafter above the porch rail. She must have seen him staring at it.

"I found it in the barn and charged the power cell, I hope you don't mind," she said.

"No," Tim answered and shook his head. "I'm sorry we're so late, we ran into a little problem with the generators."

"That's okay. Dad went to bed about an hour ago. He called me Sarah again when I was tucking him in."

"I'm sorry—"

"That's okay. I really don't mind. Would you like a cup of coffee?" she offered and stood up.

Tim glanced at Derrick. Derrick didn't say a word. He folded his arms over his chest and sat down on the porch rail, leaning his back against the support post. He raised his eyebrows as if to prod Tim. Tim turned back to her.

"No, thank you. I'm fine. Can we— can we talk to you a moment?"

Lily gave them both a look of confusion mixed with worry. "Sure," she answered and sat back down on the wicker loveseat. She pulled an afghan around her once again.

Tim walked over and sat down in the chair beside the loveseat.

"When we were at the SAC we discovered something. Everyone who woke up was what the government deemed as undesirable."

"I don't understand," she said looking back and forth between Derrick and Tim.

"Before we all went to sleep, the government had made a list of people they deemed as not fit to wake up. They were classified and labeled as Undesirables," Derrick spoke up. "The plan was that these people would be terminated while everyone else slept."

"You remember I told you about the people over sixty, how they wouldn't be woke up?" Tim jumped in.

"Yes," she nodded.

"Well, also included in that group were the homeless, disabled, gay people and inmates," Derrick added.

Tim watched Lily's face intently, looking for any reaction. There was none. She still had the same confused look as before.

"Derrick's awake because he's gay. I'm awake because of a mix up. My mother and I were put in the wrong chambers."

Lily looked at Derrick and then back at Tim. "So, what's your point?"

"I guess I'm just curious as to why you're awake?"

Lily's expression changed sharply. Her brow furrowed and she looked back and forth between Derrick and Tim.

"Okay, I confess, I haven't been totally honest with you," she said, looking at Tim. "I'm a lesbian."

Tim didn't know what to say. He had hoped she would admit to her past. He looked at Derrick.

"Maybe so, but when we searched the computer for a Lily Evers, the name you gave us, it came back with 'not found'," Derrick blurted.

"Oh?" she said suddenly looking scared. Tim's stomach tightened. "Maybe they listed me under my full name, Lillian?"

"We found you." Derrick stopped her. "Lavinia Lillian Fisher. You're not Lily Evers are you?"

In the glow from the lantern Tim could see tears well up in her eyes.

"Yes," she admitted and looked down for a moment. "I'm sorry I lied," she continued.

"Cut the tears, sister. They don't work on me," Derrick snapped coldly.

"Derrick!" Tim yelled at him. "That's uncalled for."

Derrick's expression was unapologetic. "You were with the inmates," he continued in an accusing tone.

Tim glanced at Lily. Her tears stopped and her expression went cold.

"Yes, I was!" she came back at him. "And yes, a little girl died. But it wasn't my fault. Why won't anyone believe me? I didn't know what they were going to do. I didn't know they had a gun. Do you think I'd have gotten in that car—"

"How do I know you're not lying, now?" Tim asked. His mind reeled and his heart broke. "How can I trust you?"

"Maybe you can't." Her tone softened. She wrapped her arms around her stomach. "It's just when I woke up and found everyone else was still asleep, I thought it as a sign. A sign I was being given a second chance, a chance to go back to who I was, who I am. You *can* trust me, Tim."

"So, who were the Evers?" he asked.

"My aunt and uncle. They were the only people in my family who stood by me during my trial. I used to spend summers with them on their farm when I was younger, before they moved into town. That's where I learned about cows. When I woke up I looked for them. I found the glass on their chambers cracked and they were dead."

"Or did you break it?" Derrick interrupted.

"God, no! I would never do that."

"Really? Why not?" he continued.

"Because I loved them. They were the only family I had left, the only family who believed me and would still talk to me after what happened."

"But you still lied to me, Lily. You lied about your name. Did you lie about being taken by those men, getting away from them, or were you just inventing a story so I'd feel sorry for you and take you in?"

Three were on that porch, but at that moment no one existed except the two, Lily and Tim.

"It was true," she insisted between clenched teeth. "All of it. And in six months I can prove it."

"Six months?" Tim looked at Derrick, who looked confused, then back at Lily. "You mean, you're pregnant?"

"Yes," she nodded.

"How long have you known?"

"I figured it out a few weeks ago, right around the time you showed up."

"Why didn't you say something? Why didn't you tell me?"

"Because I wasn't sure how I felt about it, I mean, I was raped for God's sake. I'm pregnant with the child of a low-life scumbag. At first I hated it. I wanted nothing to do with it and I wanted it gone.

"But then something changed. I thought, maybe this is God's gift to me. A way for me to bring a child into the world, not to replace the life that was lost because you can never trade one child for another, but God's way of saying, it was not your fault. I saw. I believe. This is vindication, Tim. This is proof that from all this bad stuff, some good can still come."

"Or it's another good story you're trying to use to convince us you're not supposed to be in a prison somewhere," Derrick spoke up.

"I don't have to convince you or anyone that I was innocent. Only God can judge me, and he already has." She placed her hands across her stomach protectively.

"So you say," Derrick remarked.

"Stop it, both of you," Tim shouted. This was all too much to sort out. His brain was on overload and he needed time to think.

"Tim, please believe me. When I met you, you were so nice to me. You didn't know me and yet you let me stay here. You looked out for me. I wanted to be the person you thought I was. I never intended to lie to you."

The three fell into silence. Tim looked at the beautiful, young, auburn haired girl. He couldn't help thinking what happened was fifty-three years ago, in a different world with different rules. He thought about the judge and the jury who convicted her. For all he knew, they were dead. He wanted to believe her. He looked at Derrick who looked as if he were still undecided.

"So, now what?" Lily spoke up. "Do you want me to leave?"

"No." Tim blurted but inside I was still struggling, trying to decide if Lily was an innocent victim or a skilled manipulator. *Which one was the Lily who had been looking after my dad?*

"What about you, Derrick?" she asked.

"It's not my house. It's not my place to say."

"But if it were?"

Tim looked at him and their eyes met. Slowly he shook his head.

"No. I don't want you to leave either," Derrick answered but continued to look at Tim.

"Thank you," Lily said. In the soft glow of the lantern,

Tim thought he saw her smile.

After giving each of them a hug, Lily went upstairs to bed. Derrick looked at Tim again. Tim could tell he wasn't fully convinced. With a loud sigh, Derrick adjourned to the sofa in the front room, leaving Tim alone on the front porch with his thoughts.

Sitting down on the loveseat, Tim wrapped the afghan around his shoulders. His head was still reeling. *Why am I having such a hard time with this? Could I have fallen for her that fast?*

Of course you did. Look around. She's the only game in town.

That's not it. She has been such a help to me with my dad and what about the chickens and cows?

So she can milk a cow. Girls are cunning and will use whatever they can to manipulate guys. She's lied once, she'll do it again.

Stop it! Just, stop it.

He looked in on his dad who was sound asleep before heading to his bedroom upstairs. The events of the last twenty-four hours weighed heavily on his mind. He lay awake, starring at the moonlit ceiling. How he longed to go back to the world he knew. Life was so much simpler then, easier. He had his condo, his job. His only responsibility was to take care of himself and occasionally help his mom out with looking after his dad. *How did everything go so wrong?*

He turned over and closed his eyes.

EPISODE V:
NEWBERG

The kitchen smelled of bacon and fried eggs, of hot oatmeal cereal with maple syrup. Philip sat across the small kitchen table with his hands folded above his plate and his elbows resting on either side of it. He looked young again. His hair was dark brown, almost black. His brown eyes sparkled.

A plate of warm toast sat in the center of the table. Tim reached for a slice and instantly his dad slapped his hand away.

"You know the rules," he said. His voice sounded stern yet playful. "We have to wait for your mother."

Tim turned in his chair and looked around. *That's odd. She wasn't there.*

"Where'd she go?"

"You know where she is," Philip answered.

Suddenly there was a knock at the door. Tim looked at his father but he didn't appear to have heard it.

There it was again, only this time it boomed louder. Surely his father heard it this time.

Philip didn't react. He just sat in his chair with a smile on his face staring at the stove by the kitchen door.

"Tim!" A man's voice called his name. "Tim, wake up!"

Suddenly the kitchen, breakfast, his dad, all of it vanished. Tim opened his eyes and was momentarily blinded by the sunlight that shone through his bedroom window.

Another knock on his bedroom door and this time he recognized Derrick's voice. "Tim?"

"Yes," he answered. "Open the door."

The door opened and Derrick stepped into the room. He was obviously upset. His eyebrows were pinched right above his nose. The look in his blue eyes reflected worry with a touch of fear. Instantly the thought that something had happened to his dad flashed in Tim's mind. Panic pounced on him and set his heart racing. He threw back the covers. Any concern he would normally have about being naked in front of another person was smothered by his overwhelming fear for his father. He grabbed his jeans off the back of the chair by the desk.

"What? What's happened?" he asked while he hopped around trying to get his legs into his jeans. Finally he pulled them on and began to button the fly.

"The Hummer's gone," Derrick blurted. "That little lying—" He grit his teeth and restrained his tongue. "She took the Hummer and left."

Suddenly Tim froze and looked at Derrick.

"What do you mean?"

"Lily stole the Hummer. It's gone," he said slowly.

"But how? When? I didn't hear anything."

"Neither did I," Derrick answered and shook his head. "How did she get the keys?"

"I must have left them on the kitchen table when I put the lantern down before I went to bed. I don't know. I don't remember. Did she leave a note? Anything?" Tim asked. He grabbed the shirt he'd worn the day before and pulled it over his head.

"No."

"Why would she leave now?"

"Because we're onto her. She can't pretend anymore. We know who she really is. Once a lying, thieving—a leopard can't change its spots." Derrick's tone rose to an angry and disgusted pitch.

"But she's not an animal, she's a person and people can change and do," Tim said.

"She's a con, Tim. She lied to you. She pretended to be this poor, sweet, innocent little girl," he mocked. "She probably was lying about being raped."

"She's pregnant, remember?"

"So she says. But even if it's true, she could have been a willing participant. Girls lie all the time for sympathy."

Tim could feel his anger building the more Derrick went on. His fingernails dug into the palms of his hands while he clenched his fists at his side.

"I'm pretty sure she wasn't lying about being pregnant. She had morning sickness all this time. I thought it was food poisoning. Guess I was in denial. I need you to just drop it," Tim snapped. "I don't want to talk about her any more. Let's concentrate on what we can control. Oh, damn, we were supposed to go to Newberg with the Bjorges this morning. Now what do we do?"

"How the hell should I know?" Derrick answered. It was obvious he was annoyed by Tim's comments.

"Maybe Lily will be back," Tim said. "Have you looked in her room?"

"No," he answered and scowled.

Tim slipped past Derrick and walked across the large

landing to the bedroom Lily used. It had been Tim's sister Sarah's room. The walls were papered in a pink floral pattern that had faded even more than Tim remembered. The full-size bed with an antique, iron frame sat with its head in front of the window just under the gabled ceiling. The bed was neatly made with Sarah's pink chenille bedspread. Across the room, on the opposite wall by the door was Sarah's dresser. A thin layer of dust covered its top along with the knick-knacks that remained from her childhood. On the chair in the corner opposite the dresser sat a neat stack of the clothes that he had lent Lily.

"She's not coming back," he realized out loud. A feeling of sadness and emptiness engulfed him.

"Great," Derrick said coldly.

Tim slipped past him and headed down the stairs. He wanted—no, he needed to check on his dad.

When Tim reached his parents' bedroom, just off the dining room, he stopped himself from entering. His parents' bedroom had always been off limits and even though he crossed the forbidden line several times already it didn't feel right entering now. Or was he just afraid? Afraid that Lily might have done something to his dad before she left. A feeling of guilt sparked and began to burn inside him. *I can't believe I thought she could actually be that evil and harm a defenseless old man?*

Why? What do you really know about her?

No, he scolded himself. He turned an ear to the door and listened. The sound his father's rhythmic snoring penetrated the door and reassured Tim that his dad was okay. He listened a little longer, letting his dad's breathing chase his fears away and with it the guilt he felt for thinking what he had about Lily.

After a few minutes Tim joined Derrick in the kitchen.

He walked over to the refrigerator and opened it.

"Well, she at least gathered the eggs and milked the cows before she left," Tim commented and closed the refrigerator door. "So, we know she left this morning. She could still come back."

"Whatever—" Derrick sounded indifferent.

"Where could she have gone? You don't think she would head back to Astoria, do you?"

"I thought you said you didn't want to talk about her? What about Newberg?" Derrick asked.

"Why would she go there?"

"I wasn't meaning her. Us, we are supposed to be going." Derrick responded.

"Well...do you mind staying here with my dad while I go talk with the Bjorges? I should probably fill them in on what's happened and see what they think we should do."

"No, I don't mind," Derrick answered.

Tim grabbed his jacket from the hook by the door.

"I won't be long," he promised.

"Whatever," Derrick said under his breath.

Day Sixty-five. The morning air actually felt cold, erasing any lingering traces of sleepiness. Tim zipped up his jacket and pulled the collar tighter around his neck. Autumn was definitely on its way. The leaves on the oak trees had already begun to change. Tim pushed his hands deeper into the pockets of his jeans and picked up the pace.

The Bjorges' two-story farmhouse was set back about a hundred feet from the road. Built in the early 1900's, like Tim's parent's house, it had a large front porch that spanned the width of the façade and overlooked the nearly one acre wide front lawn. A gravel driveway on the left separated the front lawn from their pasture. The driveway cut straight back toward the barn and widened when it reached the side of the house. The black Hummer, the twin of the one Tim "borrowed" from the Suspended Animation Center, was parked near the side door. Tim knocked.

Mrs. Bjorge greeted him with a smile. Her braided hair was pinned up in its usual large crown across the top of her head.

"Tim, come on in," she said and opened the screen door wide. Tim noticed the blue and white gingham apron that she wore over her mid-calf length house dress. It was like one his mother wore. "The boys are just finishing their breakfast."

The smell of fried eggs, hot oatmeal mush with a tinge of coffee scented the kitchen air. Tim took a deep satisfying breath and felt his stomach growl.

John and the twins, George and Godfrey, sat at the kitchen table. John looked at his watch and then back at Tim.

"Is it that time already?" he asked.

"Actually, we might have a problem," Tim answered and cringed. "Lily has run off with the Hummer."

"What?" Godfrey shrieked.

"Derrick woke me up with the news and as near we can figure, she took off sometime this morning."

"Why didn't either of you guys stop her?" Godfrey asked.

"Uh, because we were asleep and didn't hear her," Tim answered sarcastically raising his pitch. "I pretty sure she's coming back. She milked the cows and gathered the eggs before she left."

"Well, from what the boys told me you found out about her, I wouldn't be so sure," John said and took another sip of his hot coffee. "Either way, we should move forward with the assumption she is not."

"So, what do we do now?" Godfrey asked.

"First we finish our breakfast," Anna said sounding every bit the mother she was.

"That's right," John agreed. "Then we'll just have to take our Hummer. We have no choice. We have to go to Newberg today. I don't know how much longer those generators will run without being repaired."

"Sounds like a plan," George said, shoving the last bit of a biscuit into his mouth.

"There's only one problem," Tim spoke up. The three men looked at him. "I'll need to stay behind to sit with my dad."

"No, you can't stay behind. How will we get inside?" Godfrey protested.

"I'm assuming through the front door. The generator room isn't locked so you won't need a key or keycard. Besides, I'm not sure the keycards from our SAC would work anyway."

"Well, what if we run into another crazy man?" Godfrey continued.

"Really, God? You have to bring that up? I still feel bad enough about that—"

"I'm sorry," Godfrey interrupted and held his hands up in surrender. "I was only joking around. I didn't mean to upset you. I'm sorry."

"Forget it," Tim said with a shrug and stifled his regret over the old man. "I can't believe I was so gullible and stupid. I should have known better."

"About what?" John asked.

"About Lily."

"Why on earth would you think that? We all liked her, Tim. Don't be so hard on yourself," Anna spoke up.

"I wish I could, but I left my dad with a stranger. How could I have been so blind?"

"Because you fell for her," George said in a matter-of-fact tone.

"I did not!"

"Did too," Godfrey spoke up.

Suddenly it seemed as though they were all back in grade school. "We both saw the way you looked at her," Godfrey continued.

"No, I didn't."

"That's enough, boys," Anna said when she took George's plate away. "It doesn't matter now. She's gone. It's over and done."

Tim wished it were over and done but he still felt so angry inside, angry with Lily, angry with the government for not keeping their word, angry with himself for ever trusting any of them.

"I'm sorry," Tim apologized.

"For what?" Godfrey asked.

"For everything. I just want my mom and everyone to wake up and for things to be normal again. I should have known better than to trust them. Why did I let them do this to us?"

"Who? The government?" George asked.

"Will you stop? We didn't have a choice," John spoke up. "If you resisted, they would have come after you, your mother and father and forced you. Remember the Potters?"

"Yes, why?" Tim said and nodded.

"Shawn and Vivian resisted. Government men came after them with guns. They shot Shawn and his wife and hauled off their three children. When those kids wake up, they will be orphans with no one to care for them. No, we had no choice but to cooperate, Tim. This is not your fault."

"I know you're right," Tim answered. "I just wish—"

"Tim, I can stay with your father," Godfrey spoke up.

"No, Godfrey," Anna said, drying her hands on a linen kitchen towel. "You need to go and help out. I will sit with Philip and keep an eye out for Lily."

"Really?"

"Yes," Mrs. Bjorge smiled. "Just give me a few minutes to clean up the breakfast dishes, first."

"Thank you," Tim said and managed a smile. He felt a sense of relief knowing someone he actually trusted like his own mother would stay with his dad.

While Anna tidied the kitchen, John, the twins and Tim went outside to get the Hummer ready. While Tim helped load some tools, a thought occurred to him.

"Mr. Bjorge, how far do you think Lily will get? I mean, how far can she go without stopping to recharge the power cell?"

John stopped and turned toward Tim. He frowned a bit and furrowed his brow while he appeared to think about what Tim had just asked him.

"She can pretty much go anywhere. The solar tiles in the roof will help charge the power cell." He patted the hood of the black hummer that was parked between them.

"Great."

"Don't sound so sad," Godfrey spoke up, nudging Tim in the shoulder. "At least you don't have to worry about what she might do to your dad while you're gone."

"Thanks a lot, God!" Tim quipped sarcastically. "That really helps." In all truth, Tim never worried about it until this morning. Lily had always been so gentle and patient with Philip. *Was it all an act? Was she mean to him when I wasn't around to see her?* Tim shook the thought from his head. He tried to think about how she helped him find his dad, how she always spoke kindly to him. That's what he wanted to remember. Besides, his dad showed no signs of abuse, Tim reminded himself.

Minutes later the five were all standing in Tim's parents' kitchen. Anna set her basket down on the counter and began unpacking jars filled of flour, jelly and butter, packets of corn and green beans, and one larger packet the contained beef.

"When you get back, I'll have a nice dinner ready for you," she said over her shoulder.

"I'm not sure when we will be back," John warned. "It could be very late."

"That's okay," she answered with a smile and nod. "I'll keep it warm."

John gave his wife a kiss on her cheek and then headed for the back door. The twins followed.

"Mrs. Bjorge, my dad usually sleeps until around eleven or noon—"

"Don't you worry, Tim, we'll be just fine. Now, the sooner you boys get on the road, the sooner you will be back."

"Thank you, so much," Tim said and fought back the urge to give her a hug. He had known Anna Bjorge all his life. She was like a second mother to him and in the absence of his own mom a hug from her would have felt close enough. He hurried to catch up with the others.

John drove the Hummer as though it were a racecar. Seated in the backseat between Godfrey and Derrick, Tim couldn't help but lean into them whenever John swerved right or left. He was grateful for the seatbelt that kept him from sliding off the seat when John stopped out of habit at the end of their street.

John turned right onto TV Highway and headed into town. It was a familiar route; one Tim had taken countless times. When they reached 1st Street, instead of turning north toward the center of town and the SAC, John turned right again and headed south, out of town.

Tim was surprised at how well the road, Highway 219, had held up. Despite areas where grass had poked through the cracks in the pavement, it was fairly smooth, unlike Cornell Road that ran by the airport in northeast Hillsboro. Time had all but crumbled the pavement there.

Tim sat back and let himself enjoy the ride. The landscape was green and lush. Fir trees had overtaken the once barren farmlands that bordered the two-lane highway. It was almost as if they had gone back in time, to a time when Tim's grandfather was a boy according to the old photos. Everything looked wonderfully unfamiliar.

Just when feelings of being lost began to rise inside Tim's chest, they crossed the Christensen Creek Overpass with a bump. The Hummer began to shimmy and bounce. John slammed on the brakes. Everyone lurched forward. Tim threw his hands up and grabbed the backs of the seats in front of him while the seatbelt dug into his waist. The Hummer began to turn right; the back end seemed to slide around to the left. John's hands gripped the steering wheel harder, his foot pressing on the brakes. Tim could tell John felt it too. John turned into the spin to right the Hummer.

When it stopped, Tim leaned forward and looked past Derrick and through the side window. Instantly he was terrified.

Outside the once smooth pavement appeared to have been blown up. A crater that spanned the width of the two-plus lane road was only a few feet from where John had brought the vehicle to a stop. Chunks of asphalt from the size of gravel to large slabs covered the surrounding area along with dirt and unearthed rocks.

"What do you make of that?" John asked looking over his shoulder at the crater.

"I don't know," Tim breathed. A memory flashed. The rocket launcher the Naturalists used on the Aloha SAC. Tim looked ahead at Bald Peak Road.

The years of uninhibited growth had reduced the two lane road leading to Bald Peak to one snaking lane. Wild blackberry vines entwined in the branches of the fir trees and formed somewhat of a canopy above the road. *A definite trap if ever there ever was one.* The uneasiness in Tim's stomach began to grow.

"Guess we should take Bald Peak Road," George suggested.

"No!" Tim blurted before he realized he had spoken.

George turned in the passenger seat to look back at him. John looked in the rear view mirror.

"No?" John asked.

"What's the matter with you?" George sneered.

"I think we should stay on this road."

"Are you blind? Can't you see the condition, that crater?"

"I see it, George. Take another look at it, yourself. The road up to this point has been in fairly good shape. That looks as if someone intentionally blew it up."

"All the more reason to go the other way."

"Look at the road you want us to go down." Tim said and motioned toward the windshield and Bald Peak Road. George turned around and looked at the road ahead.

"Once we head down that road," Tim continued, "we are trapped. There's not enough room to turn around and with the way everything has grown over the road, backing up isn't going to work either. It's a trap!"

Slowly George shook his head.

"You're just being paranoid, Tim. Dad—"

"No," John spoke up. "I think Tim might be right."

"Okay, who would do that? Who would blow up the road?" George asked, his tone belying his growing impatience.

"Oh, let's see, the criminals from Lower Level One are all awake, pick one," Tim snapped. "Remember the Naturalists? They had a rocket launcher. Maybe they did this?"

"But they're all dead and their launcher blew up."

"That doesn't mean there wasn't another."

"Stop it!" John snapped at them both.

Derrick spoke up. "I'm with Tim on this, guys. It does look like a trap."

"Then what do you suggest?" John asked looking in the mirror again at Derrick.

Derrick looked out his window. "What if a couple of us got out and led you around the crater?"

John turned and looked outside. Slowly he nodded his head. "Sounds like a good plan."

"I'm not getting out!" George snapped and shook his head.

"That's okay, Derrick and I will do it," Tim said.

He unbuckled his seatbelt while Derrick opened his door. They both climbed out of the Hummer.

The morning air felt a little warmer in the sunlight but in the shade it still had a bite. The two carefully walked over to the crater. The crater was circular with a diameter of about forty to fifty feet. It wasn't as deep as Tim had first thought, only about five feet in the center. The blast took out the full width of the two-plus lanes and also downed a couple trees on the east edge.

"Do you think John will be able drive through this?" Derrick asked.

Tim looked at the west side if the crater. The berry vines and smaller bushes were flattened by the blast and the raining dirt and debris but there was no telling what was under it or if it was solid enough.

"I don't know. Maybe if we keep close to the outer edge he can," Tim answered and cautiously began to make his way into the crater. His heart pounded as images of war movie battlefields played in his head. He tried to stifle them but then thoughts of landmines and unexploded bombs hidden beneath the surface took over.

"The ground feels solid enough," Derrick said when they reached the other side.

Tim stood on the south rim and took a look around. The old farmhouse on the east side of the highway was gone. Judging by the shards and splintered timbers lying about, it was hit by another explosive. What may have remained of the building after the blast had burned to the ground.

"Why would someone do this?" Derrick asked.

"To keep people from leaving town?"

"But the other roads are all passable. It doesn't make any sense." Derrick said looking over his shoulder at the Hummer.

"What I'd like to know is where are they now?" Tim said.

Turning back to the road, Tim strained to see down the highway as far as his could. Dark shadows from the tall fir trees on the east side of the highway left plenty of places for someone to hide. He bent down to get level with the pavement. It was too shaded. He couldn't see any movement but that didn't mean someone wasn't there.

"It's a little too quiet, don't you think?" Tim whispered.

His stomach tightened. Neither route seemed safe. He stood up.

"Let's go back and tell John to follow us. The sooner we're out of here, the better I'll feel," Derrick suggested.

After explaining the plan to John, Tim and Derrick once again made their way across the crater. John inched the Hummer slowly along behind them. Once safely on the other side, the two climbed in the back seat. The knot in Tim's stomach loosened a bit.

"Thank you, boys," John said and stepped on the accelerator. The Hummer began moving once again down the highway.

"Let's just hope we don't run into any more of those," Derrick said. "If we do, it's you and your brother's turn to get out." He gave George's shoulder a playful shove.

Godfrey's head turned sharply toward Derrick. Sitting between the two of them, Tim saw see the fear in Godfrey's eyes and felt him trembling.

"You okay?" he whispered.

Even though Godfrey looked at Tim and nodded Tim knew better. Over the many years growing up as neighbors and best friends, he'd become adept at reading Godfrey.

"We'll be okay." Tim tried to sound convincing and reassuring, but the truth was he was afraid too. Not knowing for sure who or what blew up the farmhouse and road or why was more than just a little unsettling.

Godfrey gave Tim a slight but forced smile before he turned away to look out the window beside him.

When they came down the hill into the outskirts of Newburg, the sun had just begun to crest in the sky above them. The leaves on the trees in the fields on either side of the road were bright yellow, orange and red. The tall grasses along the roadside had already begun to brown. Fall was definitely early.

John slowed the Hummer.

"What's wrong?" George asked.

"I don't know. It doesn't look right." John answered. His head turned from side to side while he looked out at the scenery.

"What do you mean?" Tim asked and leaned forward to get a better look outside.

John slowed down even more and came to a stop. "Take a look around. See those fruit trees?"

Everyone responded that they did.

"If everyone woke up when they were supposed to, why didn't they harvest their orchards?"

"Maybe they haven't got to them yet?" George answered.

"And the fences? Why haven't they been fixed?"

"I don't know," George admitted.

"Something's wrong," John repeated.

"Let's forget it and just go back home." Godfrey's voice quivered. Tim could feel Godfrey tremble.

"No, we need those parts for the generators," John answered. He looked in the rear view mirror at his son. "We'll get the parts and then head back home. We'll be okay."

Tim looked at Godfrey whose eyes were fixed on the reflection of his father's eyes. His trembling ebbed. He nodded to his dad. John pressed on the accelerator and they were moving once again.

John rounded a bend in the highway and a housing development came into view. The wooden fence that bordered the edge along the road was weathered and broken down in places. Tall weeds and wild plants had overgrown the area between the sidewalk and curb. The houses themselves appeared neglected and in need of repair.

Tim was beginning to feel John was right. Something was definitely wrong. The closer they came to the center of town the more that feeling grew. There wasn't a soul in sight except for a pack of feral dogs. *Where is everyone?*

John turned left on North Street but still no sign of life anywhere. He stopped when they reached Meridian Street and the west edge of the George Fox University Campus, the site of the Newberg Suspended Animation Center.

Tim remembered visiting the university with his mother. People were everywhere, walking about the campus, sitting under the many trees with their books in hand, riding their bicycles, coming and going in their cars, but there was no one anywhere now. Not even a curious peek from a front room window in the many houses across the street from the campus.

John turned south and slowly drove down Meridian. The Newberg SAC was built on the site where Wood-Mar Hall, the Hoover Academic Building and Stevens Center once stood. Unlike the one in Hillsboro, this was a three story building that spread out over a three block area and still had that academic look. The façade was made of red brick. The large classroom-like windows were tinted dark. Even the entrance looked more like a school than a government building. The plan, as Tim vaguely remembered, was it would be returned to the college after there was no longer a need for the Suspended Animation Center.

When they reached Pacific Highway, John turned west.

"Where are you going? It was back there." George asked sounding a bit panicked.

"Just keep a look out for any sign of someone watching us," John answered. Tim could tell by the sharpness in his tone that John was more fearful than he wanted to let on to his sons.

Everyone looked out their window while John continued westward. When they reached the bend where the westbound lanes of the highway rejoined the eastbound, John came to a stop. He took a slow survey of the surroundings. Nothing stirred. He made a sharp U-turn and headed back into town.

"Boy, what I wouldn't give for a Subway sandwich about now," George groaned when he saw the old deserted building. Its front window was cracked and cloudy with years of dust. It was obvious that no one had been served in ages.

"Never mind that, keep looking around," John said.

"Look!" Godfrey, who had been silent for miles, gasped.

John slammed on the brakes and everyone lurched forward.

A little shaken and confused, Tim looked through the windshield at the traffic lights suspended over the two lane road at the intersection of South Main Street and the highway. They were glowing red.

"They still have power?" Godfrey said.

"So, now what?" George asked.

"Keep looking," John repeated and continued to drive.

John drove a little faster but still slow enough for everyone to take a good look around. Two blocks down, John suddenly turned into the Erickson's Thriftway. The parking lot was deserted. John pulled up to the front doors and parked the Hummer.

"Wait here," John said and opened his door.

"Dad, what are you doing?" George asked.

"Stay in the car, I want to check something out."

Before anyone could object again, John stepped down. He walked over to the store's double doors. They didn't open. He pushed against them and one gave just a bit. Glancing over his shoulder, he turned and slipped into the store.

"What do you suppose he's doing?" Godfrey asked.

"Probably doing a little shopping," George answered.

"Not funny," Godfrey said and smacked the back of the front seat behind George's head. "I want to go home."

"Will you relax," George groaned. "Put your big boy pants on and quit being a baby."

Tim looked at Godfrey. His eyes narrowed and his jaws tightened. He turned and looked out the window. Ever since they were kids, George had a way with reminding Godfrey who was the older of the two. George was only a minute and a half older, according to their birth certificates, but he treated it as if it were years. Tim turned back to look at the front of the store. John was still inside.

"Hey, Derrick, mind if I get out and stretch my legs a bit?" Tim asked.

"Not at all," he answered and opened the door. "Actually it sounds like a great idea."

The two climbed out of the vehicle. While Derrick waited by the Hummer, Tim headed back to the sidewalk to have a look around.

He stood on the corner looking back the way they came. With the exception of the faint chirping sounds from a random bird or two, it was eerily quiet. He crossed his arms over his chest and gave himself a hug. His thoughts returned to Lily. *How awful it must for her knowing she's all alone in this foreign world and pregnant.* Even though Tim had his father, it was still hard for him. Everything had changed and not just the environment. More than ever, he wanted the comfort and safety of everyone being awake, especially his mother. The responsibility of caring for his father alone weighed heavy. He just hoped when they finally reached the SAC that it held the answer he so desperately needed.

The sound of someone walking up behind him jolted him from his thoughts. He turned around so quickly it startled Godfrey.

"Hey, God," Tim smiled. He could tell Godfrey was afraid. His arms were crossed over his chest and his head was ducked down as if he were protecting himself. He scowled but Tim could still see the tears in his blue eyes.

"I don't like this," he said.

"Why?" Tim moved closer, standing beside Godfrey with his hands stuck in the pockets of his jeans.

"I have a bad feeling, like the one I had when we went to Aloha."

"I know what you mean. I admit I'm a bit creeped out too."

"I want to go home." It sounded more like a plea than a statement.

"I do too, but we'll be all right. We'll get what we came for and leave the moment we have it. We won't stay any longer than we need to, I promise."

Godfrey shook his head as though he didn't believe a word Tim said.

"Okay, boys, back in the car!" John called.

Tim turned around. George was right. His dad did do a little "shopping." Three grocery carts were filled to overflowing with cartons of packaged foods.

"The store is still fully stocked," he explained while Godfrey, Derrick and Tim emptied the carts into the back of the Hummer. "I would have taken more but we need room for the parts once we reach the SAC."

Moments later, with the groceries securely loaded in the back, they were once again headed east back toward Meridian Street and the Newberg SAC.

Still uneasy and fearful that someone might hijack the Hummer, John pulled into the SAC's southeast parking lot. The lot was crowded with cars and trucks. More than a few were resting on their rims, their tires rotted and flat. Finding no empty spaces, John parked by the curb in the farthest corner away from the SAC.

"It should be safe here," John announced. Everyone climbed out. John locked the doors and tucked the keys safely in the front pocket of his jeans. As far back as Tim could remember he had never known John to wear anything other than denim jeans with a blue, heavy cotton, work shirt and a pair of work boots. He looked every bit the stereotypical mechanic.

They walked across the parking lot weaving in and out around the cars. Tim couldn't help but glance inside each car he passed. Memories of that crazy old man stirred inside him. He didn't want any surprises.

When he glanced through the back window of an old Toyota Corolla, Tim stopped. His mouth dropped open when he realized what he was seeing. Inside, on the back seat were what appeared to be the skeletal remains of a small dog. It was curled up as though waiting for its master to return. The thought made Tim angry. *How could someone leave their beloved pet in their car as though they were just running into the store and would be right back out? Everyone was told to set them free.* He turned away and kept walking.

The five regrouped on the other side of the parking lot.

"Keep your eyes peeled. We don't need any surprises," John warned.

The walkway, wide enough for them to walk five-abreast, was still in decent shape, only a few buckled and cracked places where the roots of the trees had grown underneath. The sidewalk separated what was once a flowerbed against the building and the front lawn. The lush green lawn of the college was gone, replaced with a grove of wild maple trees and saplings. Their leaves had already begun to turn to bright yellows and reds with some littering the ground around their feet.

As they neared the main entrance George, Derrick and Tim picked up their pace, as if they were in a contest to see who would be the first to reach the door. The three kept pace, but once they were within ten feet, they broke into a run.

"Ha!" George shouted and touched the door. He turned around and held his hands up triumphantly.

Behind him the doors slid open. Tim and Derrick froze. Instantly they raised their hands, exposing their bare palms and took a step back. The grin faded from George's face and he turned around. His eyes widened and he raised his hands high. He quickly stepped back in line between Tim and Derrick.

"We mean no harm." John said when he joined the three.

Slowly a woman dressed in an old, buckskin jacket that looked home-sewn and way too big for her small frame, walked out from inside the SAC. Her dirty, mousy-blonde hair was pulled back in a rough ponytail. She squinted and glared at them through blue-gray eyes. Her lips were pinched thin and pulled down at the corners in an angry frown. Fine lines crisscrossed her face accentuated by what appeared to be long hours spent in the sun. It made it impossible for Tim to guess her actual age; that and the double barrel shotgun she gripped in her ruddy hands. Aiming the shotgun at each of them, one at a time and moving from right to left and then back again, she pushed the men back, away from the entrance. The doors closed behind her.

"Who are you?" she snapped in a raspy, dry voice.

"I'm John Bjorge and these are my sons, George and Godfrey."

She cocked her head and squinted even more while she looked at John. "Bjorge? Where are you from?"

"Hillsboro."

"Not with a name and accent like that you aren't," she snapped, her neck stretched and her shoulders lowered. "I won't ask it again." She aimed the shotgun at John's head.

"I was born in Norway but I moved to the United States when I was twenty-three," he explained.

She lowered her gun but continued to eye him suspiciously. "What are you doing here?"

"We need help," Tim answered.

"Help?" she repeated and turned her gun toward him. She took a couple steps closer.

"We're looking for the people in charge of the SAC."

"Well, they aren't here," she snapped. "So, you can go back to Hillsboro."

"They aren't? Where are they? Where's everyone?" Derrick asked.

"Don't know and don't care," she said and swung the gun around, aiming it at Derrick.

"Then what's the harm in us having a look inside?"

"Because I said you can't."

"Who are you?" George asked.

The woman swung around and took aim at George. She took a step closer.

"I'm the one who's gonna blow your damned head off if you try, that's who I am!" she hissed.

With her attention diverted away from Derrick. Tim glanced at him. Derrick gave a nod indicating he knew that they were thinking the same thing. Together they lunged at the

226

woman. Tim went for the gun; Derrick grabbed her around her waist knocking her off balance. She let out a yell as the three of them crashed to the hard concrete of the walk. On the way down she released her hold on her weapon and Tim seized it.

"Get off me!" the woman screamed and twisted beneath Derrick's weight.

Tim broke open the shotgun and removed the shells. He shoved them safely into his pocket before snapping the shotgun closed. Meanwhile, Derrick helped the woman to her feet but kept a tight hold on her arm which he held pinned behind her back. She twisted and turned trying to break free.

"Let me go!" she spat.

"Not just yet," Tim said feeling his anger replace his fear. "Who are you?"

"None of your business!" she spat.

"Do we still have that rope?" Tim said over my shoulder at George.

"Uh, yes!" he answered not sounding the least bit convincing.

"Good, go get it."

George hesitated and gave Tim a puzzled look. Tim turned away so the woman wouldn't see and winked at him then motioned with his eyes for him to start to walk away.

Turning back to their prisoner Tim continued, "We'll just tie her up and leave her here."

"No!" she shrieked and twisted some more.

"Then answer my question; who are you? What is your name?"

"Barbie," she answered in an almost child-like voice.

Tim glanced at John. He nodded as if telling Tim to go ahead.

"When did you wake up?"

Barbie cocked her head and looked at Tim as if he were crazy.

"What?"

"When did you come out of suspended animation?"

"I never did," she whimpered and grimaced, holding the shoulder of her pinned arm.

"What do you mean?"

"They never did that to me."

"How did you avoid it?" George asked returning to the group.

"My mom and dad hid my two brothers and me in the root cellar in our barn. Then they piled hay over the door to hide it. The plan was when the men came looking for us my parents would show them the three pretend graves we dug in the back yard. They'd think we were dead and we'd be safe."

"Brothers? Where are they?" Godfrey blurted sounding frightened.

Barbie grinned and looked at Godfrey. "That's for me to know and you to find out," she taunted.

Derrick jerked her arm higher behind her back. She let out a scream.

"Okay!" she shrieked. Derrick eased his grip. "They died," she said sounding as though she were about to cry. "Bertie died a long time ago from a fever. Chuck died sooner. He complained of stomach pains. He was sick for a very long time. I tried to take care of him like mama did but he just got worse. I begged him not to leave me, but he did."

"I'm sorry," Tim murmured.

"Your story isn't adding up." John stepped forward while he spoke. "If your parents buried you in the barn, how did you and your brothers get out?"

"We waited for our cows to eat the hay. It took weeks,

maybe even a month or more. I couldn't tell how long."

"Then what did you do?" John asked. Tim could hear in his voice that he doubted her story.

"We hid out in the house and waited. My parents left instructions hidden in the cupboard for me and my older brothers. We had to stay inside out of sight and leave the curtains closed at all times. We were to wait until everyone was asleep. Then we were supposed to go and get them."

"And did you?" Tim asked.

"We tried, but there were two people in white smocks still awake. They tried to grab my brothers but they were no match." Her lips curled in a smug grin. "My brothers were too smart. They could shoot, gut and skin a deer faster than anyone."

"Are you saying your brothers killed them?" Godfrey asked, his voice an octave higher than normal.

"It was either them or my brothers," she answered and looked at him. "Don't worry, my brothers were fast. Those two were dead before they knew it."

Godfrey took a step closer to his father. His hands began to tremble.

"So, what about your parents?"

"They're still inside," she answered and motioned toward the doors with her head.

"Still asleep?" George asked.

"Uh-huh."

"But they were supposed to wake up a long time ago. What happened?"

"I don't know. When we found them, Bertie wouldn't let me see 'em. But I snuck a peek. They looked so strange, sort of a pale yellowy color. Chuck, he was the oldest and smartest one. He said it was normal for people in suspended animation."

"Did you notice anyone else?"

"Yeah," she nodded. "My teacher, Miss Hertel. She was yellowy too."

Tim looked at Derrick. They both knew what happened.

"Barbie, how old were you when everyone went to sleep?" Tim asked.

"I was eight," she answered proudly.

"What about Albert?"

"He was thirteen."

"We should go take a look," John said. He started for the door.

"No!" Barbie shrieked and twisted and pulled against Derrick's grip. "You can't go in there!"

"Why?" John asked.

"'cause, Bertie said if anyone goes inside, something bad will happen to my mom and dad."

John stopped and turned back to face their captive. "Don't you want us to wake up your parents?"

She didn't answer but appeared to be thinking about what he said.

"No!" she yelled again. "You'll hurt them!"

"Why would you think that?" Tim asked.

"'cause Bertie said and Bertie never lied."

"Barbie, I promise you, we won't hurt them. We won't touch them. We only want to look around and see if there's a way to wake them up. Okay?"

She looked at Tim through squinted eyes and appeared be considering what he had said.

"Okay, but don't touch nothin'!"

They moved toward the doors. The doors opened automatically and they walked inside. Derrick brought Barbie along as well.

Inside, the lobby was open and wide. A grand spiral staircase rose in the center of the room. Around its base sat groupings of dusty chairs and sofas with fake plants for greenery, something Tim now found odd with all of the real stuff only feet away outside. Beyond the stairs was a large alcove, a counter stretched the full width of the space. It reminded Tim of the front desk at the Hilton Hotel in downtown Portland. Tim headed for it, hoping to find a directory that would tell them where the generator room was and more important to him, where he would find the offices and apartments of the two doctors who manned the SAC.

At either end of the counter was a small gate that allowed access behind it. While the others waited in front, Tim went through to search the other side. Behind the front desk, beneath the countertop, were drawers and shelves. He started opening them but they were empty.

"What happened to the stuff that should be in here?" he asked, remembering the drawers in the Hillsboro SAC had binders and papers.

"Bertie and Chuck burned it all up outside," Barbie answered.

"What?" Tim shouted, his voice echoed down in the near-empty room.

Barbie didn't react.

The wall behind the counter was papered with what looked like torn pieces of brown paper sacks. The rough edges overlapped each other and formed an interesting texture. Tim touched it. It felt smooth like it was coated in a varnish.

In the center of the wall were twelve one inch by two inch black bars; evenly spaced in a large circle with their ends all pointing toward the center. Two, large, black, metal, filigree clock hands attached to a clock mechanism stuck out of the center of the circle. The hour hand was bent and pressed flat against the wall. The minute hand was bent at an odd sideways angle. Suspecting it happened in a scuffle, Tim looked at the floor. The floor was tinted and polished concrete though dulled under a layer of dust. Confirming his suspicions, the fronts of the drawers and the bottom half of the wall were all marred by a dark, uneven stain. He looked closer and Barbie's words came back to his ears, "they could shoot, gut and skin a deer faster than anyone." *This must have been where it happened.* Tim felt sick.

"Look over there," Derrick said, pulling Tim out of his thoughts.

Tim looked at Derrick who motioned with his head toward the end of the counter.

"By the video equipment," he said.

Tim turned to look at what Derrick was talking about. Recessed into the wall at the opposite end of the counter from where Tim stood were shelves. Carefully he stepped around the stain on the floor. Even though he knew it was dry, he still didn't want any of it on him or the soles of his shoes. He quickly searched the empty spaces over, beside and behind the DVD players and monitor.

"Nothing," he announced. Right when he turned back to face everyone, a large rat jumped off the shelf beneath the counter and ran across the toes of his shoes. Tim let out a startled yell and stumbled backward, falling against the wall. The wall gave a bit.

"What's wrong?" Godfrey asked, stepping behind his father for protection, the same way he did when he was a young boy.

Tim searched around him. The vermin was gone.

"Nothing, just a stupid rat," he answered.

"That was some scream, Timmy," George teased and laughed. "I didn't think your voice could hit that note anymore."

"Very funny," Tim said in a sarcastic tone. He could feel his face flush with embarrassment. He felt so stupid for letting this woman's bizarre story, the blood splatters, and his own imagination send him into an extreme jumpy mode.

He stood up, away from the wall and heard a click. Turning around he noticed he had tripped a hidden door in the wall, like his mother's secret cupboard. The door was the width of the wooden panels but only three feet tall, cut out of the middle of the panel. Tim grabbed the edge with his fingertips and pulled it open. Fearing another rat may be inside, waiting to jump out at him, and not wanting to scream again, Tim opened the door a couple inches but stayed safely behind it. To his relief, nothing happened. He swung the door open the rest of the way and took a look inside.

On the inside of the door was a map of the Center's three floors with room numbers clearly marked. On the back wall of the shallow cupboard were rows of hooks on which keycards were hung. Each card had a name printed on it.

"Found it!" he announced triumphantly and showed the others. George hopped over the counter and joined him for a closer look. Together they located the maintenance room where the generators should be. George grabbed a card.

"Find the room?" John asked.

"I think so," George answered. This time he walked around the end of the front desk to rejoin his brother and dad. "The map says Maintenance Room is in the basement, Room B-NW9. I'm not sure if that is where the generators are but it's a starting point. There was nothing on the map marked generators."

John nodded. "Sounds good. Why don't you show me the way, then you can give me a hand."

"Sure," George answered his father.

The two headed off across the lobby to the north hallway.

Tim lingered a little longer, studying the map and trying to locate the offices and apartments of the two administrators. The map showed a hallway on the other side of the wall he was facing. It led into the core of the building where unnamed rooms were outlined. *That must be them.* He turned to examine the keys. Three were missing. One was the card George had taken. The other two spaces were labeled O'Brien and Nichols. He took the unmarked card that hung beneath the label, Master, and another one with an actual name on it just in case. Turning back to the map, he studied it one last time. *There has to be a way into the corridor on the other side of the wall.* Pressing his cheek against the papered wall, he looked down its length more carefully.

Slowly he walked back to the end of the counter where he had passed through, running his hand gently along the wall to feel for possible irregularities.

"What are you doing?" Derrick asked.

"I think I found the offices and apartments. They're behind this wall. I'm thinking there may be another hidden door somewhere."

The words were barely out of his mouth when Tim felt a ridge. He pushed against it but it didn't move. He moved over a foot and pushed again. It gave slightly and clicked a little louder than the cabinet door had. When he let go, the door panel popped ajar.

"Wow!" Godfrey gasped.

"But before we check them out," Tim said, remembering

the ID numbers on each chamber, "I think we should find where Barbie's parents are, first."

"No!" she snapped and started to lunge forward but Derrick grabbed her arm and held her back.

"Why?"

She looked at Tim and her expression softened. "'cause Bertie said never to go in there. It could hurt them."

Tim looked at Derrick while Barbie squirmed and tried to twist free. It was obvious that Bertie knew his parents were dead and was hiding it from Barbie. Perhaps he felt she was too young at the time.

"When did you see them last?" Tim asked.

Barbie stopped struggling and furrowed her eyebrows. She looked up at the ceiling while she appeared to be thinking. "I don't know. It was before Bertie died."

Again Tim looked at Derrick. He shook his head.

"If I promise not to hurt them, would you tell me where they are?"

Barbie looked at Tim. She stopped struggling to break free. Finally her expression relaxed and she nodded.

"They're upstairs," she said.

"Would you show me where?"

"Okay," she answered.

They took the stairs. Even though Tim knew what they would find, he wanted to check on the others.

Barbie led them up to the third floor. When they came out of the stairwell, Tim was surprised to see how clean it looked.

"Did you do this?" he asked her.

"What?"

"Clean."

Barbie nodded her head.

The third floor looked like any college building with a

wide hallway and several doors lining the walls on either side. The floor was the same polished concrete as the first floor. The swirls of orange-red tint gave it a terra cotta appearance. The sound from their shoes echoed up and down the corridor while Barbie led them south. When they reached an adjoining hallway she instructed Tim to go down it. He could see the end of the hall ahead.

"Which room are they in?" he asked.

"That one," she nodded toward the second to last door on the right.

The LED lights above the entry switched on when they stepped into the room. Then like ripples in a pond, the remaining lights switched on until the whole room was illuminated.

The sleep chamber room was much larger than Tim had anticipated given the spacing of the doors in the hallway. It took up the entire side of the building from the first door they passed after the turn to the last door they hadn't reached yet, but it was smaller than the rooms in Hillsboro's SAC. The room still held hundreds, possibly thousands of sleep chambers. With three floors of rooms just like this one, there would be plenty of space for the population of Newberg easily.

"Where now?"

"Down there, the row facing the windows" she answered and nodded in the direction she wanted them to go.

When Tim turned down the aisle he glanced at the first tube and his breath caught. He glanced up at the lights above the chambers. They were out. Turning back, he stopped Derrick and Godfrey before they could see what he had.

"Wait here," he told them. "How far down the aisle are they?"

"They're about halfway, on the left."

"Their names?"

"Ken and Rosa Dickson."

"I'll be right back."

While Tim slowly walked down the aisle he glanced at the names on the brass plates between the chambers. With each step he felt his stomach tighten more. When he found the names, he looked at the remains inside. His suspicion was correct. He rushed back to the three.

"What's the matter with you?" Barbie asked when she looked at Tim's sweat dampened face.

"Nothing, just a little out of breath," he lied and started for the door.

"You find them?" Derrick asked.

Tim nodded.

"And were we right?"

Again Tim nodded.

Derrick turned and looked back at the sleep chambers. He let go of Barbie. She took two steps away from him and turned sharply. Before anyone could stop her she punched him in the stomach. Derrick doubled over. Tim grabbed her arm and fended off her blows.

"Stop it!" he scolded her. "No one is going to hurt you."

To his surprise, Barbie heeded him. She stood with her head tilted slightly down like a young girl.

"Barbie," Tim spoke softly. "After your brothers saw your parents, what did you do?"

"Bertie got really mad. He and Chuck said something and then they took off downstairs."

"Then what?"

"They broke into a big room," she answered in a matter-of-fact tone.

Tim looked at Godfrey and Derrick. He was sure they

could see the trepidation reflected in his eyes.

"Where's this room? Will you show us?" Tim asked.

"Okay, but you're not gonna like it," she answered in a little sing-song tone.

"Why?" Derrick asked.

"You'll see."

Barbie turned around and the three men followed her back into the hall.

No one said a word while she led them back down the stairs to the lobby. She walked over to the end of the front desk and pulled the hidden door in the wall open.

"This way," she said and headed down the hall on the other side of the door. The corridor was wide but not as wide as the one upstairs. The doors that dotted the walls on either side were more decorative with tinted windows and painted on signs. Beside each door was the familiar keycard reader.

"Here," she said and stopped at a doorway on the right.

The door had been torn apart, leaving only a few inches of the frame and the kick plate at the bottom still attached to its hinges. The rest of the door, in splinters, littered the floor along with shards of broken glass.

"How on earth..." Derrick gasped upon seeing the destruction.

Carefully they stepped over what remained of the door and entered the outer office. The room reminded Tim of the one where he had found Dr. Dever. It was a small room with a desk facing the door. Three chairs sat against the wall by the doorway. Another fake fichus tree stood in the opposite corner. Except for the main door, the outer office appeared unscathed. Tim started to feel hopeful.

Behind the desk was another door. This door was still intact, probably because in the absence of a card reader it wasn't locked. Tim opened it and all hope drained away.

The office was larger than the one out front and matched the layout of Dr. Anderson's back home. The wall to the right was made of thick security glass with a single door at the far end that provided access to the room on the other side. The wall to the left was taped and textured and had several deep gouges and holes in it. Nails with bits of wire that once held paintings still dotted the wall. The mangled artwork lay in a heap on the floor beneath them. Against the far wall, a large bookcase spanned the room. Some of its many shelves had been chopped and reduced to kindling. The contents of the shelves, binders that matched those from the Hillsboro SAC, were scattered all over the room. Only a few remained tucked between the top of the bookcase and the ceiling, probably because they were out of reach for two young boys.

Behind them, on the wall right above the door to the front office, hung monitors just like those in Hillsboro, but many of their screens were broken and none of them were working.

In front of the bookcase sat a large oak desk. Deep gouges marred its surface and sides. Pens, paper clips and other small office items lay strewn across the desktop and spilled onto the floor. The back of a flat screen monitor was shattered and had been knocked over, face down on the keyboard.

Derrick brushed past Tim. He picked up the desk chair, sat down and then righted the monitor. He typed on the keyboard for a moment while he looked at the monitor. Scooting away from the desk, he looked under it. His expression filled with a mixture of anger and disgust.

"Did your brothers do this?" he asked and lifted up the keyboard. When he turned it over, a few of the black keys fell off. They bounced on the desk before landing on the floor.

Barbie bit her lower lip and bent her head down like a

child who had been caught doing something she knew was wrong.

"Answer me!" Derrick yelled and slammed the keyboard down on the top of the desk.

Barbie nodded but didn't say a word.

Derrick's jaw tightened and his lips became a thin line. He threw the keyboard across the room. Godfrey ducked just in time. It hit the wall with a loud crack and fell on the floor.

"What did you do?" his voice thundered. He leaned over the desk and looked directly at Barbie.

"I didn't do anything, it was Bertie and Chuck," Barbie blurted and took a step back. She bumped into Godfrey who was standing behind her. She grabbed his arm for protection.

"Why?" Derrick demanded.

"I don't know. They were just mad and crying. They wouldn't tell me anything."

"Did they do anything else? Go anywhere?" Tim asked.

Barbie looked to the right. Tim turned to see and noticed the door. Derrick did too.

"Did they go in there?" Tim asked.

Barbie nodded.

"Good God," Derrick gasped.

Tim met him at the door.

"Keep her here!" Tim said to Godfrey and nodded toward Barbie.

"No, I want to leave now," she said and started for the outer door.

"I don't think so," Godfrey said and stepped in front of her. She froze and took a step back.

"We'll only be a minute," Tim told them. He smiled to himself when he saw that Godfrey had found his courage again.

Derrick kicked at the debris on the floor, clearing a space so he could open the door wide. When they passed over the threshold, the LED lights inside the server room came on. Derrick staggered and nearly crumpled to the floor.

"Oh my God," he groaned.

The room was filled with a mountain of debris. The black metal, refrigerator-sized cabinets that housed the computer servers, the brains of the building, lay twisted, bent and dented on their sides. Smaller shards of green plastic and computer guts were scattered all over the floor. It was hard to imagine that children would have the strength to do this, but they must have.

"Those imbeciles killed them all," Derrick groaned.

Tim turned to head back to office but stopped. Across the room, lying on the floor in a corner, he noticed a discarded pick axe, the kind that was in the emergency fireboxes in the stairwell on each level. Images of two young boys, grieving, and angry, even a bit frightened, going on a rampage flashed through his mind. He imagined them knocking over the servers and swinging that axe with tears clouding their vision. They were lashing out, not knowing whom to blame or why or what they were doing. Tim's heart ached for them and for the innocent people they unknowingly murdered.

John and George were waiting with Godfrey and Barbie when Tim and Derrick returned to the office. George stood beside his brother, blocking the doorway out. John looked shocked as he surveyed the room. Godfrey looked at Tim and shook his head.

"Did you get what you need?" Tim asked John.

"Yes and more," he answered.

"We found the garage and another pair of Hummers," George added. "And twenty new power cells."

"Great!" Tim said but his voice lacked enthusiasm.

"What happened in there?" John asked glancing at the view of the computer room.

Derrick stood with his shoulder leaning against the bookcase. His arms were folded angrily over his chest. He looked up, past everyone, at Barbie seated in a righted chair by the wall between the desk and outer door.

"What?" she asked and gave a slight shrug.

"They're all dead. Every last one of them," Derrick said before Tim could answer.

"How?" George asked and took a step forward.

"My guess is the heads of the SAC took care of the undesirables while Barbie and her two brothers were hiding out in their home. When the boys found their parents and discovered they were dead—"

"They and went on a rampage," Derrick interrupted Tim. "They murdered everyone else, thousands of innocent men, women and children."

Barbie's eyes widened and her mouth dropped open. She looked back and forth at Tim and then at Derrick. Her chest heaved and she breathed faster. She began to shake her head.

"No. No. No!" she shrieked and leapt to her feet. Her fists were raised and ready to fight. "You take that back! My brothers didn't kill anybody who didn't have it coming!"

Godfrey grabbed her shoulders from behind and pulled her back down into a chair.

"When your brothers smashed those computer servers in there, they shut down the only thing keeping all of the people of this town alive. They most certainly did murder them!" Derrick spat back taking a step toward Barbie but keeping the desk between them, to lean on.

"You take that back or I'll kill you!" Barbie pulled and

twisted but Godfrey held her down.

"I see it runs in the family!" Derrick sneered.

"Stop it! Both of you," Tim shouted and stepped between them. "No one is going to kill anyone," he said to Barbie. Turning to Derrick, "Derrick, she wasn't responsible for what her brothers did. Besides, it was over fifty years ago."

"I need some air. I've got to get out of here. I can't take this." Derrick said and left the room before anyone could say another word. Tim could tell by his tone that something else was going on with him, but now wasn't the time to talk about it.

Tim looked around his feet at the pile of torn up binders and papers.

"Let's go, Tim," John said in a fatherly tone.

"Can you give me five minutes? I'd still like to see if I can find something that could help everyone."

"Okay, we'll meet you back in the lobby," John answered. "Don't be too long. We don't want to lose the sun."

"I'll be there."

"Come on," Godfrey quietly urged Barbie. "Let's go."

Barbie wiped her tears away and stood up. Tim watched the four leave the room. Again he looked at the pile and then at the bookcase. Giving up, he left the office and went back into the hall. He needed to find the other doctor's office. Rounding the corner at the end, he headed left toward the center of the building.

He stopped at every door and tried the keycards. He found a janitor closet, a linen closet, a movie theater and a workout gym. *It has to be here.* He stopped at another door. *Please, be the office.* The light turned green and the door clicked open.

The room was not an office. It was their grocery store complete with shopping carts, check-out counter and aisles of food in the governments' foil packaging. Tim grabbed a cart and loaded it up with the unopen cases of food. He pushed the cart into the hall and grabbed another cart. After loading up four heaping carts, he returned to his mission.

The next door was across the hall. It was ajar. The glass pane had been broken out. Tim found a large piece on the floor with a partial name painted on it, "Dr. Alice O'."

He found it. His heart beat faster with anticipation. He pushed the door open and his hope crashed. The office was in shambles. The boys had trashed it as well.

Papers, ripped from binders, littered the room and covered the floor and desk. Little tufts of white batting from the seat cushions of the two office chairs dusted the room like the snow in one of those winter globes. The broken and twisted chair frames poked up from the floor with dangerously sharp and pointed edges. The fake fichus tree was stripped of its leaves and pulled out of its pot. The ceramic pot was smashed; another source of hidden dangers. The large bookcase on the far wall had also received unwanted attention. Its lower shelves had been chopped to pieces. Their contents, the binders and other books, were torn apart. Only a few of them remained intact on the upper shelves, out of reach for the crazed young boys. Carefully Tim made his way over to take a closer look.

Please, let it be—here.

He looked up at the top of the bookcase, above the shelves. The edge of a binder was barely visible. Tim's curiosity took over. He had to know if that was *the* binder. He looked for something to climb on so he could reach it. Finding nothing, he grabbed the fichus tree. After several prods and almost pushing the binder further back, he managed to hook it enough to pull it out and off the top. It fell to the floor like a butterfly, pages fluttering but held together by the binder rings.

Tim threw the tree aside and grabbed his prize. He looked at the spine and read, Fourteen. *Oh my God!* He opened it to the contents page and quickly ran his finger down the listings until he found what he had been looking for. He slammed the binder closed and held it to his chest.

"Yes!" he said triumphantly. Racing back into the hall, he grabbed a cart and headed back to the lobby.

John and the twins were standing at the foot of the staircase. Derrick was off by himself near another seating area.

"What happened to Barbie?" Tim asked when he approached the Bjorges.

"She wanted to go home," John answered. "So, I let her go."

"But she's all alone," Tim protested.

"She's managed for fifty-three years, Tim. I'm sure she'll be fine. What do you have there?" John asked, eyeing the cart.

"I found their store and it's stocked. I loaded up some carts and left them in the hall back there," Tim answered. "Also, I found the binder!" He held it up. He glanced over at Derrick and his excitement waned. "We can talk about it later. Do you mind loading this stuff up in the other Hummers? I think I should talk to Derrick."

"Sounds good," John answered. He sent his sons to get the other carts while he took the cart from Tim.

Derrick stood staring out of the window. His arms crossed with his hands holding his shoulders in a self-hug.

"Are you okay?" Tim asked in a calm and quiet tone.

"No," Derrick answered. Tim could hear the tears in his voice. "It's one thing to know a whole center was wiped out by a bunch of fanatics. It's another knowing that two people a whole town trusted with their lives went ahead with wiping out those they deemed undesirable. It sickens me. I can't stop thinking about Robbie who risked his own life to save mine and so many others."

"Thank heaven for him," Tim said. "He was a true hero."

"But he's still dead," Derrick said as his grief engulfed him and tears streamed down his face.

Tim felt his own tears well up. He put his hand on Derrick's back and stood beside him not knowing how to comfort him.

"I'm sorry," Derrick apologized. "We should go." He wiped the tears from his face. "Did I hear you say you found the binder?"

"Yes," Tim answered, but the joy he felt seemed dim. He almost felt guilty for being excited when Derrick had lost so much.

"Good, now maybe we can finish Robbie's plan."

Tim and Derrick joined the others in the garage. As promised, there were two more Hummers. However, instead of being black, they were a drab olive green. Everything else about them was identical to the two Tim and John had taken from the Hillsboro SAC.

George opened the large, metal, garage door. It groaned and rattled noisily but slowly rose.

"Load up as much as you can," John instructed. "I'll go get the other one and bring it around."

When the four finished transferring the boxes to the back of the Hummer, George and Godfrey took the carts and rushed back to the store to refill them. John arrived with the Hummer. They emptied the grocery carts, filling all three vehicles to the ceiling.

"There's still a lot more left," George informed everyone when he closed the last tailgate. He handed the keycard back to

Tim.

"We can make another trip later," John said. "There's also the grocery store."

Tim put the card in his pocket. He was surprised that he didn't feel bad about taking the food from the SAC. It had sat there on the shelves for over half a century and no one touched it. Barbie obviously had found her own way.

John made the decision that Derrick would get one of the new Hummers and the other would go to Tim, to replace the one that Lily stole.

"I don't feel much like driving right now. Do you mind?" Derrick said and handed his key to George.

"No problem!" George answered.

"I'll go with Tim," Derrick said and climbed into the passenger seat and fastened his seatbelt.

Tim started the engine. It was quiet like the other. He had to look at the instrument panel to be sure it was running. After George had cleared the garage, Tim slowly backed out. He found the garage door fob and pressed the button. The heavy door rattled and groaned all the way down.

John took the lead with George and Godfrey behind him. Tim and Derrick brought up the rear. They headed for Hillsboro right when the sun began its decent.

"I'm sorry," Derrick apologized again.

"Forget it. Let's just get back home and put this whole ugly incident behind us."

"Agreed."

Driving the old road back to Hillsboro suddenly brought back a memory. Tim laughed and told the story to Derrick to fill the silence. "I was sixteen and Dad was teaching me to drive. We had gone to Newberg for something, I can't remember what or why, but Dad wanted me to drive home. I was so nervous. He had an old pickup with a stick. As long as we were on the flat, I was okay but when we started to climb, the truck started slowing down and the engine sounded funny. Dad wasn't about to tell me what to do until we nearly came to a complete stop. Then and only then did he tell me to downshift. After that, I started to relax again.

"Then suddenly we neared the top of the hill. There was a space between the trees on the cliff side to my left and I saw how high we were. My hands tightened around the steering wheel and I froze. Dad quickly slapped my hands and I looked back at the road just in time to keep from driving into the ditch on the right. All my protests and telling him that he should drive fell on deaf ears.

"'You're doing fine,' he kept telling me. 'Just relax and keep your eyes on the road in front of you.'

"I can't tell you how glad I was to get home. I nearly kissed the ground. Now that I think of it that was the last time dad let me drive his truck. I had to use my mom's car for my driving test."

The story brought a smile to Derrick's lips.

"I remember my driving test," he said. His voice sounded less depressed.

"Yeah?" Tim urged.

"It was in the middle of winter, Chicago winter," Derrick said. "There was snow everywhere. I had put off the test as long as I could but the snow wouldn't melt. So, I did the test in the snow. I even parallel parked for the first time."

"Wow! Did you pass?"

"By one point," Derrick admitted. "But, hey, I passed and got my license."

"That's funny; I passed by one point too." They both laughed.

The caravan passed the Christensen Creek Crater without incident, other than Derrick laughing when Tim dubbed it that. *It was good to hear him laugh*, Tim thought.

Crossing Jackson Bottom and back into Hillsboro Tim felt the tension in his shoulders and neck ease. He was home again, back to what had become familiar: vandalized buildings, deserted streets and the comfort of knowing that in the safety of their homes the undesirables of Hillsboro were still alive.

Tim glanced at Derrick. He was looking through the binder.

"Was I right? It's there?" Tim asked.

"Yes, it's all here," he answered with a nod. He closed the binder and looked at the road ahead.

Tim turned down 331st Avenue, his parents' street. *Almost home.* Thoughts of Lily flashed in his mind. Silently he found himself hoping she hadn't come back. *Life would be less complicated.* Immediately he felt a sadness sweep over him. He had fallen for her. She was everything he thought he was searching for . . . or was just that she was there?

John was the first to pull into Tim's parents' driveway. Struggling with a mixture of excitement and anxiety, Tim craned his neck to see around John's Hummer. The space in front of the barn was empty. Tim felt his body relax and slip into depression. Lily was really gone.

Anna and Philip met the returning men at the back door. Tim left the food in the hummer and rushed over to give his dad a hug. Philip's body tensed.

"It's me, dad, Timmy," he whispered in his dad's ear.

Philip relaxed and hugged Tim back.

"So, how was your trip?" Anna greeted her husband with a quick kiss and hug.

"Not good," John answered. "They're all gone."

"Gone? Like Aloha and Forest Grove?"

"I'm afraid so."

"Oh, dear God in heaven," Anna gasped and made the Sign of the Cross. "What has happened to this world?"

"I wish I knew." John shrugged and then glanced over at the Hummers. "At least we have the parts for the generators. And we even managed to pick up a couple more vehicles and solved our food worries."

"Wonderful."

Tim brought his dad over to show him the new Hummer.

"What do you think?" Tim asked, silently wishing his dad would say he did good at last.

Philip didn't say anything. He just looked in back when Tim opened the door, but his eyes only registered confusion.

Tim, Derrick and the twins took the boxes of food from the back of Tim's Hummer and stacked them on the floor in the corner on the back porch. When they were finished they went inside.

The kitchen was filled with the aroma of fresh baked biscuits and Anna's vegetable beef soup. Tim's stomach growled, letting him know he was alive and hungry.

"So, how was my dad while we were gone?" Tim asked Anna who had donned her oven mitts and opened the door on the stove.

"He was fine, Tim. We listened to some of the old records. He seemed to enjoy that. Then we went for a little walk to check on the cows and chickens."

"He didn't mention my mom or anything?"

"A few times but we got through it." She smiled at Tim and set the cookie sheet on top of the stove before closing the oven door. The biscuits were a golden brown and made his mouth water.

After washing their hands, everyone sat down at the dining room table. Tim looked around and tried to recall the last time he and his parents had used the dining room for anything other than a hallway. Then he remembered. It was the Sunday before Sarah ran away. The four of them had sat down to a nice dinner his mother had made. They were halfway through the meal when Sarah received a text message on her phone. It wasn't until she answered it that Philip lost his temper. He had told them both not to bring their phones to the dinner table. *It was family time.* No TV. No phones. No radio. It was a time for them to connect with each other. Sarah said she was finished anyway and pushed away from the table. Tim ducked while he tried to keep eating. Philip told her if she was through then she could go to her room for the rest of the night and week, for that matter.

Tim looked at his dad and wondered if he remembered. Philip didn't appear to. He sat down in his usual seat at the head of the table. Tim sat beside him, to his right.

Anna brought in the steaming pot of soup and sat it on the trivet in the center of the table in front of Philip's plate and bowl. She rushed back to the kitchen and returned moments later with a large bowl of biscuits wrapped in a kitchen towel to keep them warm. Tim noticed a small bowl of fresh butter in the center of the table and realized she must have made that too.

"I hope you're all hungry," she said and sat down across from Tim, in his mother's usual chair.

"I'm not hungry," Philip said.

"Oh, that's okay, Phil, you can sit with us anyway," Anna said and patted his hand gently. "Let's say Grace."

Everyone bowed their head. Tim looked at his dad. Philip had bowed his head. When Anna finished her prayer, Philip said amen along with the others. Tim smiled to himself, happy that some of the dad he knew was still in there.

Philip watched Anna dish up bowls of soup for everyone and then he handed her his bowl. She smiled at him, filled his bowl and set it on the plate in front of him. He just looked at it. When the biscuits were passed around the table, he took one and set it on his plate.

"Would you like some butter?" Tim offered.

"Where's the jam?" he asked.

Tim looked at the table. They didn't have any jam or jelly. What his mom had made and stored in the pantry didn't survive the fifty-three years while everyone slept.

"I have some apple jelly," Anna spoke up. "I made it last week. I'll get it."

Before she could stand up, Tim stood. "I'll get it."

She settled back in her chair. "It's in the basket. Bring a teaspoon for it, please."

"Sure."

When Tim sat back down, he handed the small jar of jelly along with the spoon to his dad.

"What's this?" he asked.

"Apple jelly," Tim answered.

"I don't want that." He set the jar on the table by his plate and looked around.

Tim suppressed his feelings of pain and loss with a bite of soup. The salty, vegetable and beef broth tasted so good. His stomach instantly growled for more. He took another bite before putting butter on his biscuit.

Tim glanced at his dad. Philip was staring back at him with a question in his eyes.

"What?" Tim asked.

"Where's your mom?"

Tim felt a tug at his heart. He hated lying to his father but he knew his father wouldn't understand the truth and it would upset him if he did. He finished with the butter and set his knife down.

"She's out with friends," Tim answered and prayed he would accept that answer.

"When's she coming home?"

Tim glanced at John and then Derrick and the twins. They all had the same expression on their faces, one that told him he was on his own.

"Soon, Dad, soon. Would you like some milk?"

"Please," he answered.

Tim poured a glass and set it down by his plate. Philip picked it up and took a drink. Then he began to eat his dinner. The moment had passed but Tim couldn't relax. He began to worry about what he would say the next time his dad asked about his mom, and he would ask, of that Tim was certain.

After dinner Philip retired to his chair in the front room. Tim turned the stereo on and played an old, *Sons of the Pioneers* album. Philip began to rock in time with the music. Tim knew when his dad closed his eyes it wouldn't be long before he was asleep. Tim covered him lap with the afghan from the back of the sofa and went back to the kitchen. He needed to talk with John and Derrick.

Anna stood at the sink washing the dishes. She handed them to John who dried them and in turn, gave them to Derrick for him to put away. Tim watched them for a while, enjoying their precision, before he finally spoke up.

"Where did George and Godfrey go?" he asked and leaned against the doorpost.

"I sent them out to give the cows some grain and to milk them," John answered.

"So, when did you want to go to the SAC in the morning?"

"Early. I need to get those generators fixed before the others quit or break down from being overworked."

"Well, if all goes as I hope and if the book I found is right, we won't have to worry about the generators much longer."

John stopped drying. He put the towel down and turned to face Tim.

"Tim, come and sit down, I'd like to talk to you about that," he invited and directed him over to the table. "You should join us, Derrick. This involves you, as well."

The three of them sat down at the kitchen table. Anna finished washing the dishes and moved on to drying them.

"I know you want to wake everyone up, especially your mother," John began when they were all settled. "But you can't."

"What? Why not?" Tim heard the biting tone in his own voice and felt his anger spark to life from somewhere deep inside of him.

John held up his hands and gently lowered them at the same pace that Tim felt his anger ebb.

"First of all, winter is fast approaching. We woke up too late to plant any crops, let alone a garden. You've seen the stores in town. They've been stripped bare. Even with the food in the Newburg SAC and the stores there, there simply isn't enough food available to feed the whole town for a minimum of eight months. We'd be waking them up only to have them starve; and desperate people soon become violent people when they are trying to save their families. It wouldn't be fair to them."

Tim opened his mouth to object but John raised his hand,

silencing him.

"What I'm saying is some people will have to remain asleep a little while longer."

"So, how do we decide who to wake up and who to let sleep?" Derrick spoke up.

"We go by, who is essential. That book you boys found lists everyone's name, occupation and address, right?" John asked. He glanced at Derrick and then Tim.

"Yes," Tim answered.

"We use it to wake up the people who worked for the power company and get them working on restoring the power to the town. We also wake up mechanics and farmers. The mechanics can get the farm equipment running and the farmers can start making preparations for planting. We need to also wake up doctors so they can be ready to help in case they are needed."

"Makes sense," Derrick said and nodded in agreement.

"But wait, what about my mom? My dad—"

"We will wake her up."

"And Henry's family?" Tim asked.

"I know you promised him," John said. "So, yes, we wake them up as well. So, are we all in agreement with this plan?"

"Yes," Tim answered.

"As long as the book tells us how we can do it, then I'm in." Derrick answered.

"Fine, you and Tim get started on figuring out that book and make a list of the people for the first round."

Tim looked at Derrick but Derrick seemed to be avoiding eye contact. He was looking at his hands and his expression was the same he had back in the Newburg SAC.

"Okay," Tim said. He put his hand on Derrick's shoulder.

Derrick looked up and nodded.

That night, with Derrick soundly asleep in Sarah's old bedroom and Philip asleep in his, Tim stood on the front porch with a heavy quilt wrapped around his shoulders. The sky was clear. The stars sparkled and the moon, just a sliver, shone overhead. He watched his breath fog in front of his face and felt the cold air against his cheeks.

How did this happen? How did everything go so terribly wrong? Why?

He leaned against one of the posts that supported the roof over the porch.

"Please, God, if you are still listening, I need your help. I can't do this alone anymore. I love my dad so much, God, but I'm just not strong enough to take care of him on my own. I don't know what to do for him and I hate lying to him. He needs my mom again. I need her. At least when she's here, together we can face whatever. I miss her so much. Please, let her wake up tomorrow. Let what's in that book work."

Tim stared at the sky not sure what he expected to see but hoping for some sign to tell him that God heard him and was still out there.

What a hypocrite you are! You gave up on God years ago and now you are asking for his help?

That's not true!

It is true. After Sarah died, you couldn't bring yourself to pray anymore. You avoided even a conversation about God.

No, I didn't!

Remember when those people came to your door? You shut it in their faces but not before ordering them in no uncertain terms to leave. That was real Christian of you.

You know nothing!

Tim pushed away from the post and walked back into the house. He was tired of arguing with himself and yet, he knew he was right. He had stopped praying and believing in God after Sarah died. Seeing the pain in his mother's eyes and weighing on his father's shoulders, how could God allow that to happen? Was it punishment for some past sin? That's what the priest said. Sarah died because she sinned against God and against her own body. Tim wanted nothing to do with a god like that. Still, he pretended to believe and went to church until his father was diagnosed with Alzheimer's.

He paused by his parents' bedroom door and listened. Inside his father snored softly. He was sleeping peacefully, blissfully, unaware of the mess the world had become. Sure, it had renewed itself just as the government had promised, but at what expense? At the expense of the populations of Forest Grove, Aloha and Newberg, and God only knew how many other towns and cities had been sacrificed.

Tim walked up the stairs. When he reached the landing he looked at his sister's bedroom door. He didn't know why he felt at ease around this stranger. Perhaps knowing that he was connected to the head of the SAC gave Tim strength and courage. His being a nurse was a bonus and relief when it came to caring for his dad.

Leaving his disquieting thoughts on the landing, Tim headed for his bedroom. He undressed and climbed under the covers. The bed was cold at first but quickly warmed from the heat of his body. Tim turned on his side and faced his desk under the window. The binder sat opened to the page with the instructions on setting a wake up date. He felt excited, nervous and scared all at once about tomorrow.

Please let it work.

The room grew darker. Tim looked up at the window. Outside, clouds had moved in, blocking what little light there was from the moon and stars.

Figures!

He turned over, closed his eyes and willed himself to sleep.

Day Sixty-six. Tim woke up to sunlight streaming through his window and the sound of someone pounding on the front door below.

"Tim!" he heard George shout.

Tim jumped out of bed and grabbed his jeans. Pulling them on he headed for the door, grabbing the shirt off the chair along the way.

Derrick was just coming out of his room. His eyes still half closed. His blonde hair was mussed and sticking out at all angles. Tim wondered if his hair looked the same.

"What time is it?" he asked with a yawn.

"Don't know, but I think we're late," Tim answered, equally tired. "Throw some clothes on."

Tim rushed down the stairs. George was still knocking but at least he had stopped yelling.

Tim threw the front door open. "Are you trying to wake up my dad?" he asked.

"Why aren't you ready?"

"What time is it?"

"It's half past seven."

"Seven! Ugh, don't you guys ever sleep in?" Tim looked past George at the Hummer parked in the street in front of the house. Anna waved when she saw him. Tim waved back.

"I thought you'd be up all night."

"I was. That's why I was asleep. I was awake reading that binder until my eyes crossed and I couldn't see anymore."

"Did you find the instructions?" George asked.

"I think so. I'll be right back."

Tim rushed back up the stairs while George went to get the rest of his family. Stopping at Derrick's bedroom door, Tim leaned in. Derrick was tucking in his shirt. The bed was already neatly made.

"The Bjorges are downstairs. It's after seven," Tim informed him.

"Okay," Derrick said with a nod. "Be right down."

It didn't take Tim long to finish getting dressed. He grabbed the binder from the desk and stopped by the bathroom to splash a little water in his face and run a comb through his hair. Derrick was helping Anna unload her basket in the kitchen. The coffee was already brewing on the stove. She disliked coffeemakers, preferring to use her old coffee pot instead.

"Morning," John greeted.

"Morning, Mr. Bjorge," Tim answered back. "Where are George and Godfrey?"

"Milking the cows and tending to the chickens. They aren't going with us today. They can be a better help doing some things around here. We need to get a more weather proofed shelter built for the cows. As well as get the hay in that field across the street cut and stored."

"Oh," Tim answered, surprised that he hadn't thought of that.

John looked at the binder when Tim set on the table.

"George said you were up all night reading that?"

"Yes, I found the instructions. They're written step-by-step so it's pretty straightforward."

"Good. We'll head out after you have some coffee."

"It's ready now," Anna announced. She seemed extra cheerful. Tim wished he could be, that this would be the day he would wake up his mother, but John had insisted they make

259

a list of the vital people first.

Half an hour later, John parked on Main Street in front of the SAC building. He handed Derrick and Tim the boxes of parts from the back and grabbed his tool kit before locking the doors and activating the alarm on the Hummer.

The three made their way down to Lower Level Five. Derrick and Tim set the boxes down.

"Do you need a hand?" Derrick asked John.

"Sure. That would be great."

"Is it alright with you if I go check on my mother?" Tim asked but didn't know why. Perhaps it was John's fatherly tone that made him feel the need.

"Yes, go on," John smiled at him.

"Thanks."

Tim left them and started up the stairs. It had been two days since he last visited her. His irrational feelings of guilt had made it impossible for him to face her. Even though he knew it wasn't his fault that he was awake instead of her, he couldn't shake it. But today he had good news to tell her.

Butterflies still found their way into his gut when he rounded the end of the aisle on the fifth floor. He spotted her immediately and out of habit, looked at the blinking lights above her chamber for reassurance that she was all right.

She still looked the same as the day she entered the sleep chamber fifty-three years ago. Her hair was still pulled back in her usual manner. Her cheeks were still a rosy pink. Her hands were folded in front of her, her fingers intertwined.

"Hi, Mom, it's me, Timmy." Tim didn't know why he said that. He had tried for years to get her to call him Tim. For some strange reason, it just felt right at that moment. "I found the book." He touched the cold glass that separated them. "I now know how to wake you up."

"You do?"

Tim jumped and stumbled backward, tripping over his feet and falling against the empty chamber behind him. His knees bent and he slid down until he was sitting on the floor. He put a hand over his chest. His heart thumped wildly deep inside. He looked down the aisle.

"Henry?" Tim gasped and climbed back to his feet. "Don't do that!"

"You know how to wake them up?" the eighteen year old, Hispanic boy asked. His dark brown eyes sparkled with excitement and hope. He rushed at Tim who took a step back.

"Henry, I— what are you doing here?"

"I was looking for you. I wanted to know if your offer was still open, for me to stay with you, I mean. I ran out food and I don't have any heat where I live. I can't pay you or anything but maybe I could work or do something for you."

"No, Henry—"

"I knew it! You're just like all the others! You say you want to help me but then you take it back."

"No, Henry, you're wrong. The offer is still there. You can come and stay with me but you don't have to pay me back."

"What about my family? Can you wake them up too?"

"I...I..." Tim glanced at his mother, part of him hoping she would help him somehow. "Henry, here's the deal. Before we can wake everyone up there's something we need to do first."

"I want my family back. Please."

"I will wake them up. I promise you, just not today."

The disappointment was clear in Henry's expression. Tim felt his own.

"Derrick and I will be working on it today. We'll see

what we can do," Tim said and heard his father's empty promises echo in his ears. "But you can definitely stay with us."

"Thanks," Henry said. His disappointment was evident in his expression and tone.

They walked down to Lower Level Four. With every step, Tim's words echoed in his head. He wondered how long it would take Derrick and him to make the list before they move forward.

Derrick was waiting for him in Dr. Anderson's office.

"Is John finished already?" Tim asked.

Derrick looked up from his seat at the desk. He was already typing into the computer. He spotted Henry immediately and slowly stood.

"Who is this?" he asked in a matter-of-fact tone.

"This is Henry. He found me upstairs. He's the boy I told you about, the one who saved my life. Henry, this is Derrick. His partner was the one in charge of this Center."

"Hi," Henry greeted. He stepped forward and held out his hand to Derrick.

Derrick reached over the desk and gave Henry's hand a polite but quick shake and then let go, all the while looking at Tim.

"Tim, I need to show you something in the other room."

"Okay," he answered and turned to Henry. "Have a seat over there and don't touch anything. I'll be right back."

Tim followed Derrick into the computer room. He walked across the room to where he could see through the glass wall that separated the server room from the office and keep an eye on their guest.

"What is he doing here?" Derrick snapped.

"I told you, he was looking for me and found me talking

to my mom."

"No. I mean, here, in this office?"

"He wants to stay with us."

"What? Why?" Derrick gave me a suspicious but confused look.

"Because his family is still asleep upstairs and I offered to let him come and stay with us at the farmhouse. He has no food or heat and he's all alone."

"Are you serious?" The tone of Derrick's voice raised a pitch.

"What was I supposed to do? Say no? He saved my life, Derrick. I couldn't just turn him away."

"What about your mom—"

"Uh, that's another problem. He heard me telling her I found the book and was going to wake her up. He thinks we can do it now, today."

"I suppose you told him you would?" Derrick began to look and sound more and more angry.

Tim was a bit taken aback and confused.

"No. I told him I couldn't because we have to make that list first."

"Good," Derrick nodded. "You did good."

Tim suddenly had a strange feeling stir in his chest. A feeling he hadn't felt in a long time. It was a cold, empty feeling. He remembered. It was the day he landed the job with the law firm in Portland. He was excited and couldn't wait to tell his parents the news. Instead of being happy for him, his dad just nodded his head. "Finally, something good comes from all that money I spent on your schooling. Good job, Timmy."

"Are you coming?" Derrick asked.

Tim was momentarily confused, lost somewhere between

the memory and the present.

"What?" he answered.

"Are you planning to stay in here all day?"

Tim realized the Derrick was standing by the door into the office waiting for him.

"Oh, sorry," he said and followed him.

Derrick took his seat again and pulled the binder closer. He stared at the page with the instructions and then at the screen. "This doesn't make sense," he said.

"What?" Tim asked and looked over his shoulder.

"The instructions say to open this program." He moved the cursor to an icon on the screen and clicked. Instantly a small pop-up window appeared asking for a password. "We're locked out."

"What?" Tim felt his hope start to fade.

"It needs a password."

"Well, don't you know the doctor's?"

"I've tried all the passwords he used. None work."

"Oh my God, you don't think it wants Dr. Dever's password?"

"It's possible."

Tim remembered the note that fell out of the journal he found in Dr. Dever's office, "Oh God, what have I done." Finally it made sense. Dr. Dever had returned to her office, discovered Dr. Anderson on her computer. She intentionally shot through her computer, stopping him and ruining his attempt at whatever he was trying to do. His hand slipped and he mistyped the year. He grabbed his gun and returned fire, killing her. When he saw the monitor was destroyed and realized he was shot, he knew was dying. He wouldn't make it to his office in time to finish setting the date for everyone else.

"Now what?" Tim asked.

"We search for the password." Derrick answered.

EPISODE VI:
AWAKE

Winter, like fall, seemed to arrive earlier than normal; but then again, what is normal? Before being placed in suspended animation the seasons were all messed up. Winters were dry and warm, summers were cold and wet. People used to blame it on El Nino and Global Warming but stopped short of actually blaming it on man's interference. *People never seemed to take responsibility for their actions.*

Perhaps, this was the way winter was supposed to be, cold with the overcast skies and dreary rain for days on end. Whatever the case, the Tualatin River had flooded its banks and the lowlands south of town. Tim had a memory from when he was a young boy of seeing his dad's lower field flooded. In fact, Godfrey, George and he built a raft of plywood and a couple of old wooden fence posts. They dragged the raft down to the lower field and tried to paddle across the big expanse. However, the raft snagged the wire of a submerged fence and the three ended up in the slimy, smelly water. That short adventure earned them all a round of Tetanus shots from Dr. Nachtigal, their families' doctor. Tim looked across the kitchen table at his dad and wondered if he remembered that? *Probably not.*

Philip's Alzheimer's seemed to have worsened over the last two months. He rarely spoke at all, not that he did before but lately he would go days without a word. Tim became even more determined to wake his mother. She needed to be with his dad.

The only thing stopping them was the missing password. Tim, Derrick, the Bjorge twins and even Henry searched everywhere in the SAC for the password but found nothing. Tim frustration mounted.

Other than Philip's memory failing, he seemed to be in good health. He didn't complain about being cold, but Tim noticed that he grabbed the blanket from the sofa in the front room whenever he sat in his chair. Tim turned up the heat in the house for him and hoped the power cell on the generator would keep it working.

Day one hundred thirty (December 23, 2095). The rain finally stopped but the temperature felt colder. Walking back from milking the cows, Tim glanced at the sky above Hillsboro. For a second, he wasn't sure what he was seeing. It came to him all at once. In an otherwise cloudless sky, a plume of dark black smoke rose from somewhere in town.

"Derrick!" Tim shouted and rushed to the house, nearly spilling the bucket of milk. Setting it on the kitchen counter, he quickly searched the house. Tim's father was still sound asleep but neither Derrick nor Henry was inside. Tim heard talking outside on the front porch.

"Didn't you hear me calling?" he asked and let the screen door slam shut behind him.

"Sorry," Derrick answered. "Look!" He pointed toward

town.

"I know! We need to go." Tim looked at Henry. "Can you stay with my father?"

"No, I want to go too," he protested.

"Fine, stay here and wait. I'll be right back."

Tim jumped off the porch and took off in a run for the Bjorges' house next door. John and his family were on the front porch of their two-story farmhouse staring at the smoke in the distance.

"Get ol' Bessie going," John told George when Tim stopped at the foot of the front steps, out of breath.

"Why Bessie?" George hesitated.

"There could be other people around. It's too risky taking the vehicles. No one is going to try to steal ol' Bessie. They wouldn't know how to start her even if they wanted to."

Apparently satisfied with the answer, George took off for the barn in back.

"I'll grab my basket and stay with Philip," Anna said. She quickly loaded up her handbasket with a jar of preserves and biscuits. "A little something nice for when Philip wakes up," she volunteered when she climbed up onto Bessie and sat on the old bench.

John was right. Bessie was basically the chassis of an old Ford pick-up with its engine exposed in the front. A wooden floor extended to the back past the tops of the back tires. An old buckboard bench seat, pulled from a junkyard heap, was bolted to the floor behind the steering wheel. It resembled a giant go-cart more than an actual car.

Tim, George and Godfrey huddled close on the flat bed behind the bench seat. The old gal creaked, rattled and bounced as John drove next door to Tim's parents' farm.

After helping Anna down, Henry and Derrick hopped on.

George and Derrick took the seat next to John while Henry slipped between Tim and Godfrey, their backs pressed against the back of the driver's seat.

"Hang on!" John called over his shoulder and they were off once again.

"Please don't let it be the SAC," Tim said under his breath when they turned east onto TV Highway.

Godfrey carefully turned around and knelt behind his father, holding onto the back of the seat to steady himself. "Can you tell where it's coming from?" he asked, shouting over the noise from the old springs and creaking boards.

"It looks like it's near the courthouse," John answered.

Tim's stomach tightened. He quickly turned around and climbed to his knees. With no padding on the floor and the jostling of ol' Bessie, Tim's knees responded in pain instantly but he had to see. Without a windshield to protect anyone, the cold air stung Tim's face and bare hands. There was just enough space between Derrick and George for him to get a better look. To his relief, the smoke appeared to be to the west of the courthouse when John turned north on 1st Avenue.

When they approached the intersection of 1st and Washington Street, George shouted.

"Stop!"

John slammed on the brakes and everyone lurched forward. Tim was pressed against the wooden back of the bench.

"What?" he asked, rubbing his chest.

"We should grab some equipment," George answered.

He nudged Derrick and the two hopped down and headed toward the building to the right, the Hillsboro Fire Department.

John stayed with Bessie and kept her going while Tim and the other two joined Derrick and George.

The large glass and metal garage doors were locked shut. Derrick found a hunk of metal pipe from somewhere around the side of the building. He used it to break out one of the panes in the garage door. There was enough room for George to get through. He quickly retrieved a couple fire hoses, a large wrench, and a first aid kit from inside. He handed them through the broken window and then came back outside. The whole stop took less than five minutes.

When John reached Main Street he stopped in the middle of the intersection. He shifted gears. Bessie's metal parts groaned and bucked nearly knocking Godfrey off. Tim grabbed Godfrey's arm just in time.

"Thanks," he said. He held on tighter to the back of the seat as his father turned west onto Main.

The smoke cloud appeared larger than it had from the front porch. Tim could smell the thick, unmistakable scent of a house ablaze. It wasn't the same odor as a campfire. It smelled of burning shingles, insulation, wood and memories.

John slowed Bessie down when they neared the intersection with Bailey. He pulled into the parking lot of the old American Legion Hall. The one story, cinderblock building sat abandoned, its doors and windows boarded up even before everyone went into suspended animation. However, there was something new; a section of the roof had caved in with decades of decay. Another sad reminder of how time had continued while everyone slept.

John pulled in front of the building and shut off Bessie's engine.

"We walk from here," he announced. "I don't want to risk getting any closer with the old girl. It's best not to draw too much attention."

Tim was actually relieved to get off his knees and onto

solid ground.

Derrick looped one of the fire hoses over his arm and let it rest on his shoulder. George did the same with the other hose. Tim grabbed the first aid kit while Godfrey took the wrench.

The six of them walked back to the cracked sidewalk along Main Street. They rounded the corner onto Bailey Avenue and headed north. In the distance Tim saw several people had gathered on the west side of the street. John made the right call with Bessie.

Without the roaring sirens, the rumbling of the firetrucks and rescue vehicles engines, it seemed eerily quiet. Just the sounds of shattering glass, snapping timbers and crashing beams could be heard.

The group crossed the street to the west side when they came to Lincoln. The building on fire was the third house from the corner, an old two-story craftsman. It was completely engulfed by flames. Despite the efforts of the elderly men and women manning garden hoses aimed at the flames, the fire kept advancing. Even the tall oak tree and the overgrown shrubs around the house were ablaze.

Tim turned to say something to John but John, Derrick and George were already busy attaching the fire hoses to the fire hydrant on the curb at the corner.

There was the loud crack. Tim looked back at the once beautiful house just in time to see the roof collapse onto the second story. He felt so helpless standing there holding the first aid kit, but he didn't know what else to do.

He spotted Dr. Nachtigal. He was standing with his arms around his wife while tears ran down her aged cheeks. Tim slipped past a small group and made his way over to them.

"Dr. Nachtigal, are you both all right?" He asked in lieu

of a greeting. Neither of them took their eyes off the burning home.

"Yes, we're fine," he answered and nodded. His voice was different than Tim remembered. It sounded weak and frail.

"Was anyone living in there?"

"Albert Newman and his wife, Gloria," he answered.

Tim's jaw dropped open. "I know them, I mean, my parents know them. They are all friends. Did they get out okay?"

He shook his head and closed his eyes. A tear squeezed out and dampened his eyelashes.

Tim's head turned sharply toward the burning building. His stomach felt hollow and nauseous at the same time. He surveyed the crowd, all elderly, wrapped in blankets and heavy coats. He looked at the man he had known for nearly all his life. Dr. Nachtigal was old, his face was crisscrossed with fine lines and his eyes were greyer. His once skilled hands were thin making his knuckles appear larger and gnarled. With his back bent and worn down with age, he appeared smaller than Tim remembered, less godlike. He was just an old man.

Another loud crack followed by a crash came from the house when an unseen timber gave way somewhere in the back. Images of Mr. and Mrs. Newman, frightened, choking, trapped inside their burning home flashed in Tim's mind. He thought about his father and mother. How would he tell them? He looked at the Nachtigals.

"Does anyone know for sure if they were home?"

"Gloria was," he answered. "She was ill. Al asked me to have a look at her. As near as I could tell it was pneumonia. Without the ability to run tests and without access to the proper medications, I wasn't able to help her. I just told Al to keep her warm and hydrated as best he could.

"Last night when I checked on them, her condition was worse. I caught Al trying to light a fire in their bedroom fireplace. I told him not to, that the chimney had fallen in on the side of the house. I suspect he may have tried to light it anyway, after I left."

"Oh no," Tim sighed.

Dr. Nachtigal closed his damp eyes and tightened his arms around his wife.

"Can we get some help?" Godfrey's voice shouted from the distance.

Tim turned to look. George and Derrick were manning one of the fire hoses, spraying water on the south side of the house. John and another man were using the other to shower the north side. Godfrey was knelt down beside a bush toward the back of the house away from the flames. The mist from his father's firehose kept the heat and flames from him. It wasn't until Godfrey stood up, pulling a body with him, that Tim realized what was happening.

Dr. Nachtigal rushed across the street.

"Julia, get me my bag!" he shouted over his shoulder to his wife.

Tim gripped the handle on the large first aid kit tighter and followed him.

One of the men who had been using a garden hose on the fire was the first to come to Godfrey's aide. Together they brought the injured man to the sidewalk and helped him sit down at the curb. All three were drenched by the water and shivering.

"Albert!" Dr. Nachtigal gasped when he knelt down in front of the man. "Open that up," he said to Tim, motioning at the first aid kit.

Tim set it down and did as instructed.

"Let me see what we have to work with." He pawed through the packages of sterile gauze pads and bandage rolls. There were tubes of ointments and salves as well as syringes and small bottles of clear liquid. "Ah," he said and tore open a package that contained a large gauze pad. He turned to Albert Newman and began to gently dab his soot covered forehead.

"Albert, what happened?" Doctor Nachtigal asked while he continued to clean the wounds.

Albert's face and hands appeared to be badly burned and covered in black soot. When he shivered, his entire body shook. Julia arrived with a blanket and the doctor's black medical bag. Her years of being a nurse hadn't left her. She took a pair of scissors from the first aid kit and cut Albert's shirt off. She then draped the dry blanket around him to help him get warm.

Tim stepped back so he wouldn't be in their way and watched them tend to their patient. All his years of working in a legal office hadn't trained him for anything remotely like that.

By the time the fire was reduced to smoldering embers, the sun had already begun its descent. Two men had picked through some of the rubble toward the back of the house and carried something out, wrapped in a sheet. Tim assumed they had found what remained of Mrs. Newman's body.

George shut off the hydrant and rolled up the hose. He looked like a real fireman. The training he received helping at the station one summer during high school had stayed with him.

John walked over and stood beside Tim. He watched the doctor.

"Martin," John said quietly.

When Dr. Nachtigal looked up, John beckoned him away

from Albert. The three took a few steps away.

"What happened here?" John asked.

Dr. Nachtigal shook his head. "John, I don't know, exactly. Albert isn't talking. What I do know is they ran out of food a while back and heat. Gloria became sick. I suspected pneumonia. My guess would be Albert started a fire in their fireplace to try to keep her warm." He paused and looked around at the people still gathered on the sidewalk watching. "What worries me is how many of these other people are in a similar state. The government really did a number on us this time and we all just let them."

John looked at Tim. Tim could tell he was forming a plan in his head. His brow was pinched and his eyes reflected concern. He turned back to the doctor. "How much food do you and Julia still have?"

"Oh, I don't know," he stammered. "Maybe enough for a couple weeks or a month at best."

"What if we could pool all the food and set up a soup kitchen?"

Dr. Nachtigal turned and looked at his wife who was still attending to Albert Newman. He turned back. "I don't know if you could get all of these people to agree to it. They're old and scared. They don't trust anyone, especially when it comes to their food."

"Try to convince them. I'll talk with the boys and see if we can find a building to house it. Please, tell everyone, no more fires in their fireplaces. We don't need to lose any more homes to chimney fires."

"Okay, I'll try," Dr. Nachtigal answered. "By the way, how'd you get here so quickly?"

"The boys got ol' Bessie running," John said.

Tim's jaw dropped in shock. He thought they were

supposed to keep it a secret.

Dr. Nachtigal chuckled and shook his head. "That old bone rattler, I don't believe it."

"Yeah, she's a rough gal but the boys love tinkering on her. They even converted her to solar power."

"Solar power," the doctor repeated. "How'd they learn to do that?"

"Remember when the city built that new junior high school on the site of Hare Field? It was to be Hillsboro's first totally green school complete with solar panels for electricity— hey, I've got an idea." John suddenly looked at Tim. "Grab the boys and let's go. Martin, take care of Albert and I'll get back to you. I need to check something out."

Tim and John left Dr. Nachtigal standing in the middle of the street with a confused look on his face. After gathering up Derrick, Henry and the twins, the six of them hurried back to Bessie.

"Before we head for home, I want to make a little detour," John said still being vague.

"Where?" Tim asked.

"Hare Junior High," he answered.

"Before we go, I'd like to stop by the SAC," Henry spoke up. Tim could tell by the look in his eyes that the fire and Mrs. Newman's death had left him shaken. Tim had to admit, it had its effect on him as well.

"Sure, we can stop for a few minutes," John said and nodded.

"I think I'll just walk to the SAC," Henry announced.

"I'll walk with you, if you don't mind?" Tim said. Part of him feared Henry would disappear again. After all, he was only eighteen and this sort of thing is hard to process even for an adult. The other part of him wanted a break from being bounced and jarred by ol' Bessie.

Henry shrugged his shoulders indifferently in answer.

The pair headed east on Main. The SAC was only a couple blocks away but standing at fifteen stories tall, it was clearly visible over the tops of the Post Office and other buildings.

"Are you okay?" Tim asked while they walked.

"I don't know," he answered. "I just wish I could talk to my mom."

"I know. I do too."

They stopped outside at the base of the front steps and waited for the others.

"Do you hear that?" Derrick asked when he and John walked up.

"Hear what?" Tim asked and looked around.

"It sounds like it's coming from inside the SAC," Derrick answered and rushed up the steps.

Everyone quickly followed. Tim had to admit, he didn't hear a thing until he caught up with Derrick at the stairwell. When Derrick opened the door to the stairs a pulsating high-pitched beeping sound filled the lobby.

"The four of you go up and start checking the floors. Make sure all the lights above the chambers are still working." Derrick took command. "John and I will check the computers and generators below. Meet us in the office."

"Okay," George answered.

Tim and Henry started up the stairs behind the twins.

"I going to check on my mom, first," Henry said and pushed past them, taking two steps at a time.

"I'll go with you but slow down or we'll never make it to the thirteenth floor," Tim shouted and chased after him. "You guys start on the second floor and work your way up," he called behind him to George and Godfrey.

"Got it!" Godfrey answered.

By the time Tim reached the eleventh floor, the muscles in his thighs burned. His legs protested with each step, threatening to stop moving. Still Tim pressed on and made the other two flights. He arrived at the door winded and sore. The only comfort was he could rest a bit before having to climb the last two flights.

Henry seemed unfazed by the climb. *Probably because of his youth and his determination to reach his family,* Tim reasoned. He quickly led the way to the sleep chambers.

The lights overhead flickered and threatened to go out but thankfully the daylight that streamed in from the outer windows made up for the dimness. Tim followed Henry straight to the row where Henry's parents slept quietly in their suspended animation tubes.

Tim looked at the young girl asleep in the tube across from Henry's mother. The pink in her cheeks was gone. Her head drooped slightly her shoulder and her hands hung limply by her side.

"No," Tim quietly moaned.

"What?" Henry asked and looked at him.

Tim looked away from the child and took a deep breath. He felt his strength return.

"Nothing. Just tired," Tim answered. He spotted a cart at the end of the row just beyond Henry. "Be right back." He slipped past Henry and searched the cart. Finding a pad of paper he tore off the top, dust covered sheet. In the drawer, beneath the flat surface, Tim found a pen. It didn't work. Digging in the back of the drawer he found a pencil.

"What?" Henry asked again.

"We need to write down the numbers of your family's

chambers. We can't trust the lights above the tubes."

"What's so important about the lights?"

"The lights indicate the chamber is working. Normally, if the lights are out it means…"

Henry turned sharply and looked at the lights above his mother's chamber.

"No!" he yelled and his body began to tremble. Tim could see tears starting to stream down Henry's cheeks.

"Henry, it's okay. She's still asleep. Look at her face."

Henry wiped his eyes. He looked at his mother and slowly his trembling ebbed.

"The lights on this floor for whatever reason aren't working properly. Derrick can check on the chambers when we get back to the office," Tim explained.

Suddenly Henry turned toward Tim with fear and anger blazing in his eyes. He grabbed the lapels of Tim's coat and pushed him back against the glass of the little girl's chamber across the aisle.

"Wake them up!" he demanded in a guttural tone.

"We will, I promise," Tim answered. "I mean it. But first we need to get the numbers and then get back down to the office."

Slowly Henry released his hold and stepped back. Tim quickly wrote the numbers down on the paper right when the lights flickered again.

"We have to check the upper floors before we can—"

"No!" Henry shouted. "I don't care about those other people. Wake my family up!"

Tim was shocked by Henry's outburst. Even though he felt a measure of the same, hearing this boy verbalize his total lack of concern for others was numbing.

"You go then, I have to check," he said to Henry.

Henry appeared afraid of leaving alone. He looked around while he seemed to think about what Tim said.

"Fine, I'll go with you, but you have to hurry," he relented.

Tim quickly rushed up to the fifteenth floor, everything appeared normal. The lights above each tube were still blinking. They checked the fourteenth floor and then made their way down checking each floor. They met up with George and Godfrey on the eighth floor.

"Everything's okay so far," Godfrey reported.

"Same for the upper floors," Tim said.

"Come on! What are you waiting for?" Henry demanded. Not waiting for the rest, he took off down the stairs.

"What's up with him?" George asked.

"I'll tell you later," Tim answered. "Let's go."

While they made their way down the stairs, the pulsating horn grew louder. When they emerged on Lower Level Four, the sound was almost unbearable. The three caught up with Henry who was waiting by the locked door with his hands over his ears.

Tim unlocked the door and Henry pushed his way inside. The lights were on in Dr. Anderson's office.

"What's going on?" Tim asked when he saw Derrick behind the desk.

Derrick glanced up from looking at the computer monitor. The expression on his face was frightening. He didn't say a word but Tim could hear his fingers on the keyboard.

He glanced through the windows on the wall to the right at the computer servers that maintained the sleep chambers in the building. Nothing appeared to be out of the ordinary.

"Where's John?" Tim asked.

"Generator room," Derrick answered.

Tim turned and started for the door right when the annoying beeping sound quit. He stopped and looked at Derrick.

"Did you do that?"

Derrick shook his head. "I don't think so." His voice appeared to be more relaxed.

"What's happening?" Henry asked still sounding panicked.

Derrick stood up and took a step back, away from the desk. He leaned against the wall of built-in bookcases and crossed his arms over his chest.

"I wish I knew," he answered. "We're losing power to the computers. I have rerouted as many floors as I can but it's putting a strain on the system."

"Okay," John interrupted when he entered the office. His forehead dotted with beads of sweat. He wiped his hands on an old rag. "We've got trouble."

Those words sent a chill throughout Tim's body. He felt his pulse quicken. "What sort of trouble?"

"The generators are failing."

"Can't you fix them?" Henry asked. Tim could hear the fear in his voice.

John shook his head. "I've done all I can to put a band aid on them—"

"What about going back to the SAC in Newberg? You could get more parts there," Henry blurted.

"We've already harvested every useful piece from their generators. I'm afraid this is it. When they break down next time…" He shook his head.

"What about the SAC in McMinnville?" Tim asked.

"We wouldn't make it back in time." John answered.

"You have to wake up my mom!" Henry screamed and

rushed the desk. Tim grabbed him and pulled him away before he could damage the computer.

"We will, we will," he assured him. "Please, try to stay calm." Tim heard a voice in his head telling him to heed his own advice. "Derrick?"

Derrick looked at Tim. "I can't." Derrick he said. "I don't have the password, remember?"

"Boys, think," John said. "You have searched this woman's apartment. There has to be a clue. What did you find?"

"She liked to read romance novels," George answered.

"She wore lacy underwear," Godfrey answered.

John gave him the look.

"Wait a minute!" Tim gasped, remembering the photograph on her nightstand. "I'll be right back!"

Before anyone could stop him, Tim ran back to the stairs and up two flights to the residence level. He took Dr. Dever's keycard out of his pocket and held it to the reader by the door. Once inside, he rushed to her bedroom and grabbed the picture.

He was out of breath by the time he walked back into the office. Everyone looked at him. "Here," he said and handed the framed photograph to Derrick.

"What?" he asked looking at the picture of the soccer player and then back at Tim.

"This was on her nightstand. It's her husband, Isaac Dever. He played for the Portland Timbers and wore number twenty-eight. Maybe she used him as her password. Try Isaac28."

Derrick glanced at John and shrugged. "Okay." He typed in the password and pressed send. He frowned. "Nothing." He then started typing again and again. "Nothing." He looked at the photo again, staring at something in the lower right corner. He pulled the back off the frame and took out the photo. Turning it over, he smiled and began typing. "Bingo! I'm in."

Tim picked up the photograph and turned it over. In the lower corner was written what appeared to be a date. "This?" he asked.

"Yes," Derrick answered.

Tim looked at the date again. It meant nothing to him but evidently it meant something to the doctor. Whether it was a birthdate, anniversary or date her husband died, it didn't matter. Derrick was now able to wake everyone up.

"John?" Derrick asked. "We need to begin right away."

John looked hesitant, something Tim didn't understand. He then stepped forward.

"Forget the list. Start with Mrs. Stone and Henry's family and then wake everyone up as quickly as you can," John started ordering.

"I'll get on it," Derrick said. "You two may want to get back upstairs. The process takes an hour," he said looking at Henry and Tim.

"Here are Henry's family's tube numbers," Tim said and handed the piece of paper to Derrick.

"Once I begin, I'll start waking the rest of the people on those floors. So, be ready to help them," Derrick added.

"Bring them down to the lobby," John instructed. "I'll talk with them there."

"Got it," Henry said and hurried out of the office.

John turned toward his sons.

"George, I need you to take Bessie home, grab a Hummer and check out Hare Junior High. See if the solar power is working. If it is, I need you to come back here immediately."

"Why?"

"Because if it's operational, we can use it as an emergency crisis shelter."

"Be right back," George said and rushed off.

"Hey, John, what if we cut off the power to the floors that don't need it? Like lower level one and two and the lobby?" Derrick asked. "Would that take some of the burden off the generators and buy us some more time?"

"It might. Do it," John said.

Derrick began to type rapidly. In less than a minute he looked up, "Done. The power is off. I'll shut the power down on each floor once everyone is awake."

"Good," John said. "Tim, what are you waiting for? Get upstairs to your mother."

"Okay." Tim answered and headed off.

Walking up to the fifth floor wasn't bad. Tim managed to make it without being exhausted and too out of breath. He started down the hall and turned back to the reception desk. Taking one of the chair with casters, he pushed it toward the sleep chamber room where his mother was about to wake up.

It felt so surreal. In just a few short minutes he would have his mother again. She would be able to help him with his father. Life would start to return to normal. Tim wondered what would be the first thing he would do. Would he hug her? Would he tell her how much he missed her?

He pushed the chair down the aisle. As he had done every day since he woke up, he glanced at the lights above her chamber. They were still blinking but one light had turned solid. He glanced at his chamber. No lights. He set the chair in front of his father's chamber ready to grab it should his mother need to sit for a while.

Another flashing light turned solid above her chamber. Tim stood right in front of the glass. His breath fogged the glass in front of him. *Oh! I'm too close.* He took a step back. He didn't want to startle her.

He looked at her face, still no signs of waking. He glanced at the lights. The last blinking light changed to solid. He took a deep breath and looked back at his mother. Her hands were still clasped in front of her. *Shouldn't she be breathing by now?*

He heard the sound of rushing air. A strand of her hair came loose and fell in front of her face. Still no sign of her waking. *Oh God! No!*

Tim's eyes began to tear. *This can't be happening. Please, God, no.* He stepped forward and touched the glass chamber. The glass vibrated and then slid open with a hiss as the pressure inside was released. Tim jumped and took a step back. He wiped the tears from his eyes so he could see clearly.

His mother stood motionless against the cushioned wall. Her eyes still closed.

"Momma?" Tim said. His voice strained. He reached out and touched her cheek. It was soft but cold. Tears streamed down his cheeks. He took her hands. They were cold too. "Momma, please wake up," he sobbed.

He felt her fingers move. He looked at her through his tears. She took a deep breath. Her eyelids moved.

"Mom?"

Della opened her eyes and blinked a few times.

"Timmy?" she said. "Why are you crying?"

Tim threw his arms around her and gave her a hug.

"Okay. Okay. That's enough," Della said in a firm tone.

Tim knew she hated public displays but he didn't care. She was awake.

"Stop it, Tim," she snapped.

"I'm sorry. It's just that I've missed you."

"Oh, nonsense, I just closed my eyes." She looked at the empty tube next to her. "Where's your father?"

"He's at home. We've been waiting for you."

The hiss of another glass chamber door sliding open caused Tim to look down the aisle. Another person was awake.

"Come on, Mom," Tim said. "I have a chair for you. So you can sit down."

"I don't need a chair. Let's go home," Della said and took a step out of the chamber. Her knees buckled and she collapsed into Tim's arms. He lowered her to the chair. "What's wrong with me?"

"It's okay," Tim assured her. "You're a little weak from being in suspended animation. In a few minutes you'll be fine." Tim glanced up the aisle and saw someone starting to move. "Mom, wait here I'll be right back."

Tim rushed to the open chamber just as the woman inside took a step and started to collapse. He caught her and helped her sit down on the floor of her chamber. "Rest a bit and you'll be fine," he told her.

All over the floor the sound of chamber doors opening every few seconds erased the silence. Tim rushed from one chamber to the next, instructing the people to sit on the floor of their chambers for a while until their strength returned. *Come on, Derrick. Can't you wake them one row at a time?* They were waking up too fast. He wondered if Henry was having the same trouble on his floor.

After several people had regained their strength, Tim gathered them at the door.

"Please, I know you have a lot of questions but I need you to take the stairs down to the first floor. Please, use the handrail and go single file. The weakness you feel will go away. John Bjorge is waiting in the lobby for you and will tell you what has been going on."

While each person passed by him, Tim looked at their confused expressions. Even though several were older than him, they all seemed to obey his directions without question.

"Timmy," Della said standing beside him. "What is going on? Why are you helping everyone? Where are that nice man and the people who run this place?"

Tim looked around at the people left in the room. They were dazed but no worse than any of the others. He took his mother aside.

"We over slept," he said. "Instead of waking up after twenty years, we slept for fifty-three years."

"What?" Della gasped. "Are you sure?"

"Yes, Mom. Positive."

"And your father?"

"He woke up before me, as near as I can tell, maybe two days before I did. But he's home and Mrs. Bjorge is with him."

"Anna?"

"Yes," Tim answered and nodded.

Della looked more confused the more Tim tried to explain.

"Mom, please wait here." Tim said. "I'll gather up the rest of the people and then we'll head downstairs. Mr. Bjorge will explain everything."

"Okay, son," she said.

Several minutes later, with all the chambers emptied, Tim led the group down the stairs to the lobby. All the useless furniture, the end-tables, lamps, and fake plants, were stacked against the outer walls. The broken glass had been swept up. The chairs and sofas were positioned in theater row style, all facing the large, dark TV screen.

"Della," John smiled and opened his arms when he saw

her.

"John," she said and let him give her a hug.

"So, good to have you back."

"Well, I don't know what to say," Della answered, still looking a bit confused. "It doesn't feel like I was gone."

"This is the last of them from the fifth floor," Tim informed John.

"Great," John answered. "Where are the others?"

"The others?"

"The people from the thirteenth floor."

"No one has come down yet?"

"No," John said, sounding concerned.

"Oh no," Tim said. "Mom, please stay with Mr. Bjorge. I'll be back."

Before she could respond, Tim rushed back to the stairs. The first few flights up were easy. Tim climbed them in no time, it seemed. However, when he reached the eighth floor, the muscles in his legs began to burn. He rested them for a moment then pressed on. By the time he reached the thirteenth floor, his legs felt weak and wobbly. He leaned against the reception desk to rest and to catch his breath.

The chamber room was noisy when Tim walked in. People were dazed and walking around. Tim began to direct them to wait by the door.

"Henry?" he called above the noise.

Henry didn't answer. Tim made his way to aisle nine. When he turned down it, he saw why. Henry stood in the middle for the aisle with his mother and sister. His mother was weeping and sobbing uncontrolled. Henry was trying to console her.

"Henry?" Tim said when he walked up on them. "What's the matter?"

Henry looked at him with tears streaking his cheeks. He held his mother while she held onto his younger sister. Slowly he shook his head and looked at an unopened chamber.

Tim stepped behind them to see. Henry's father was slumped against the side of his chamber. His skin was pale and mottled. "But how?" Tim asked while his gaze fell to a crack in the glass near the bottom of the chamber. He looked at Henry who continued to console his mother and sister. "You need to take everyone down to the lobby," he told Henry in a firm tone.

"Come on, mama," Henry said and pulled her away from her husband's chamber. She wailed louder when they reached the end of the aisle.

Tim looked at the crack in the glass. *That wasn't there a few minutes ago. That glass was fine.* He looked around and noticed the wrench from the fire station tucked between two chambers across from Henry's father. A cold chill came over him. He left the wrench and headed down to the lobby.

When he reached the door to the stairs, the power went off on the floor. He headed down to the office.

By the time he reached the third floor, the alarm sounded again. Tim picked up his pace and was joined by John when they reached Lower Level Four.

"Where's my mom?" Tim asked while they headed for the office.

"She's with Godfrey."

They burst into the office and found Derrick frantically typing.

"What's happening?" Tim asked.

"We lost power to the top two floors."

"Lost power? What does that mean, exactly?" Tim asked.

"It means that they're all gone," Derrick answered.

"Dead."

The word echoed in Tim's ears. He was just up there. The floors were filled with families, mothers, fathers and children.

"Can't you try to wake them?" he asked.

"I started the wake up process immediately but without power—"

"What about the other floors?" John interrupted.

"I'm starting the eleventh and twelfth floors now."

"What about the alarm? Is there any way to shut that off?" Tim asked.

"I'll take care of that," John said. "Grab Henry and get up those floors."

"Henry's not going to help," Tim said.

John stopped in the doorway. "Why?"

"I'll fill you in later."

"Fine."

"The twelfth floor will wake up first," Derrick said. "Go there."

By the time the sun started to rise the next morning, the SAC had lost a total of five floors, a third of Hillsboro's population. Derrick shut himself in the office and wouldn't let anyone in.

Before the first group had awakened, George had returned with good news. The power system at Hare School was operating fine. John then explained to everyone who woke up that we were setting up a shelter at the school and everyone who wanted could bring their bedding and whatever food they had stored. He sent George and Godfrey to get another Hummer and drive Tim's dad and Anna to the shelter. Anna and Della would start setting up the kitchen with whoever else wanted to volunteer.

Tim sat on the floor in the room outside the Dr.

Anderson's office. He was exhausted and his head felt numb. The craziness of the last twelve hours had caught up with him. He just needed to rest.

"Tim, wake up. It's time to go."

The sound of John's voice pulled Tim out of a dreamless sleep. He looked around the room and stuck between sleep and awake, he was disoriented. He looked at Derrick and John standing in front of him. Slowly his mind caught up and he sat up.

"How long was I asleep?" he asked.

"Just a couple hours," John answered. "We best be getting over to the shelter. Your mom and dad are already there and waiting."

Godfrey sat behind the steering wheel of the green hummer. He didn't look the least bit tired. Tim and Derrick climbed into the back while John rode shotgun. Godfrey drove up Main Street and turned north on Fifth Avenue to Grant. The school was five blocks ahead.

The closer they came, the more excited and awake Tim began to feel. It seemed like an eternity since he spent time with both of his parents. Finally, they were together and he would see them.

When they arrived, George was waiting for them outside the main entrance.

"Dad, just to warn you, several of the men are asking if you would fix their vehicles. They are pretty demanding, even threatening to take the Hummers."

"You two take the Hummers back home and lock them in the barn. You can come back on Bessie." John said. "I'll deal with the men. You haven't told them about the power cells have you?"

"No way," George answered.

"Fine. Go."

John led the way down the main hall toward the noisy cafeteria. Before they reached the doors, Tim could already smell pancakes and eggs along with brewed coffee. His stomach sprang to life.

Opening the doors, Tim was shocked by the sight of the crowd. People were seated around every table and standing against the walls. It was definitely more than the posted fire code would permit but no one seemed to care. Everyone turned to look the three of them. The room became silent. Tim, John and Derrick stood just inside the door. Tim wasn't sure who started it but the room slowly erupted in applause. Some even whistled and cheered.

Tim glanced at the food counter and spotted his mother smiling proud and clapping with several other women. They all wore white aprons. *Probably from the staff closet somewhere.* When Della saw him, she motioned for him to come behind the counter.

Tim rushed to her and gave her a hug, careful not to lift her off her feet. She hugged him back but patted his back. "Okay, Tim, that's enough."

The surprise of hearing her call him, Tim, was enough to get him to let go and step back.

"Come in here," she said and led the way to a quiet table set up in the corner of the kitchen.

Philip sat at the table sipping his cup of coffee and watching a couple women wash the pots and pans. Tim sat down beside him. Della gave Philip a kiss and sat down across from Tim.

"John filled me in on what happened. I'm so proud of you, Tim."

"Thanks, Mom," Tim said. "I couldn't have done

anything without the Bjorges, Derrick and—" he stopped before he mentioned her name. Even though it had been two months, he still wasn't over her.

"Here you go," Anna said and set a plate of scrambled eggs and pancakes in front of him. She set down two more just when John and Derrick joined them.

"Looks like things are running smoothly," John said.

"Fred Jensen has been a huge help," Anna admitted. "I guess if he can run a restaurant he should be able to organize this motley crew."

"Where is he?" John asked and looked over his shoulder.

"He went to get some rest. We've turned the classrooms into makeshift dormitories. That way people can get some rest away from the noise."

"That's wonderful," John said.

"Hey, John," a man by the door called. "We have a couple guys out here who worked for the power company. They were wondering if they could get a lift out to the substation north of the airport. They want to see if they can get the power back up."

"I'll have George give them a ride. He should be here shortly."

"I'll let them know."

Tim watched the man leave and then he turned to John. "But you sent George to get Bessie."

"They can ride out on Bessie. I'm not risking losing another vehicle," he said and took a bite of his food.

Day one hundred thirty-eight (December 31, 2095).

Eight days had passed since everyone was awakened. As the temperatures dropped, the population in the school grew. More and more people who at first went home decided to come to the shelter. The addition of more mouths to feed and the overcrowding in the classrooms had begun to weaken the peace.

George located the multimedia classroom and found they had a small newsroom for closed circuit TV broadcasting as well as a fully functional radio station. When his voice came over the speakers throughout the school, everyone was startled and went silent. When music began to play, they cheered. George tried his best at being a disc jockey but was grateful when one of the professional crewmembers for KSSN radio took over.

While the music helped to calm some people, it did little to stop others from becoming suspicious and paranoid. Tim could feel the anxiety inside him grow while he looked around the cafeteria. He was glad his mom had taken his dad home after one night in the shelter. Staying there was not an option for Philip. He needed to be around things more familiar to him.

Tim took a sip of his coffee and looked across the table at John and one of the electricians. They were looking at a map of sorts and talking about what caused the power outage.

"We need to clear some of these trees but in order to do that, we need some of our heavy equipment working," the man told John.

"I'll have some of the mechanic take a look at it and see what we can do."

"Thanks, John," he said and rolled up the map.

"John," Fred called while walking over to the table.

"I think you should look at this," he said. "Come with me."

Tim jumped up along with John and followed Fred to the room where the crates and boxes of food were stored. Walking over to an opened box, Fred pulled out a package of stew and opened it. "This stuff is no good."

"But how?" Tim asked. "This was supposed to stay good for twenty years."

"Exactly," Fred answered. "Not fifty years. These packages must have frozen and then thawed several times. That's not good for meats. The flour and other dry goods are fine but a lot of this is useless. Where did you get this?"

John looked at the box. "We found it in a grocery store in Newberg."

"I see." Fred acknowledged and turned around to inspect the other boxes. "What we should do is sort through these and separate out the stuff you found from the store."

"I'll get George and Godfrey to help," John said.

"Wasn't the government supposed to have a food storage bunker?" Fred asked.

"If they were telling the truth," Tim said. "So far we haven't been able to locate anything that tells us where it is. With all the lies they spewed I wouldn't be surprised if this was just another one."

"Well, we need to find it if it exists. If even a fourth of this food is bad, we won't have enough to last us five weeks."

Tim looked at John and remembered John's words that starving people become desperate and chaos would ensue.

"Dad," Godfrey said while he stood in the doorway trying to catch his breath. "You need to come quick before a fight breaks out."

"Where?" John asked.

"The gymnasium."

Tim felt his pulse quicken. The gym is where John and several other mechanics set up shop to restore necessary vehicles. He quickly followed John and Godfrey. Before they reached the gym, they could hear raised voices.

John threw open the door. "What's going on here?" he demanded, his voice echoing off the walls.

The small group of men, about ten in all, turned around to face John. One of them stepped forward.

"We've come to get our rigs fixed," the man with short cropped hair and dark, coal black eyes, demanded.

"As we announced when we started this," John said in a calm but firm voice. "Vehicles will be fixed based on the needs of the town. Right now we are working on trucks that are needed to restore power to the town."

"Then give us your rigs," another one standing in the back of the group shouted.

"Yeah!" the others joined in and took a step forward, fists ready at their sides.

John held out his arms in front of Tim and Godfrey and backed them up. Suddenly a loud blast behind them caused everyone to duck. Tim looked over his shoulder.

Derrick stood with a pistol in his hand. "That's enough!" he shouted at the group of men. "If it weren't for these men, your sorry asses would be rotting away in those sleep chambers. So, show some gratitude. If not, fix your own damned cars and quit acting like a bunch of spoiled babies."

"Who are you?" one of the men challenged.

"The one who woke your sorry ass up, that's who," Derrick snapped.

"That's just a starter pistol," another man shouted.

"Are you sure?" Derrick aimed it at the man.

The man cowered and ducked his head.

"Now, I suggest if you want to stay here you'll quit this nonsense and help out," Derrick said.

The men looked at each other and then dispersed. Tim had a feeling this wasn't over.

"Thanks, Derrick," Tim said and smiled. "Is that a starter pistol?"

"No," Derrick answered. Tim's eyes widened. He looked at the pistol in Derrick's hand.

"Where did you get that?" John asked.

"It was in the Robbie's safe. The partner to the one he used on that Dever person."

"You've had this all along?" Tim said.

"Yes."

"Why?"

"This is why," Derrick said and spread his arms out in a gesture toward the gym.

"Well, this opens up a whole new problem," John said.

"What sort of problem?" Godfrey asked.

"The threat of gun violence," John said. "Now that they saw you have a gun, they will find their own. We could all be in danger."

No one said a word. The sound of the mechanics returning to work replaced the silence.

Day one hundred sixty-one (January 23, 2096).

A foot and a half of snow covered the ground outside. So far the solar panels were able to keep up with the demand for heat inside. Tim sat in the cafeteria and looked out the window at the young children playing in the snow and building snowmen.

"Hey, Tim." Godfrey sat down across him. "Have you heard the news?"

"What?"

"The men working on restoring power just told Dad that they should have it back up this afternoon."

"Really?"

"Yeah," Godfrey answered. His smile faded. "What's the matter?"

"Nothing," Tim said sounding worried.

"What is it?" Godfrey insisted.

"I don't know. It's been three weeks and we still haven't located the food bunker, and with the snow on the ground, we can't get out to search. Fred said he found more boxes that had gone bad. So, we have a week's worth left."

Godfrey looked worried. He leaned forward. "The Hummers can still get through this stuff. Maybe you, Derrick, George and I could sneak off."

"What? Walk three miles back to the farm in this?"

"It beats sitting here fretting about it."

"Let's run it by Derrick and George," Tim said.

They located George in the electronics room. He was working on a couple of old two-way radios.

"What are you doing?" Tim asked walking up to the table.

"I'm trying to get these radios to work."

"Where'd you find these?" Godfrey asked and picked up a microphone the size of a computer mouse. He pressed the button on the side. Static and a high pitched sound poured out of the speakers sitting on the table.

"Will you stop that," George snapped and grabbed the mic from his twin.

"What are you using for power?" Godfrey asked.

"I found some small power cells that were still good. I've wired them together and connected it to the power intake."

"But why?" Tim asked.

"Since the phone lines and cell phones aren't working, I thought we could use these old two-way radios I found in some utility trucks that were junked. We could use them in case we need to drive to Portland or something."

"Funny you should mention that," Tim said. "Godfrey and I thought we—you, Derrick, Godfrey and me—could walk home and get the Hummers and then see if we couldn't find another food supply in Beaverton or even Forest Grove?"

"Are you guys nuts?" George protested. "It's cold out there and—"

"We have to. The food supply is running out," Godfrey snapped. "Fred thinks it'll run out by the end of next week."

George looked at them. "Let me finish this. I'm almost done. We can take it with us."

"Good," Tim said. "We'll go get Derrick and then tell your dad. It's best he knows the plan."

An hour later, after explaining their plan to Derrick, George was finished with the radios. The four walked into the gym. An old school bus and a few pickups were parked down the center of the gym. Each mechanic was working on one vehicle. John was working on the bus in the center. He stood up and wiped his hands on a rag.

"Hi boys," John said. "What's that?" he asked eyeing the backpack in George's hands.

"Dad, we want to walk home and get the Hummers," Godfrey said.

John looked at the other mechanics and then ushered the four away to a more private spot. "What's this?"

"Fred said that the remaining food will last a week," Godfrey said.

"Yes, I'm aware of that."

"Well, the Hummers are able to get through the snow, so we thought we could take them and see if we can't find more food in Beaverton or even Forest Grove."

"I fixed this radio," George stepped forward and handed the backpack to his dad. "We can keep in contact with each other with these." George turned so his father could see the backpack he had strapped on.

John looked at the bags and then nodded. "Okay, but be careful. We can't afford to lose any of those vehicles."

"We will. We promise," Tim assured him.

The sun was shining and the sky was a clear sapphire blue. Tim pulled the collar of his jacket tighter around his neck. Walking home sounded like a good idea but trudging through snow had slowed everyone down. By the time they reached Main Street, all four were out of breath. They stopped and rested for a moment.

"We should walk down to Baseline," Godfrey said.

"No, if we head up Main all the way, it runs into TV Highway near the bottom of the hill. Plus, with the buildings and trees, there will be less snow to walk through," George insisted.

"Sorry, God, I have to agree with George." Tim spoke up.

"Fine. We'll do it your way," Godfrey snarled and started walking up Main.

"God, don't be like that," George said and hurried after him.

"Are they always like that?" Derrick asked.

"Yeah," Tim said and nodded. He wrapped his arms around himself to keep warm. "George was born first. I think that has a lot to do with it."

After a few blocks Tim and Derrick caught up with the twins. George was right about the snow. Even though the buildings were dark and without power, the sun warmed the façades and melted the snow enough to make walking easier.

When they reached the SAC, Tim suggested they go inside to rest and get warm. He didn't tell them he wanted to take another look at Dr. Dever's office. Even though they had gone through it several times, the thought never occurred to him if Dr. Anderson had a safe in his office, she might have one too. The only problem was, with the generators not working the only light left was from the emergency lights, and those were dim. Still, Tim had to try.

"Guys," he said while they rested on the sofas in the lobby. "I want to go check on a hunch."

"What?" Godfrey asked.

The radio in George's backpack squawked. "George, can you hear me?" John's voice came through.

George grabbed the mic and pressed the button on the side. "Yes, Dad."

"How are you boys doing?"

"We've stopped at the SAC for a minute."

"Don't be long. You won't have a lot of daylight left."

"Okay."

"Call me when you get to the farm."

"I will."

The radio went silent.

"I won't be long," Tim assured them.

"I'll come with you," Derrick said.

The two headed to the stairs and then down to Lower Level Two. The hallway was nearly dark. The emergency lights were beginning to run out of power.

"What are we looking for?" Derrick asked while he followed Tim down the hall.

"I want to check to see if Dr. Dever had a safe in her office," Tim answered. "One of them had to have known where the government's food bunker is located. We didn't find anything in Dr. Anderson's office, so she would have to be the one."

"Haven't you checked her office several times?"

"Yes, be we were looking for a binder or some clue to her password, not a safe," Tim explained.

They stopped outside her office. The emergency light in the hall had gone out but the one in the outer office was still bright enough to see.

"I'll check her office," Tim said.

"Then I'll check the outer office, here." Derrick volunteered.

Tim went into the dimly lit interior room. He looked at the bookcase to his left. Dr. Anderson's safe was behind his, but the wall behind the Dr. Dever's bookcase wasn't thick enough. The safe would stick out into the outer office. If there was a safe it would have to be on the back wall.

A large painting hung in the center of the wall. Tim walked over to it and lifted it off its hook. He held it aside and looked at the wall. *Too easy and too cliché.* He set the painting on the floor and looked around. All the other pictures had been taken off the walls. He had searched the desk thoroughly when he was looking for her password. *Where could it be?*

A floor safe! The thought popped into his head. *All-night stores had floor safes, why not her?*

He looked around at the carpeted floor but the light was too dim to see. He took a step toward the desk and the lights came on, startling him. They blinked a couple times and stayed on.

"Hey!" Derrick shouted. "The power's back."

"I thought you shut it off," Tim said a little confused but still appreciative.

"Only power from the generators, Derrick clarified.

Now that he could see, Tim walked around to the back of the desk. *I wonder . . .* He pulled the chair out of the way and thought about finding Dr. Anderson sitting at the desk, dead and the stains on the carpet. He pushed the thought from his mind and knelt down. Looking at the carpet he searched for any irregularities.

"Nothing out here," Derrick announced and walked into the inner office. "What are you doing?"

"Looking for a floor safe," Tim answered and brushed his hand over the smooth but crusted carpet. "I think I found something," he gasped and stood up. "Help me move this desk."

The desk was solid and heavy but between the two of them they pulled it out far enough to let more light shine on the spot.

"It's right here," Tim said and felt the carpet again. He pinched some of the nap and pulled. Nothing. He tried it again and this time he felt the carpet move. He pulled harder and a circle about ten inches in diameter came loose to reveal a combination safe.

"Oh great!" Tim groaned. "Any idea what she would have used for the combination?"

"Why don't we try the same one she used on the computer, except make it numbers instead?" Derrick suggested. "Start with eight." Derrick watched while Tim turned the dial. "The next number is also eight." Again Tim spun the dial. "And the last one is 36."

Tim slowly turned the dial. Once the number lined up with the arrow on the outer part of the wheel it clicked and the spring in the door pushed it upward.

"We're in!" Tim announced. He opened the door to the safe and looked inside. The contents were shadowed. He stuck his hand in and grabbed the first thing he felt and pulled it out. Once the safe was empty, the picked up the treasures and carried them over to the desk to get a better look.

Tim spread them out. He opened a small jewelry box and took out a gold chain that was strung through a pair of gold wedding bands. There was also a folded up paper that appeared to be a birth certificate. Tim's eyes skimmed over it.

"Oh my god," he gasped. "They had a son named Christopher."

"What?" Derrick asked.

"Doctor Dever and Isaac Dever had a son," Tim repeated. "He was born in 2038, and would have been four years old when everyone went to sleep."

"Was he here?" Derrick asked.

"I don't know," Tim answered. He tried to remember if he saw a lone four year old boy wandering around after waking up. There were so many children. He couldn't be sure. "We could look in the binders in Dr. Anderson's office."

"It'll have to wait," Derrick said. "John said we needed to hurry up and get to the farm before nightfall."

"Right, we can check tomorrow," Tim agreed.

He sorted through a handful of papers. "Here's her will, the deed to her house, the title to her car, aha!" he nearly shouted. "I think this could be it!" Excited, he tore through the seal on an envelope with an official government seal on the front. He pulled out a paper and quickly scanned it. "Found it!" he announced. "They didn't lie about the bunker. Here's the address in black and white." He showed it to Derrick. "Let's go."

Derrick looked at the paper and then folded it up. He handed it back to Tim.

Tim stuck it into the inside pocket of his coat and put the rest of the treasures into his messenger bag. "We can give them to her son when we find him," he said when he noticed the questioning expression on Derrick's face.

After telling the others they decided to head back to the shelter and tell John in person. They didn't want to risk broadcasting it over the radio and having the other mechanics hear.

Excited over their find, they made it back to the school in record time. The sun was beginning to set. They found John and Fred sitting in the cafeteria over a cup a steaming coffee. Tim slipped into the chair beside John. The others sat down as well.

"You're back already?" John asked and appeared concerned.

"We didn't make it," George answered.

"We stopped at the SAC to have one last look around," Tim explained and pulled the letter from his pocket. "We found it," he whispered.

"What?" Fred asked.

"The food bunker," Derrick answered.

"Really?"

"Yes," John said and grinned while he looked at the letter. He folded it up and tucked it away. "We'll wait until morning. Then we'll take some trucks and see what we can find."

Tim didn't sleep much. He was too excited about the bunker. He wished he could radio his parents to let them know but they didn't have one. When the sun came up the next morning he was waiting in the cafeteria. Fred was behind the counter, filling a thermos with coffee. John, Derrick and the twins walked in, dressed and ready to go.

"We have two pickups," John said. "I think we should keep this as low key as possible so we don't have a riot on our hands.

"I'll take one of the trucks out for a 'test drive' and I'll tell the other mechanics that Fred is taking the other. We'll meet you boys on the corner at Cornell Road. That way we won't draw any suspicion."

"Got it," everyone answered.

The plan worked flawlessly. John stopped and picked up Tim and Godfrey. George and Derrick rode with Fred. They headed out of town toward Orenco. According to the address in the letter, the bunker was located in the old Tanasbourne area. The government had taken over the athletic center there.

They parked the pickups near the main entrance. The building still looked like the athletic center from the outside. Even when they went inside the main floor had retained its original look.

"Are you sure this is the place?" George asked and looked at Tim.

Tim took the letter out of his pocket and looked at it again. "That's what it says." He showed George the address.

"Well, let's have a look around," Fred said. He and Derrick paired off and headed toward the office.

"George, you're with me," John said. Tim watched them head down a corridor toward the saunas and swimming pool.

"Guess that means it's you and me," Godfrey told Tim.

"Yeah," Tim agreed. "Let's check upstairs."

They walked over to the elevator and pressed the button. When the doors opened, they stepped inside.

"Hey, look," Godfrey said, pointing at the card reader. "Do you still have the doc's keycards?"

"Yes," Tim answered and pulled them both out of his pocket. He tried Dr. Dever's first, since the letter was addressed to her. He held the card up to the reader. The red light turned green and three icons below the floor buttons lit up. He touched the first one. The elevator car started down.

Godfrey grabbed the handrail on the wall and looked at Tim with widened eyes and a grin.

The elevator stopped and the doors opened. The two took one step out and froze. Lights clicked on automatically illuminating a vast underground warehouse. The ceiling appeared to be at least twelve feet high. There were rows and rows of pallets filled with crates and boxes of government foods.

"I think our worries about food are over," Godfrey said.

Day two hundred thirty-one. (April 2, 2096) Spring had arrived. With the discovery of the food bunker and the restoration of power to the town, everyone returned to their homes and began to rebuild their lives.

Tim slipped into a dark depression. For nearly seven months he had focused all his energy and time trying to wake the town. Now he didn't know what to do with himself. He sat in his condo and stared at the television screen. There was still nothing being telecast. The radio stations were still not broadcasting. The walls felt like they were closing in on him.

He decided to pack a bag and go back to his parents' farm. At least he would be around people.

Driving into town Tim reminded himself to obey the traffic signs. No longer could he drive the wrong way on one-way streets or blow past stop signs and lights. There were more vehicles on the road, though not as many as before this ordeal started.

The drive was more pleasant. Trees and flowers in bloom brightened the once barren landscape. The cloudless sky above with its bright shining sun and brilliant blue began to raise Tim up, out of his depression.

He pulled the Hummer into his parents' driveway and noticed Dr. Nachtigal's SUV parked by the back door. He pulled up next to it and jumped out.

"Mom?" he called out when he walked into the kitchen.

"Timmy? Is that you?" she called back.

"Yes." he answered. *Who else calls you, mom?*

Della came out of her bedroom. Her eyes were damp with tears. She gave Tim a hug. "Thank God, you're here."

"What is it?" Tim asked. An overwhelming feeling dread engulfed him but he didn't know why.

"It's your father," she answered. "He's had a stroke."

"What?" Tim gasped. "How do you know?"

"Dr. Nachtigal is with him," Della said, not answering her son's question.

Tim heard a noise and looked across the dining room to the foyer doorway. John walked into the room with Godfrey and George behind him.

"Oh, good, you made it." John said.

"Made it?" Tim looked confused.

"Come here," Della said and held out her hand.

Tim took it and let her lead him into the bedroom. He frowned. Tim looked at his father. He lay on his back with his arms at his side. His head was propped up with pillows. His eyes were closed and his mouth, open to help him breathe. Dr. Nachtigal looked up and removed the stethoscope from his ears.

"His pulse is slow and growing weaker," he reported.

"What does that mean?" Tim asked. He looked at his mother. Della shook her head. "He's—" Tim couldn't bring himself to say the word. He turned around and walked back into the dining room.

"Tim, sit down," Della pulled the chair away from the

side of the bed. "Talk to your father."

Tim looked at his mother and did as she said. Carefully he took his father's hand. "He's burning up," he said and looked at the doctor. "Should we open a window? Get some damp cloths and cool him?" Tim asked.

"Sure," Dr. Nachtigal answered.

Tim jumped up and rushed to the kitchen. He grabbed a dishtowel and damped it with cool water. Returning to the bedroom he handed it to his mother. Della gently wiped Philip's forehead and cheeks. He didn't respond.

Tim noticed that his dad's breathing had become more labored and slower. *No! Breathe, dad, breathe.*

Dr. Nachtigal put his stethoscope in his ears and stepped up to the side of bed. He listened to Philip's heart and lungs. He stood up and took the stethoscope out of his ears. "He could go at any time. I'm so sorry, Del."

Della nodded slowly. "It's okay, Martin."

"Mom?" Tim said. His throat tightened. His eyes teared. He struggled, determined not to cry. *This isn't happening. This can't be it! I'm not ready. There is so much I want to say to him and to hear him say to me. No!*

"It's okay, Timmy." He heard his mother's voice over the voice in his head. "Sit with your father for a while. Talk to him. We'll wait out in the kitchen to give you a moment."

Before Tim could say anything, Della escorted Dr. Nachtigal out of the bedroom. Tim was alone with his falling hero.

He sat down in the chair beside the bed. His legs felt weak. His heart was breaking. He took a deep breath and took his father's hand. It was no longer hot. He looked at his Superman, now so frail and helpless. He wanted to wrap his arms around his father and make it all better as his father had done so many times for him when he was a boy.

"Dad, it's me, Timmy."

Philip didn't respond.

"I'm here, Dad. I won't leave you," he said even though at that moment he wanted to run fast and far away from the pain he felt. "I love you, Dad."

Memories filled in where words failed Tim. The memory of his father teaching him to tie his shoes; another of his dad and him on a deep sea fishing trip when Tim caught his first salmon; and another, when Tim passed his driving test and Philip beamed proudly, came flooding into his mind. Memories he'd forgotten.

"Tim, are you doing okay?" Della's voice pulled him from his thoughts.

"Yeah, no, but…"

"I know, honey." She put her hand on his shoulder.

"Here, you sit down," Tim said and moved so she could take her place beside her husband. Della smiled at him.

Quietly Tim slipped from the room to give them their privacy.

Tim glanced into the kitchen while he stood at the door of his parents' bedroom. Godfrey looked at him. Tim could see the concern and sympathy in his eyes. Tim nodded and turned toward the front room. He didn't want to be around anyone. He didn't want to have to put on a brave face. Inside he felt like a little boy, lost, frightened and confused. He wanted his dad.

"Timmy," Della called. Her voice sounded so calm.

Immediately Tim turned around. "Yes, Mom?" he answered when he reached the bedroom doorway.

"I think you should come here."

Tim understood what she meant. He walked into the room

and stood behind her chair. He reached down and put his hand over hers while she held onto his dad's. Philip's breathing slowed, the time between breaths increased. Tim watched his father's chest intently, trying to breathe for him.

Philip's chest stopped lifting. Della continued to hold his hand. Tim's hand trembled and slipped off theirs. He choked and gasped. Tears blurred his vision.

"He's gone," Doctor Nachtigal said softly.

Tim looked across the bed. The doctor stood holding Philip's wrist, feeling for a pulse.

When did he come into the room?

Tim turned around. The Bjorges were standing at the door.

"Mom?"

"It's okay, Tim. I want to stay with him a little while longer. Go on outside." Her voice was calm.

"Okay."

Tim took a step. His legs felt weak. He started to fall. George and Godfrey grabbed his arms before he hit the floor. They helped him into the dining room.

"I need some air," Tim whispered.

The twins helped him to the front porch. Tim sat down on the wicker loveseat. Godfrey sat beside him. George sat on the rail. No one said a word.

Day two hundred thirty-five. (April 6, 2096) Time seemed meaningless to Tim. He felt as though he were walking around in a fog. John and the doctor took Philip's body to the mortuary in town. The mortician found a nice polished wooden coffin for in the showroom. The cemetery caretaker had dug a grave beside Philip's mother at some point, but Tim didn't know when.

"Are you about ready?" Della called from the bottom of the stairs.

"Yes," Tim answered and stared at his reflection in the mirror above his dresser. He straightened his tie and looked at his hair and face. He didn't recognize the man staring back at him. He looked so lost and alone. Tim fixed the lapel of his suit jacket and turned away from his reflection.

Riding in the backseat of the Hummer Tim watched blindly while the scenery passed by. He felt numb. He didn't notice when Derrick turned off the paved road onto the gravel road of the cemetery.

"We're going to be okay," Della's voice touched my ears.

Tim looked at her and thought he smiled. She looked so pretty. *I don't remember seeing that dress before.* It was a soft powder blue and had a matching blue jacket. Her hair was pulled back as usual in a twisted bun. She looked so calm, so confident.

"I love you, Mom."

"I love you, too, Tim."

The car stopped. Tim looked out the window again. A short distance away, on the lawn, a large group of people had gathered. He didn't see any of their faces. His eyes focused on the casket in the center.

The car door opened. A hand reached in to help him out. He took Godfrey's hand and tightened around the walking stick with his other. He stepped out onto the side of the road. Della walked around the back of the Hummer and joined him. She took his arm. They walked across the lawn and stood at the foot of the casket. Someone said something, Tim didn't know what then the people around him had bowed their heads. He did too.

When he looked up, everyone began leaving. A few

stopped and said something to Della before they headed down the hill.

Della let go of Tim's arm. She walked over to the casket. She said something, bent down and kissed the wooden surface. She placed a single, long stemmed, red rose on its top.

Where did she get that? I don't remember seeing it in the Hummer?

"Are you ready, Tim?" she asked when she walked back to him.

Tim nodded and turned around. He looked up at the Hummer and stopped.

Standing beside the vehicle, with a blanket in her arms was a woman. Her long auburn hair was pulled back in a ponytail at the base of her neck. Her eyes were damp.

"Lily?" Tim said.

She nodded. He rushed to her while tears filled his eyes. He wrapped his arms around her and heard a baby squeak. Instantly he let go and tried to clear his eyes.

"A baby?"

"Yes," she answered and smiled. "A boy." She moved the blanket and revealed a tiny, fair-skinned face. He turned his head and continued to sleep. "I heard about your dad," she continued. "I'm so sorry."

Tim looked back at the casket. Godfrey, George, John and the caretaker were lowering it into the grave. Tim turned back to Lily.

"Who's this?" Della asked and Tim realized she had a hold of his arm again.

"Mom, this is Lily. The girl I told you about. Lily, this is my mom."

"Hi, Lily."

"It's nice to finally meet you, Mrs. Stone," Lily smiled

313

sympathetically and gave a nod. "I'm so sorry. I really loved Mr. Stone. He was such a sweet man."

"Thank you," Della said. "Who have you got there?"

"This is my son," Lily answered and showed him to her. "I hope you don't mind, I named him Philip, after your dad." She looked at Tim.

"That's sweet of you," Della answered.

"Are you ready to go home?" Derrick asked while he stood holding the passenger door of the Hummer open.

Tim looked at Lily. She nodded.

"Yes," Tim answered.

ABOUT THE AUTHOR

James M. McCracken is the award winning author of *The Millionth Year,* and *Secrets* as well as the short *Running* and *Ellensburg.*

He currently resides in Central Oregon and is a member of the online writing group Becoming Fiction. He currently serves as the president of the Northwest Independent Writers Association.